THE BLUEGRASS FILES: THE BOURBON BROTHERHOOD

THE THIRD IN A SERIES OF MYSTERIES SOLVED BY THE AGENTS OF BLUEGRASS CONFIDENTIAL INVESTIGATIONS

F J MESSINA

Enjoy!
F J Messina

Lexington, KY 859.608.4236

Blairbrookepublishing@gmail.com

ISBN: 978-0-9998533-4-4 (Soft Cover)

PCN: pbi1503

❀ Created with Vellum

AUTHOR'S NOTE AND ACKNOWLEDGEMENTS

For those of you who have read my earlier works, it comes as no surprise that this is yet another book set in my well-loved home, Lexington, Kentucky. I love writing stories set in places I know so intimately, and those readers who are familiar with this region seem to love reading about them as well.

As you may have surmised from the title, this story will be soaked in the lore and reality of Kentucky's most famous libation, bourbon. However, in order to maintain a certain level of authenticity, while at the same time steering clear of any copyright, patent, or brand name challenges, the names of all significant bourbons and distillers are entirely fictional. In fact, I would direct readers to the admonition on the copyright page, that points out that this is a work of fiction. In other words, ***I'm just making this stuff up!*** The only exception is the tragic fire that occurred at the Heaven Hill Distillery in 1996 and is described later in the book.

On the other hand, I hope I have accurately described certain elements of bourbon production as it exists in Kentucky today. In addition, some of Lexingtonian's favorite places are mentioned by name, but as .you'll probably notice, only in the most positive of lights.

Now, as to the people who have helped me bring this story to life, my gratitude goes out to a group of special people—special in the help they gave me, special in who they are. I thank my sister (and partner in crime), Judy Thompson, for reading this work while in progress. So many twists and turns in this plot were held up to the "believability test" by her keen mind. Some made the cut and some didn't.

Then there is my daughter, Jennifer Al-Rikabi, who can spot an extra space or a missing quotation mark with the best of them. More importantly, it was her input that kept Sonia working at the highest possible level in her quest to be a true professional private investigator.

It is my daughter, Kristin Morford, who took on the responsibility of being my feminist filter as well as a critical evaluator of events and character motivations. I am grateful to both Kristin and Jennifer for helping me bring Sonia, Jet, and Tee to life as vibrant, authentic female characters.

Thanks also go out to Alex Vangellow, Mary Roycraft, and George McCormick for their willingness to read the manuscript looking for those little errors that sometimes drive readers to distraction.

As always, I must point out that, although she did not work with me directly on this book, the fingerprints of my mentor, Edie Maddox Torok, are all over this and any other book I write.

Finally, I thank my wife, Denise. Without her patience and support, this book and the ones that surround it in the series could and would never have been written. When I write about a man truly loving and cherishing a woman, I write what I feel about her.

1

It was the kind of crowd you would expect on a Wednesday morning—twelve or thirteen, maybe fourteen folks—almost all of them retirement age. That's who normally showed up for the eleven o'clock tour at the Horatio Blevins Bourbon Distillery, just west of Lawrenceburg, Kentucky, on a Wednesday in mid-May. Soon, kids would be out of school and families would be on vacation. In June or July, Earl could sometimes get twenty or more folks following him around the rustic setting, learning everything they could about how bourbon is made. For some folks, it was just a pleasant way to fill a morning or afternoon. For others, it was a way of feeling more deeply attached to something that was a big part of their everyday lives, enjoying bourbon. Of course, for the folks from Horatio Blevins, it was just one of many things they did to enhance the community's knowledge and appreciation of the heritage and tradition of this important part of Kentucky culture. In other words, to sell bourbon.

Earl, six feet tall, a little cragley in the face, a little paunchy in the middle, was dressed in khaki pants and a red polo shirt with an *HB* logo emblazoned on the breast. For him, leading the tours of the distillery three days a week was simply a way to fill some of the empty days of a retirement that was already becoming something akin to a burden. His wife, Jolene, had passed just after Earl had put in his last days as a history teacher at Woodford County High School. Now in his sixth year of retirement, Earl had done all the fishing and hunting he cared to do. He still did those things with some of his friends on occasion, but it had a lot more to do with not wanting to be alone than with the catching of fish or the bagging of a few unlucky ducks.

That's what Earl enjoyed most about this part-time job, being around people. Somehow, walking around the beautiful Blevins facility, with its rolling campus, ancient brick walls, and tall column stills made of copper—teaching these somewhat-interested folks about a process and a product that was truly enmeshed in the DNA of his beloved Bluegrass state—he felt alive, useful.

Earl finished the part of the tour in which he showed folks the charred white oak barrels that were such an essential, in fact mandatory, part of the production of bourbon and led his little group along the brick pathway that sat next to a simple two-rail system. It was along those rails the 520-pound barrels of bourbon would be rolled to their destination, the nine-story wooden rackhouse in which twenty thousand barrels, or roughly one million gallons of bourbon, sat aging.

As Earl entered Rackhouse Number 2, he was joined by his colleague, James—another retired school teacher, another older man in khaki pants and a red polo shirt, another proud purveyor of the history and lore of Kentucky bourbon. Earl explained that the bourbon would sit in the barrels that surrounded them for anywhere from two to twelve years or more. He then shocked many of the listeners by telling them that when the barrels were opened, some of the bourbon would be missing.

"That's right." Earl puffed himself up a bit as he spoke, running his hand through his seriously thinned hair. "You see, during the aging process, some of the bourbon actually evaporates out of the barrel." He leaned forward dramatically, speaking in a hushed tone. "We call that the Angel's Share."

As if on cue, James walked over to one of the barrels on the lowest level. Bending his wiry body down a little, he struck the barrel near the bottom with a small hammer. Smiling, as he listened to the solid thumping sound his tapping elicited, he spoke in a surprisingly high-pitched voice. "Full. Full of the most beautiful amber liquid your eyes would ever want to behold." Then, standing taller, James went through the same process near the top of the barrel. The looks on the faces of Earl's acolytes made it quite clear that they could hear a distinct difference. Although there was no visible sign, it was obvious that the barrel was less than completely full.

Since this was one of Earl's favorite parts of the tour, he stepped forward to repeat the process with another barrel. Tapping near the bottom of the barrel with his own small hammer, Earl drew out the same satisfactory thumping sound that his colleague had elicited in the first demonstration. Then, smiling confidently, Earl knocked near the upper part of the wooden cask. Confusion tingled in the muscles of Earl's face though he tried his best not to let it show. He couldn't resist the temptation to turn to James ever so briefly, though what he saw on James' face gave him no comfort. Still, this was a great part of the tour and he wasn't about to let it slip away. He smiled broadly. "Full at the bottom, empty at the top. The Angel's Share."

He could see some of his students nod weakly. Others just seemed confused. "Okay, then," he picked up the pace, "let's head on back to the main building. There, each of you will be able to sample one of our delicious bourbon balls." He swung his arms open wide magnanimously. "*Aaand,* you'll be able to taste just a little bit of some of Kentucky's finest libation." Leaning forward and smiling knowingly to the tiny gaggle, each of them clearly over sixty, he winked. "That is if you're old enough."

As soon as he had offered his group a final, "Y'all have a great rest of the day," Earl headed straight back to Rackhouse Number Two. James was waiting for him. Earl walked right up to the barrel he had knocked on during the tour, the one that had given him trouble. "Did you hear that, James? Did you hear what I heard?"

James was standing nearby, his hands behind him, stuck into the back pockets of his khakis. "You bet I heard it. Sounded like the barrel was still full. You sure you knocked on it good and solid?"

Earl gave him the, "*Done this a million times,*" look. "Come on, James, I conked it a good one, just like you. Here, give me the hammer. Let's try this again."

James handed him the hammer and watched as Earl tapped, first, near the bottom of the barrel, then near the top. James shook his head. "I don't get it. Sounds the same, don't you think?"

Earl was shaking his head as well. "I'll be damned if it doesn't. This is the right barrel, ain't it? I mean, this isn't a new one that got put here for some reason is it?"

James ran his fingers over the coded numbers burned into the rough-sided barrel. "Nope, I already checked. This is right where it's supposed to be. Six years old. Should have given up the Angel's Share just like every barrel around it." He slipped off his baseball cap, scratching his almost hairless head. "But it don't. Sounds full to me."

Earl stepped back, pondering the situation. He stood motionless. After a solid fifteen seconds, he responded like any good teacher would when he or she felt the principal should know about something that had happened in the classroom. "I don't get this, James, but I think we've got to call Mr. John. He's got to be told about this."

~

It was seven-thirty that evening before John O'Neal, the distillery's general manager, finally made it to Rackhouse Number Two. It had been a long and busy day, and the notion that some of his tour guides couldn't tell a full barrel of bourbon from one that had already given up a portion of its bounty to the angels was a bit frustrating to him. Nonetheless, he had asked one of his long-standing employees, Bobby Ray, to walk with him down to the rackhouse to check out this "big mystery," as he had put it disparagingly.

Earl and James had been very clear in their messages to Mr. John as to which barrel was the one in question. He had no trouble locating it. Looking around the rackhouse in the semi-darkness of evening, he motioned to Bobby. "Give that thing a couple of good whacks and let's both get on home."

Bobby Ray, a short, slight man, thin but muscular in a dark red T-shirt and jeans, walked up to the barrel. He picked up the small hammer that Earl had left lying on the cask's lid and tapped. Near the bottom first. Appropriate sound. Then near the top. Not so much. Bobby Ray knocked again. Same results. He gave O'Neal a strange look, shaking his head curiously.

John O'Neal, a big man with a freckled face and a shock of red hair that made obvious his Irish heritage, walked over to the barrel and followed suit. Knock near the bottom. Solid sound. Knock near the top. Same sound. O'Neal shook his head as well. "Just not right, Bobby."

Bobby Ray cocked his head. "You sure this barrel is where it's supposed to be?"

O'Neal ran his fingers through his wiry hair. "Earl Williams said he checked and double checked. It's six years old." A long moment went by. Finally, O'Neal motioned to Bobby Ray. "Look, I don't know what's going on, but we can't take a chance that something is wrong with that product. Let's tap that thing and see what we get."

It took a few minutes for Bobby Ray to set up a tap and a pan into which the bourbon could flow. When he was ready, he looked up to O'Neal one last time.

"Go ahead, Bobby. Let's do this."

With a few quick moves, Bobby had the amber liquid flowing out of the barrel and into a pan. Several moments later he turned the spigot, shutting down the flow. "There you go, Mr. John."

John O'Neal was no master distiller, but he had smelled and tasted literally hundreds and hundreds of samples from hundreds and hundreds of barrels in his time. It took him only a moment to know that something was off with this batch. "I don't get it, Bobby. Something wrong with the barrel itself? Something else going on?"

Bobby just looked up at him, not willing to venture a guess.

Finally, John O'Neal had had enough. "Hell, Bobby. Open the top. I want to get a good look in there."

There being no way to lift the lid off a bourbon barrel without loosening its metal hoops, thereby releasing fifty-three gallons of bourbon onto the floor, Bobby was forced to do some creative thinking. Drilling a circle of two-inch, concentric holes in the lid itself, he created a round disc that could be lifted out of the top of the barrel without the barrel falling completely apart.

John O'Neal, General Manager of the Horatio Blevins Distillery, bent down to take a careful look at some of his finest product. He shined a flashlight into the amber liquid. What he thought he saw at first was a reflection of his own face. It was only after he looked more closely, that he realized the eyes looking back at him from under the surface were never going to see light again.

DAY ONE

2

"Sixteen, seventeen, eighteen. Made it." Sonia Vitale stood on the landing outside the offices of the firm she and her partner owned—Bluegrass Confidential Investigations. She didn't normally count the steps of the wooden staircase that rose to the second story without a turn-around landing and constituted the only access to their domain, but it hadn't exactly been a normal week.

The act of getting into the BCI offices had always had its own unique charm for Sonia—turning the ancient handle and pushing the heavy, old, wooden door open, her purse and a steaming hot cup of coffee in her hand. On many days, the process was even more challenging, as it often included a white, paper bag filled with an almond croissant as well. This morning the challenge was even greater than usual.

Sonia got most of her news from cable TV. She would watch as she ate breakfast and then listen as she moved around her tiny apartment getting dressed. This morning, however, she had a copy of the local newspaper, *The Lexington Herald-Leader*, tucked under her arm. As she'd purchased it, she'd smiled and shrugged, speaking softly to herself. "You can't blame a girl for buying the paper when her picture is on the front page, can you?"

Sonia walked into the BCI offices and saw her partner, Joyce Ellen Thomas, Jet to everyone who knew her, sitting at her old wooden desk. The firm's offices filled the converted attic over a bakery. It consisted of a large waiting room, half the size of the entire space, and two glassed-in offices overlooking East Main Street. The waiting room provided only one large leather couch and a small table with a modern, but not-very-large, television—plans for an equestrian motif having been put on hold until finances allowed. The two offices were built with wood and glass walls that afforded privacy, while at the same time offering a sense of security when the girls were meeting with clients, especially males. They hoped the security factor was enhanced by the photos of them at a shooting range and copies of their concealed deadly weapons licenses hanging in each of their offices.

Jet looked up from her desk. "What's that you've got under your arm, sweetheart? It wouldn't happen to be today's newspaper, would it?"

Instead of replying directly, Sonia walked all the way into Jet's office. Putting the items she was carrying down on Jet's desk, she pointed to the date on the newspaper already lying in front of Jet. "Hmmm. Friday, May 20th." She gave Jet a snarky smile. "Seems like we're both reading today's paper."

Jet gave her a coy shrug. "Looks like we made it to the front page." She slipped briefly into one of her many accents—southern belle. "My, my, my. Now isn't that just somethin'. You and me both standing there givin' a press conference." Her mood quickly changing, Jet lost the accent and let out a long slow breath. "Can you believe it's been almost a week? I still feel sick when I think about it."

Sonia was unable to stop herself from thinking about the terrible things they had learned and faced in the previous weeks. "At least we opened a lot of eyes while we were at it."

Jet pushed her rolling chair back from her desk, locked her hands, and lifted her arms over her head, stretching. "That we did, honey, that we did."

It being May in Kentucky, Sonia had skipped her signature pea coat and cloche hat. Instead, she had on the blue jeans she almost always wore to work, the ones that hugged her bottom so nicely, a white knit top that was modest yet still accentuated her shapely figure, and a rakish, little blue scarf tied into a knot around her neck. Her red Chuck Taylors completed the ensemble.

Jet looked her up and down. "My, we are looking pretty patriotic today, aren't we?"

Sonia checked herself in the full-length mirror Jet had recently installed on the side of the ancient armoire she used for closet space in her office. "Oh, I guess so. I hadn't noticed," she said coyly. She turned back to Jet. "And what about you? You're looking a bit more dressed *down* than usual."

Jet was in jeans and a loose-fitting chambray shirt, a phony gas company logo colorfully embroidered on the front. Her long blonde hair, in its perpetual ponytail, hung over her shoulder. Her lean, five-foot-six-inch body was slouched in her chair. "Yeah. Well, I'm still not sure I've recovered from everything that happened on Monday." Though her attitude was breezy, the unusually heavy makeup she was wearing was barely able to camouflage the large, hand-shaped bruise on her face.

"Right." It saddened Sonia to see Jet's bruise, but she picked up her coffee, moving on. "So, what's on our agenda for the day?"

Jet reached out and pushed around some of the clutter on her desk. Lifting up a yellow legal pad, she flicked it with her fingernail. "Well, it looks like being major players in the solving of a local crime has once again brought out a number of folks who simply cannot," she shook her head, "and I mean *cannot*, live without our services in the immediate future."

Sonia put the coffee down on Jet's desk without having taken a sip. "Serious cases?"

"Sure. He's cheating on her. She's cheating on him. The neighbors must be stealing our newspaper every Sunday morning while we're at church." She looked at Sonia over the glasses she wasn't wearing. "Real J. Edgar Hoover stuff to be sure."

Shifting her attention to the white bag Sonia had brought into the office with her coffee and newspaper, Jet became suddenly indignant. "Well, are you just going to let that pastry die a slow death in that bag, or are you going to give it its freedom, thereby allowing me to help a small piece of it complete its mission in life?"

Sonia unrolled the top of the white bag. She pulled out an almond croissant, tore off a large piece and held it, looking for a clean place on Jet's desk to put it down.

"Oh, give it here." Jet reached out, grabbing the morsel, and popping a good-sized portion of it into her mouth. "Now wasn't that easier?" she said out of the side of her mouth while she brushed crumbs off her fingertips.

Sonia slid a much more ladylike piece of croissant into her own mouth, then chewed and swallowed. "So, have you prioritized any of those clients for us? Do we know who public enemy number one is?"

Jet pulled her ponytail through her hand, her beautiful blue eyes shining in her very attractive face. "Not yet, but I can tell you we're going to be one extremely busy private investigation firm for the next few weeks."

Sonia was just about to say, "Well, isn't that what folks in the PI business are hoping for?" She never got the chance.

3

Without a knock, the old door at the back of the room opened. A man walked in. Though he couldn't have known quite where he was going, he moved with confidence, the confidence of a man who always felt like he was in charge.

"Good morning. The ladies of Bluegrass Confidential Investigations I assume?" His black hair, clipped short, gray at the temples, were accented by his pale blue eyes and tanned skin. His voice was quiet, gentler than one might have expected given his stature. At six foot or more, easily two hundred pounds, his polite manner seemed a contradiction to the confidence Sonia had sensed as he'd entered the room. His clothing, on the other hand, fit the image. Dark blue slacks, light blue polo shirt, embroidered belt, brown tasseled loafers. He carried a soft-sided, zippered briefcase at his side—weathered brown leather. Clearly, he was a large, confident man, but one with a sense of southern culture. A gentleman.

"Can I help you?" Sonia was the first to rise, Jet following suit.

"Well, I certainly hope so." He moved quickly across the room and was in Jet's office before Sonia had really adjusted to his presence.

His hand reached out to Sonia, "Mason Holiday." He shook hers firmly. Then he turned to Jet, reaching across her desk. He shook Jet's hand as well but said nothing.

Jet looked around her office, suddenly seeming aware of the clutter on top of her desk. Sonia stepped to her rescue. "Sonia Vitale, Mr. Holiday. This is my partner, Jet." She waited for the customary look of surprise, ready to say, "That's what everyone calls her."

The look and the question never came. "Nice to meet you, ladies. Is this a good place to talk?"

Sonia decided to remain on point. "Well, Mr. Holiday—"

"Mason." He gave them each a quick smile.

"Mason." Sonia smiled. "Listen, we've been plowing through a pile of notes this morning. Why don't we move to my office where we can spread out a bit? It's right through there." She pointed through the glass wall to her office, the one with the "neat-as-a-pin" desk.

"Sure." Holiday motioned to the ladies to lead the way—as if the offices were his domain and not theirs.

A moment later they were all seated in Sonia's office, Sonia behind her desk. Jet had headed toward the wooden chair in the corner of the office, leaving the red, padded one for the client. But Holiday had deftly motioned her into that seat, taking the wooden chair for himself and sliding it to the side of the desk, between Sonia and Jet. A gentleman to be sure, but used to being in charge. He placed his briefcase on the floor next to him.

Sonia sat tall, crossing her hands on her desk. "Well, Mason," her voice was firm, professional. "How can we help you?"

Mason Holiday gave them each a serious look, then he began. "Ladies, I've heard on the news, and of course in today's paper, that you two were recently instrumental in bringing a somewhat well-known person to justice." He didn't wait for them to respond. "I must say that I was very impressed, not only with your ability to bring that case to a satisfactory conclusion but also with how you handled yourself in the aftermath. No grandstanding. No publicity seeking. No unnecessary besmirching of people or factions on the periphery of the proceedings."

He stopped, pausing. Sonia acknowledged his comments with a quiet, "Thank you."

After a beat, he began again. "It turns out that I am currently in need of some professional help, help that will be both that effective," he looked intently at Sonia, then at Jet, "and that discreet."

Jet gave Holiday a cordial smile. "That's what we are, Mason. Effective and discreet."

Seated too far away from the desk to lean on it, Holiday simply sat tall, his hands pressed on his thighs, the effect of which was to enhance his already significant presence. He took a quick breath. "Alright then. But before I begin, I must ask for your cooperation in one small matter."

Without waiting for a response, Holiday bent over and retrieved his briefcase. He unzipped it and pulled out a two-page document which he handed to Sonia. "This, ladies, is a non-disclosure agreement that I will need you to sign before I go on. It states that anything I say to you is in the strictest confidence. It also indicates that whether we continue to move forward with a business relationship or not, you will, under penalty, have to refrain from disclosing the contents and the spirit of our conversation without the express permission of myself or the others I represent."

Sonia looked briefly at Jet and sensed an emotional response on the way, one that might or might not be appropriate. She turned back to Holiday. "Listen, Mr.—ah, Mason. We at BCI are used to maintaining client confidentiality when appropriate, but I'm not certain we would commit ourselves to that agreement without a pretty clear understanding of what we were getting involved with."

Mason Holiday smiled, his voice reserved, controlled. "Very

wise. And I do understand. However," he looked at them, his tanned face crinkling just the tiniest bit, "my colleagues and I are in grave need of your assistance in a matter that is, well, very delicate." He leaned in. "I'm hopeful that when you hear what I'm about to tell you and realize who and what it is that we are attempting to protect, you will be willing, as citizens of our community, of our commonwealth, to abide by this agreement."

Sonia was really at a loss about what to say. She looked at Jet, who nodded, indicating Sonia should read the document. Several minutes of silence went by, Sonia moving her fingers slowly over each word, making certain to grasp their import. Mason Holiday waited patiently. Finally, taking a deep breath, Sonia looked back to Jet and shrugged. "I think we should take the chance." She got the silent response she expected from Jet.

Sonia pulled a pen out of the black, wire basket on her desk and signed the second page of the document. She slid it toward her partner. Jet leaned over the desk and signed it as well. Then she turned to Holiday, holding the document out to him. "Okay, Mr. Holiday, sir," her tone was a bit surly, "what's the big deal?"

4

Mason Holiday took the form and slipped it into his briefcase. He seemed to relax a bit. Sitting farther back in his chair and placing the case and its contents on the floor, he let out a deep breath. Before starting, however, he sat up tall in his chair again. Sonia felt her own body tense in anticipation.

"Okay, then. The group I represent has no particular name. It's not an official group of any sort. Really," he shrugged gently, "we're just a bunch of men with a common interest." He paused again and looked downward as if he were reflecting on the nature of the group or thinking through the ramifications of what he was about to say.

Sonia nudged. "And what is that common interest?"

Mason Holiday looked directly at Sonia. "Bourbon. We all make bourbon."

Sonia turned to Jet, then back to Holiday. "And?"

Holiday shook his head. "We all make bourbon and something has happened that could really disrupt things for us." He stopped again.

Jet was clearly getting antsy. "Come on Mason. Get it out

there. We certainly can't help you if we don't know what the heck you're talking about."

Holiday leaned forward, his hands turning upward as if in supplication. "Look, I know everyone here in Kentucky has always been all about bourbon, but it's no longer a local phenomenon. Now, I'm not here to talk about bourbon sales, but ladies, all you have to do is look around you. Bourbon is hot, really hot. There are bourbon bars, bourbon recipes of all kinds, ales aged in bourbon barrels. It's crazy. And we don't want anything to get in the way of that going on for a very, very long time."

There was a moment of silence as Holiday became reflective again. Sonia glanced at Jet and then cleared her throat. "And, Mason, what would that 'anything' be?"

Holiday reached down and picked up his briefcase again. He rifled through a page or two then pulled out an eight-by-ten glossy photograph. "Do you all know who this is?"

Sonia took the photo out of Holiday's hand and quickly showed it to Jet. It was a photo of a man in his early fifties, broad-faced, blonde, with one green eye and one blue. He was smiling his professional smile, but there was no warmth in it. She shook her head. "No. I don't believe I do." A quick glance at Jet told Sonia her partner didn't recognize him either. She held the picture out to Holiday.

Holiday waved her off, indicating she should keep the photo. "His name is Victor Rasmussen. He's a local businessman turned racehorse owner. Not a guy who many people like, but lucky, damn lucky. He's got this horse named Sultan Aly Khan. Won some big races, and now he's kind of rolling in money."

Jet leaned forward in the red chair, putting her forearm on the desk, turning a bit sideways to address Holiday. "And the reason you're showing us this guy's picture is?"

Holiday let out a breath. It was obvious to Sonia that he was struggling to get his story out. He sat up taller and continued. "A couple of months ago, Victor Rasmussen held a press conference on his farm." He pursed his lips. "I don't know the name of the farm. It's small, no big deal." He continued. "Anyway, he holds this press conference and announces that's he going to be bringing a new bourbon into the marketplace. Called it Sultan's Choice, like with that racehorse. Said it was going to be super high-end."

Sonia looked at him. "How high end are we talking here?"

Holiday rocked back just a bit, his eyebrows lifted. "Well, I don't know how high he was talking. A bottle of twenty-two-year-old *Woodland Acres Reserve* sells for a hundred and fifty bucks. James Bennington's *Double Black* goes for a hundred and ninety-five dollars a bottle, not to mention Pappy VanWinkle's twenty-three-year-old stuff. Its suggested retail price is fourteen hundred and fifty dollars a bottle, but there are guys paying upwards of two thousand dollars to get their hands on one." He grinned at Jet. "Ma'am, bourbon may be a beautiful amber liquid, but there's gold in those bottles."

"So," Sonia squinted just a bit, "this Rasmussen is going to bring out a new bourbon and you and your friends are upset because of the competition?"

Holiday let out a soft chuckle. "No, that's not it. There's lots of competition already and, honestly, there seems to be plenty of money to go around. Bourbon is the new 'in thing.' Instead of flashy bottles of wine, the big hitters are now serving rare bottles of bourbon. And it just seems that whoever spends the most money on it wins. No, competition is not the big deal. But there *are* two significantly big deals."

Sonia watched him run his hand through his short, black hair. She could almost feel the soft bristliness of it in her own fingertips as he spoke. "First, think about it. All those prices I just quoted, they weren't for four-year-old bourbon. They were for bourbons that had spent years and years aging in charred oak barrels. Let me ask you. How's this guy who hasn't been in the business two lousy months going to bring out a high-end bourbon?" His voice grew sardonic. "His grandmother been distilling it and aging it in her basement? Listen, none of the distillers I know would sell him their best stuff and let him put his name on it. And I know everybody."

Jet jumped in. "Well, what *is* he talking about?"

Holiday's voice fell away. "Honestly, we don't know. But it's got to be at least twenty years old."

"And second?" Sonia's middle finger was tapping quickly and quietly on the desktop.

Holiday swallowed. "And second, we just found Victor Rasmussen floating in a sealed barrel of Horatio Blevins' finest bourbon."

5

"Dead?" Sonia's eyes opened wide.

"Dead." Holiday's voice had become almost a whisper.

A long moment went by as Sonia and Jet tried to digest what had just been said. Finally, Sonia asked. "What do you mean, 'floating in a barrel of Horatio Blevins' finest?' "

Once again, Holiday sat up taller, bracing himself. "Okay. Let me explain. I think that by the time I'm done, you'll understand why we needed to do the NDA." He swallowed and huffed out a short breath. "Do either of you know what the Angel's Share is?"

Jet jumped right in. "Listen. You're talking to two women who know their bourbon. We know all about the Angel's Share."

"Good." Holiday went on to explain about Earl and James' experience in the Horatio Blevins rackhouse and how Victor Rasmussen had been found dead and submerged in bourbon. "You can imagine how shocked John O'Neal and Bobby Ray were."

Sonia watched Holiday take another breath before continuing. Clearly, there was something more coming.

"So, I can assume that what you're imagining is that the first thing they did was call 911, call the police." He hitched, then went on. "But think about it. The world of bourbon is exploding. Business simply couldn't be better. There seems to be no limit as to how good things could become for all the different people involved—distillers, workers, drivers, retailers, advertisers, even the state's revenue flow. It's a big, big deal."

"Then this guy comes along," Holiday twisted his lips again, "a guy nobody really cares for, a guy who hasn't gone through all the low times of the past twenty or thirty years, and says he's bringing out this high-end bourbon. What's he mean by that? Where the heck is he going to get it? Next thing you know he's dead." Another quick breath. "Not only dead but dead in a barrel of bourbon." Holiday's pale eyes searched first Sonia's face then Jet's for a reaction.

Sonia stirred in her chair. "So," she paused, "what you're saying is that you and your colleagues are afraid that this might cause a scandal that could upset the applecart for the whole bourbon industry. Is that it, Mason?"

Again, Holiday's hands opened as if in supplication. "Of course. You've got to understand. Bourbon is more than just a drink. It's a tradition. It's history. It's a way of life, an attitude. When people drink bourbon, they're wrapping themselves up in all of that for the moment. It's all part of the experience. Do we want that tainted by some scandal?" His eyes locked in on Sonia's. "And think about this. Do we want rumors and urban myths flying around about some decomposing body floating around in a barrel of bourbon, bourbon that people wind up drinking? That could ruin us." His last words were strong, animated, almost fervent.

Sonia leaned forward, her elbows on her desk, her palms together in front of her face as if she were in prayer. "So, tell me, Mason. What *did* John O'Neal do?"

Mason Holiday sat back in his chair, his eyes going to the ceiling for a moment. "Listen, John O'Neal is a good man. Good family man. Good Christian man. Kind of guy who would give you the shirt off his back before you asked for it. But he's a good businessman, too. Been in the bourbon business all his life. Understands everything we just spoke about." Another deep breath in. "So, once he realized exactly what it was that he'd discovered, he told Bobby Ray to close the barrel back up, nail a second lid on it. Told him to use the forklift and put it on the back of John's own pick-up. Then he made Bobby Ray swear that he would keep all of this to himself, at least until they'd figured everything out."

"Put it in his pick-up?" Sonia asked, incredulous. "Where is it now?"

"At his place." Holiday's voice had become level, matter-of-fact. "He lives on a small farm. Got a good-sized barn, though. Told Bobby Ray to just put it in that barn, near the back. Nobody's going to find it. Not right away."

Jet cocked her head. "How did Bobby Ray get it off the truck? It's like five hundred pounds or something, right?"

"Oh, that's easy." Holiday still seemed blasé about it all. "John's got a forklift on his farm. Bought it used from the distillery, I think. Uses it for putting hay up in the barn."

Sonia fought to keep her eyebrows from crawling up her face. Here was this nicely dressed, polite gentleman, telling them how his friend had told an underling to simply put a barrel with a dead body in the back of his barn. Try as she might to hide her shock, her eyes were wide as she continued to look at Holiday.

He noticed. "Oh, you're wondering what John did next. I get that. Well, after he sent Bobby Ray off to deal with the body and the barrel, he got on the phone. Started calling all the key players in the bourbon industry. Not the big corporate guys. He called the guys who make the stuff, the guys whose families have made bourbon for over a hundred years. He called the people in the bourbon brotherhood. Told them all we had to meet at his place the next morning, that there was something urgent and confidential that had to be discussed in private. Told them not to tell anyone where they were going—not anyone—not even their wives."

Sonia looked over at her partner. Jet, queen of the funny accents and instant quips, was mute, speechless. A moment of silence went by. Sonia nudged. "Mason?"

He plowed on. "So, at that meeting, John tells all of us what's going on. He asks us all to consider the implications. Then he asks everyone for their opinion, what they think we should do. Well, of course, some of the men thought he was crazy for not just calling the police first thing. Others were quick to see things John's way and thought that we should avoid being reckless as we moved forward." His gaze went back and forth between Sonia and Jet. "I won't bore you with the details. All I can say is that, after a very extensive discussion, we kind of came to an agreement, a sort of consensus."

Holiday was rocking gently back and forth in the wooden chair, but no words were coming out. Sonia knew she had to push him over the edge. "We're waiting, Mason."

"Okay, here it is." Holiday sat up tall again, his hands back on his thighs, unconsciously making himself as tall as possible. "We agreed that we could try to keep the whole thing secret for one week, seven days. After that, we would have to go to the police and let them know what was going on."

"Are you kidding?" Jet's voice rose. "You're waiting seven days to go to the police?"

Holiday looked at her, somewhat apologetically. "That's what we decided." He went on quickly. "But we also decided that in those seven days we would do everything we could to figure out what happened, who killed Victor Rasmussen."

Jet wasn't backing down. "*You?* You were going to solve the murder?"

Holiday didn't hesitate. "Well, not us, someone we would hire."

Sonia stated the obvious. "And you want us to figure out who did it, right?"

Holiday smiled. It wasn't the confident smile he'd brought into the room when he first arrived. It was a lame, apologetic smile. "Makes sense, doesn't it? You took care of that other culprit. In fact, Ms. Vitale, weren't you involved in another serious case earlier this year?"

Sonia nodded gently, remembering.

Holiday arched his back, ran his thumbs inside the waist of his pants, and tugged. He seemed to regain his original composure. He was once again a man in charge. "Well, ladies, whether you agree with our decision or not, you now know our situation. The question is whether or not you are willing to help us in our time of need." He didn't give them time to respond. "I want to remind you of everything that's riding on this, for our whole bourbon community, in fact, for the whole Commonwealth of Kentucky. Are you able to put your doubts aside and help us find out what happened to Victor Rasmussen, or do we simply file the NDA and go our separate ways?" He paused for just a moment. "I can assure you that your compensation will be more than considerable, and we'll cover any expenses you might incur."

Sonia and Jet had a private, silent consultation, each one searching the other's face for an indication of their feelings. Eventually, Sonia took a deep breath and turned to Holiday, believing she understood Jet's position. "It seems we are willing to do our part, to do the best we can to figure this out. Before we agree to move forward on this, however, I have one question." She looked directly into Mason Holiday's eyes. "When did all of this happen?"

Holiday gave a quick nod. "Wednesday. You have five days left."

6

The door at the back of the BCI offices closed. Mason Holiday was gone. Sonia remained seated behind her desk, Jet across from her in the red, padded chair. The only sound in the room was the muted traffic noises from down on East Main. Sonia picked up her coffee, long gone cold after the lengthy meeting with Holiday. She took a tiny sip, shook her head, and put the paper cup back down.

Jet didn't even bother to try hers. "We going to be okay on this, not reporting a crime?"

Sonia ran her fingers through her hair. "You read the study guide for the licensing test. You passed the exam. According to Kentucky statutes, we are no more responsible to report a crime than the average citizen, and they have no responsibility to do so unless they are actually witnessing a violent crime."

Jet's eyes opened wide. "And murdering someone then sticking the body in a barrel of bourbon is not a violent crime?"

Sonia took a deep breath. "Technically," her voice softened, "we didn't actually witness the crime." She thought for a moment. "In fact, even John O'Neal didn't," she wiggled her fingers in the air, "witness the crime."

Jet looked at Sonia, her chin lowered. "So, you think O'Neal and Holiday and all those other guys are in the clear?"

Sonia shrugged. "I guess, but they're dancing awfully close to the lines of tampering with evidence and obstruction of justice, don't you think?"

Jet spoke, her voice all down-home country. "Close as a turkey walkin' past a butcher shop on Thanksgiving morning."

Sonia chuckled then twisted her lips and closed one eye. "But, now that we're into it, exactly how do we go about figuring out who plopped this guy into a barrel of bourbon—*and do it in five days?*"

Jet simply shrugged.

Sonia stood and walked out from behind her desk. "I know one thing. We start with some fresh coffee. I'm going downstairs to get some. You look over that list of names Holiday left us. I'll be back in a couple of minutes."

For the ladies of BCI, "downstairs," meant the bakery over which their offices were located, Magee's. Opened in 1956, Magee's had become somewhat of an icon in Lexington. Many a retirement cake, birthday cupcake, and Sunday-morning-family-tradition donut had come out of the place. It had quite an assortment of regulars, and that certainly included Sonia and Jet. For them, one of the few things that offset the heat of the summer and the cold of the winter that plagued their upstairs offices was the sweet and inviting aromas of freshly baked pastries and rich, hot coffees that emanated from Magee's and wafted into their workspace. The other things, of course, were cheap rent and an opportunity to put their Bluegrass Confidential Investigations sign right over one of the best known and most-often-visited places in town.

Sonia walked to the counter and was greeted by Hildy, the same older woman who greeted her every morning. Hildy's face was a question mark. "Back again so soon?"

Sonia shrugged. "Just had a heck of a meeting. Never did get a chance to drink the coffee before it went cold."

"Don't you worry. You just go get yourself a nice hot cup on the house." Hildy gave her a wink. "We guarantee the best hot coffee in town, even if you're the one who lets it get cold."

Sonia tipped her head in a "*You're so sweet*," kind of way. "Thanks, Hildy." She turned and headed for the coffee bar, which had recently been moved to the back wall of the bakery.

Hildy called out after her. "And get a cup for that partner of yours. I'm sure she could use one as well." Sonia put the lids on two steaming hot cups of Southern Pecan coffee brought in from Lexington Coffee & Tea Company, a popular local institution that actually roasted and ground the beans right in town at the back of the Coffee Times Coffee House.

A warm breeze crossed Sonia's face when she stepped out of Magee's and turned left then left again at the bottom of those wooden stairs. She didn't know if it was the climb in front of her or the weight of having only five days to figure out who had done in Victor Rasmussen that made her feel weary. One way or the other, there was no spring in her step as she began the long climb back to the BCI offices.

When she stepped inside, Sonia saw that Jet was still sitting in the red, padded chair at Sonia's desk. "Thought I'd stay in here to work. My desk is covered with all kinds of stuff from those other cases."

Sonia moved to her own desk, chuckling inwardly. Like there's ever a time your desk isn't one big pile of other stuff. Fully aware that they were going to have to temporarily set aside all of those new cases, she asked, "So, what've we got, partner?"

"Well, here's the list of people Mason Holiday thought we needed to look into." Jet tipped her head and twanged. "It ain't short." She held a yellow pad out to Sonia.

Sonia put the coffee cups down on her desk, took the list, then plopped into the rolling chair behind her desk. "Whew.

You're not kidding. There must be twenty or twenty-five names here."

Jet nodded. "Right, but look. Holiday put stars by seven of them. Those are the seven he wants us to talk to first."

Sonia sat up straighter, "Why these seven? I mean, I recognize most of the distilleries they represent, but . . . ."

"And that's why. Those seven are the big boys, the ones who would have the most to lose if the murder of Victor Rasmussen managed to screw things up for the bourbon industry."

Sonia furrowed her brow as she looked at Jet. "And Holiday wants us to talk to these folks? The guys in his own group? Does he think one of his own guys murdered Rasmussen?"

Jet just shrugged.

Sonia tapped on the yellow pad, "I guess he's thinking that in the best-case scenario these folks can send us in the right direction to find out who killed the guy."

"And in the worst case?"

Sonia leaned back in her chair, letting out a short breath. "In the worst case, it turns out that it really *is* one of these guys who did it." She shook her head slowly. "Tough stuff." Taking the lid off her coffee, Sonia took a cautious sip. "So, where are we headed?"

Jet took back the pad as Sonia turned on her laptop. A few moments later she was reading from it as Sonia made notes on the computer. "Okay. Looks like we'll be talking to almost all the folks on the Bourbon Trail. We've got the master distillers at Bald Knob Trace, Settler's Pride, Johnston Srpings, Elk Horn, Woodland Acres, Sandhill Crane, James Bennington—they're the ones who make Bartholomew Hughes and Kendall Run as well—and of course, Horatio Blevins."

Sonia shook her head. "Wow. That's a bunch of folks to talk to, and surreptitiously, at that. Holiday made it clear that we can't raise a bunch of suspicion by asking the right questions in the wrong places."

Jet reached out and took the lid off her coffee. "We could do it over the phone."

Sonia raised her hand, her index and middle fingers pointing upward. "Two things we learned last week. First, if you're afraid someone might not be completely honest with you, you've got to talk to them face to face."

Jet nodded. "You're absolutely right. If you hadn't made us drive down to Danville last week, who knows if we would have been able to get to the bottom of that mess. What's number two?"

Sonia took a deep breath. "I never told you this, but after we got trapped in that apartment, having left our guns in the car, I made a promise to myself. Never again am I going to get caught working without a weapon on me." She slowly took a sip of coffee and paused a moment. "Trust me, before we go talking to any of these folks, you and I are going down to see Ray at the gun shop down on Regency. He gave us a good deal on the Glocks we bought, and I'll bet he's got something small that can work for us as well. You know, something easily carried, but something with a little punch, if you know what I mean."

"Alright, Annie Oakley. If that's how you want to play it, I'm in. Right after lunch you and I are going gun shopping, and God help the man who gets in our way after that."

7

By three o'clock that afternoon, Sonia and Jet had finished their shopping trip. They had gone to Evans Firearms on Regency Road, local but not small, and had a pretty lengthy conversation with the owner. In the end, Sonia had walked out with a sweet little Smith and Wesson *Airweight.* It was a five-shot, .38 special snub-nosed revolver. Not as small and hip as the Sig Sauer P938 Jet had purchased, but it had one advantage over any semi-automatic pistol. It never jammed.

Sonia had also chosen a simple holster that allowed her to wear her Smith on her ankle, hidden from view if she was wearing boot-cut jeans. Looks still mattered. If she wore anything tighter, she would have to be content with carrying the gun in her purse or in a small holster she could attach to her belt and would have to cover with a top.

After making their purchases, Sonia and Jet had driven out to an indoor shooting range in Brannon Crossing. They'd each fired twenty-five rounds with their new weapons just to familiarize themselves with the guns and to get some real experience with how they felt in their hands when fired. As Jet drove them back to town, Sonia started a new line of conversation. "You know, I've been thinking."

"Well, there's a news flash." Jet turned and smiled. "Honey you're always thinking." She looked back at the road. "So, what've you been thinking about?"

Sonia kept her eyes forward as well. "Okay. We've got five days to try to figure out what happened to Victor Rasmussen. Mason Holiday thinks we should talk to seven different men from distilleries all over the state, men who might have nothing at all to do with this and who may know nothing more about it than Mason Holiday himself."

"Uh huh."

"Don't we also have to talk to other people, his family, other people who knew him?"

"Absolutely." Jet paused, then went on. "Look, it's obvious that some people in the bourbon industry are pretty upset about Sultan's Choice coming out soon. But that doesn't mean it wasn't someone else who pickled the poor bastard in bourbon."

"I know, right?" Sonia brushed a wisp of hair out of her face. "And before we left the office, I did some quick research and dug down into his family background. Guess what that does to the list of people we've got to talk to?" She started ticking names off on her fingers. "There's his father, his mother, his sister, wife number one, wife number two, his son. That's six. Now we're up to fourteen and we haven't even followed any leads, you know, spoken to someone who told us there was a someone else we should talk to."

Jet checked her rearview mirror. "And what about folks at the Blevins distillery? We should be talking to them, right? I mean, somehow, somebody got onto the property and dropped the fool into that barrel."

Sonia twisted her lips. "I don't know. Maybe not at first. Remember, Holiday needs us to be discreet, and I don't think anyone out there, other than O'Neal and Bobby Ray, knows anything about this. We don't want to start arousing suspicion, at least not at first."

Jet was silent for a moment then glanced quickly at Sonia. "Still, that's an awful lot of folks to get to in five days. What about your hunky fiancé? Any chance he can help us?"

"I called him while I was downstairs getting coffee. He was blown away by what those guys had gotten themselves into, and he was concerned about us getting caught up in it too. But he said that whatever we get involved with he would always have our backs. I did, however, make it clear that it's our investigation." She paused. "Still, this is one hell of a time press."

"You bet your dang hushpuppies." There was just a trace of southern belle in her voice. "That's an awful lot of face to face, and it's got to be done by someone who knows what they're doing."

Jet drove on, and it wasn't long before she was pulling into the parking lot at Magee's. As she did, an old, blue Chevy Caprice with Ohio plates and a banged-up front fender caught Sonia's eye. Hmmm. When they reached the bottom of those steps, Sonia looked up. There, sitting on the top step in the warm, Friday afternoon sun, blue jeans, sandals and a burgundy, flouncy top floating on her body, was her sister. The words "drop-dead gorgeous" ran through Sonia's mind.

"It's about time." The words fell down from above. "I've been sitting here for over an hour. Don't you guys ever work?"

Sonia didn't say a word as she climbed the stairs, but if the sun hadn't been out, the smile on her face would have lit up the parking lot nonetheless. Just a touch breathless at the top of the steps, she reached out her arms. "Tee, come here, you. Give me a hug." There was a special joy that flowed through her body as she held her baby sister, smelled the fragrance of her shampoo, felt the softness of her hair. "What are you doing here?"

"Oh, I don't know. It's Friday afternoon. The stock market is closed and I won't be called on to make any earth-shattering decisions as regards the national debt. I'm letting some of my friends use my yacht for the weekend, and my polo match got canceled because nobody was willing to play my team, which, by the way, never loses. So . . . ."

"Who's the wiseass?" It was Jet.

Sonia smiled back and forth between the two. "Oh, that's right. You two have never met. Tee, this is my partner, the one, the only, Jet, a legend in her own mind if I do say so myself." She turned back to her sister, smiling. "Jet this is Teresa, Tee to most of the world. She's down here from Cincinnati."

Jet gave Tee a big smile. "I'm glad to see that not all Eye-talians are wound as tight as your sister, here. Welcome to the Bluegrass." The two women hugged while Sonia unlocked the door and led them inside.

Tee's eyes roamed through the space, her artistic sensibilities pleased by both the rugged earthiness of the brick walls and unfinished floor and by the modern glass and wood walls that created the private offices. "Nice. Very nice. I like it. I could do great things in this space."

Sonia gave Jet a quick look as if to say, "*Apparently, we haven't done anything of note with the place so far.*" She took Tee by the elbow and led her toward her own office. "Come, see the view. It's pretty cool."

They moved to the large window in Sonia's office and looked out over East Main. "That brown-brick building across the street is the school district's Central Office. That's where I used to work when I took a job here in Lexington as a technology specialist. Brad's company, Semper Fi Investigations, is in the white house that's next to it."

Tee scanned the scene. "What's that little restaurant on the corner like?"

Jet chimed in. "Seems like it changes hands every few months. If you like French food, go this week. If you want Cajun, just wait a month, another month later it'll be something else."

Sonia took hold of Tee's elbow again. "Come on. Let's go downstairs and get some coffee and maybe a little treat. Then you can tell us all about what's going on in your life."

Jet opened the door and nudged them out onto the landing. "And then we've got to get back to work."

8

It was her first visit to Magee's, and like most folks, Tee was immediately taken by the warm, inviting atmosphere, not to mention the smells of the pastries and coffees. Sitting across from Sonia and Jet at one of the larger tables, she wolfed down her almond croissant and most of her first cup of coffee. As she did, she told them both about her life immediately after graduation. A degree in studio art hadn't exactly put her on a path to a job in upper management, and it had turned out that her boyfriend, Ricky, had the perfect look for a rock star but none of the commensurate talent.

Sonia wasn't far behind in finishing her pastry. "So, you're just here for a weekend visit with your big sister?" She licked some sugar off her fingertips.

"Weekend, maybe longer." Tee batted her eyebrows blatantly. "If that's alright with you."

A tentative smile crossed Sonia's face. "Of course, it's alright with me, I love having you down here with me."

Tee glanced over to Jet and then back to Sonia. "Are you sure?" There was real concern in her voice. "I don't want to intrude. I could go back home tomorrow."

Sonia's hand was on Tee's forearm in an instant. "No, no, no. I want you to stay, please stay."

Tee cocked her head, asking a silent question.

Sonia leaned forward. "It's just that we've recently taken on a case, a real tough case, one with an incredibly short time frame, and I'm afraid I won't have a single moment to share with you."

Jet had been waiting patiently for the right moment to say something. "She's right, sweetheart. Trust me, I know your sister, and the only other time I've ever seen her light up like she did when she saw you at the top of those stairs was when Mr. Hotstuff from across the street first came into her life. As a matter of fact," she stuck her finger in her mouth, feigning gagging, "that still happens every time she sees him."

Sonia tossed her head back gently, ran her fingers through her hair, and grinned. "Well, you can't blame a girl, can you?" She turned to Tee. "Listen, I really do want you to stay, and you can, you'll just have to understand, you know?"

Tee seemed to be thinking beyond the immediate question. "So, what's the deal with this case? Tell me more about it."

Sonia started. "So, this morning—"

"Ahem," Jet lifted a hand to her mouth.

Sonia was confused for an instant, then grasped Jet's meaning. She turned back to Tee. "Well, I've just been reminded that this case is so hush-hush that we had to sign a non-disclosure agreement with the client. I'm afraid I can't tell you anything about it."

Tee gave Sonia the look that young folks give adults when they think they're taking things way too seriously. "Come on. I'm your sister. You can tell me. Who am I going to tell?"

"Listen, cupcake," Jet wagged her finger gently, "this is no joking matter. If we tell anyone outside the firm what we're doing or why we're doing it, we could face some serious legal trouble. Heck, they could put us out of business if they wanted to."

Silence enveloped the table for a moment as each one of the

three took a sip of coffee. Eventually, Tee nodded her head in agreement. "Still, I'd like to stay, if you don't mind. It's just good to be away from home and all that stuff back there. I'll just hang out here and chill for a while."

"Sure. There are lots of neat things to do around here, especially since it's gotten warmer." Sonia found herself sounding more like Tee's aunt than her sister.

Tee responded. "Neat." It sounded to Sonia like Tee was somehow making fun of her. After a moment, Tee poked again. "I really would love to know what that big case is about." There was a bit of mischief in her voice, a silent request for a breach of confidentiality.

Jet must have sensed that it was hard for Sonia to say, "no," to her sister. She jumped in. "Honey, not only can't we tell you about it, we don't even know how in the world we're going to deal with this case."

Sonia put her cup down and started. At least that was something she could share with her sister. "That's right. We've only got five days to solve this thing, and right now we've got thirteen people—"

"Fourteen," Jet corrected.

"Right, fourteen people we've got to talk to, and that doesn't even count all the follow-ups that could come from those first conversations."

"Fourteen," Tee twirled a lock of her long, black hair around a finger, "that's a lot, isn't it?"

Sonia let out a big sigh. "You bet it is. And what's worse, we have a pretty good idea what the core of the case is about, but we haven't decided on how to get started putting the pieces together. Brad will be home tonight. We're going to put him to work talking to some of the people we won't be able to get to."

Tee's head kept nodding. She spoke softly. "Brad's coming home and you're going to ask him for help?"

Jet smiled and tipped her head. "Trust me, girl. He's a sharp one. I'm sure your sister told you he spent twenty years in the Marines, lots of them with NCIS. He's almost as good as your sister at figuring things out, and we can use all the help we can get."

Tee's shapely body seemed to get even smaller as she spoke—softly. "Yeah, I'm sure Brad's sharp. And I'll bet you can use his help."

There was a moment of silence as everyone at the table seemed to ruminate on the situation, then Tee continued. "And he'll be able to help because you'll, what do they say on TV, read him into the case?"

Sonia looked at Tee, sensing she was missing something. "Well, yeah. He can't help us if we don't tell him what's going on."

Tee lifted her coffee cup to her lips speaking over it to her sister. "And why is it okay if you tell him about it?"

Sonia looked at Jet, then back to Tee. "Well, I guess it's because we have a special relationship with him and his firm. We work together sometimes." She turned to her partner. "Right, Jet?"

"That's right." Jet sat up taller, her body language conveying confidence. "When we need some muscle for something or need to tap into some old connections he has, we can go to him for help."

Sonia followed quickly. "And sometimes he needs help from us. An extra pair of eyes, or maybe some task a woman is better suited to." She smiled confidently as well.

Tee put her cup down. "So, your non-disclosure agreement allows you to share information with another firm, Brad's firm?"

Sonia's eyes opened wide. "Now wait a minute. Brad would really be working *for* us as a consultant. He'd be an employee, not just some stranger."

Tee's energy level was subtly rising. "But that does mean that BCI can have more people on staff than just the two of you."

Sonia looked at Jet and shrugged. Jet shrugged as well and looked at Tee. "Well, yes. I guess you could think of it that way."

"Okay then. I'll just sit around being useless and doing *neat* things in Lexington while you guys are killing yourselves tracking down more leads than you could possibly get to—unless . . ." Her palms turned up; she lifted her shoulders.

"No, no, no." Sonia was shaking her head. "I see where you're going with this."

Tee plowed on, the words flying out of her mouth. "Unless, of course, I become a temporary employee of BCI and help you guys accomplish all this work you've got to do and have no chance of completing in five days." The smile on her face was somewhere between smug and joyful.

Jet picked up her paper cup and started tapping its bottom ridge on the table. She spoke to Sonia while looking over her non-existent glasses at Tee. It was pure southern belle. "Well, well, well. Sure 'nuff looks like smarts run in the family." She turned to Sonia. "Smarts and wiseass." She turned back to Tee. "Looks like somebody has figured out a way to worm herself into the firm and us with no reasonable way to say no. Ain't that true, Miss Sonia?"

Sonia's response was just the opposite and just as emphatic. "No. No way I'm letting you get involved with this. Somebody got killed. This could be dangerous. You're not getting anywhere near this thing, Tee."

Tee picked up her all-but-empty cup for effect. "Might as well let me now. You already broke your fancy agreement. I now know that somebody got killed, that you've got more than fourteen people to talk to, and that you have a pretty good idea what the case is about. I'm pretty sure it's your job to figure out who done it. Right?"

Sonia's head was shaking, her toe tapping like mad. "Ab-so-lutely not. You don't know anything about being a PI. We're licensed."

Jet kept her eyes on Tee. "Well, she's smart enough to have just sandbagged the two of us, isn't she?" The accent was gone. "And Lord knows, we sure need the help."

"Really," Tee's tone of voice shifted, cajoling. "I can help. I know I can. Just give me a chance. I'll do anything you ask. Even if you just need somebody to go along with one of you to record stuff or share perspectives."

Jet's eyes were still locked on Tee, but her hand reached out and touched Sonia's arm. "I'm afraid she's right, honey. We need all the help we can get. And I do think that if we make her an employee, we'll be okay with the non-disclosure thing. Heck, if we're not, we can't even get help from Brad, and there's no question we need that."

Sonia looked at her sister through squinted eyes. Part of her was so pissed she could spit. She certainly didn't want her sister getting involved in a dangerous case—a murder case. The other part of her was darn proud of Tee. She chuckled silently. She led us right down the primrose path and sprung her trap just as smooth as silk. Sonia let out a short breath. "Okay, employee number zero-zero-three. You start right now. We'll do the paperwork tomorrow, get you some sort of ancillary standing with the board since you don't have a license. But you do exactly what I say. EX-ACT-LY."

Tee smiled a Cheshire cat smile. "Great. Listen. I'd pay for the next round coffees but I don't have any money. By the way, can I get an advance on my first paycheck?"

9

At seven twenty-two on Friday evening, Sonia and Tee were at Blue Grass Airport, meeting the Delta flight coming from Omaha, Nebraska. They were waiting for Brad Dunham—formerly, Captain Brad Dunham of the United States Marines, assigned to NCIS, the Naval Criminal Investigative Service—the man to whom Sonia Vitale had recently become engaged.

Before meeting him, Sonia had heard a lot about Brad, the sole proprietor of Semper Fi Investigations. In fact, she'd had a pretty negative impression of him. Their first encounter had been in Magee's, where she'd noticed a big man, maybe six-three or six-four, who had to weigh at least two-twenty, all of it lean muscle. But what she had noticed most were his bright, blue eyes, set in a rugged, attractive face. Over the course of several weeks, Brad Dunham had gone from an almost mythical local figure to an adversary, then a partner, and finally, the first man she had cared about since she had been left at the altar by John Eckel three years earlier. After a pretty rocky period, including some revelations about Brad's past, they had finally worked things out, and Sonia had accepted Brad's proposal of marriage.

Waiting at the bottom of the escalator that led to the baggage claim area and the front of the terminal, Sonia was jittery. She couldn't tell if she were more excited about seeing Brad after his having been gone a week or telling him that Tee was in town and would be staying for a while. When he appeared at the top of the escalator, she was certain it was the former. Her chocolate brown eyes radiated joy.

"There's my girl." The sound of Brad's voice was deep and rich, almost as if it came directly from his well-muscled chest. He pulled Sonia's face into his body, smiling. As he did, he looked over her shoulder. "And who's this attractive waif? Anyone I should know?" He closed one eye. "Oh, wait a minute. Didn't I attend your college graduation recently? Aren't you that famous artist, Teresa Di Vitale, painter of the ceiling in the Sistine Chapel?" He closed his other eye instead. "Or was it the painter of the ceiling in her own bedroom?"

Tee gently used her middle finger to scratch her nose.

"Get over here and give me a hug, future sister-in-law." He grabbed her by the wrist and pulled her to him, winding up with both women in his arms. "What are you doing here in town?"

Tee extricated herself from his bear-hug. "Just came down to see my sister. Heard she had gotten in with a bad crowd. Hoping to talk some sense into her."

Sonia stood silently beaming, enjoying the easy relationship that had formed between two people she loved.

"Well, before you get on her for that," Brad picked up the overnight bag he'd dropped at his feet, "this member of that bad element hasn't eaten since he left Omaha. How 'bout I take you two beauties out for dinner? We're just a hop, skip, and a jump from Malone's, and they've got some of the best steaks in town."

There was a huge grin on Sonia's face. "Sounds wonderful. You don't have any real luggage, do you?"

"Never have, Babe. You know that. Now let's get this show on the road before I start rummaging through that huge tote your sister has hanging over her shoulder. God knows what I could find to eat in there."

AFTER A DELICIOUS STEAK dinner and a few glasses of wine, Sonia, Tee, and Brad left Malone's and headed to Brad's home in a nice neighborhood off Tates Creek Road. On the way, Sonia put in a call to Jet and told her to meet them at Brad's place in half an hour. By nine-thirty, though the May evening was comfortably warm, they were all sitting in comfortable chairs around the fireplace in Brad's spacious family room. Brad and Sonia sat next to each other on the couch. Each of the four had a glass of Horatio Blevins Single Barrel Bourbon in their hand. Sonia, Tee, and Jet were drinking theirs on the rocks. Brad had his bourbon neat—no ice, no water, no anything. He had already been told about the case and Tee's new role in the firm.

There was a warm, cordial feeling in the room when Sonia shifted gears. "Okay, enough family and friends." She looked across the faces of her three partners. "We've got five days to solve this case and Day One is almost over. Let's get to work."

"Yes, sir, ma'am." Brad gave her a smiling salute, but then he got down to business as well. "Okay, Jet, did you bring that list of folks that constitute our starting point?"

Jet reached in her purse and took out the list that Mason Holiday had given them. She read off the names of the general managers and master distillers that Holiday had highlighted. "Then, of course, we've got the former wives, the son, the sister, the father."

Brad furrowed his brow. "What about his business relationships? Anyone we can talk to there?"

"Actually, there is." Jet reached for her purse again. "I made a call while you all were out at dinner and I found out the name of his business manager. Turns out it's a woman, Missy Charles.

Apparently, she's been with him for years. Knows everything there is to know about his business dealings." She twisted her lips. "Of course, she may not be willing to tell us *everything*, if you know what I mean."

Sonia sat up tall, indicating she had something important to say. "Which brings me to something that's been bothering me all day. John O'Neal and that guy who helped him—"

"Bobby Ray," Jet interjected.

"Right. O'Neal and Bobby Ray didn't tell the police that they'd found Rasmussen dead, and neither did any of the other bourbon guys." She lifted her shoulders. "But hasn't anyone reported him missing?"

Tee jumped in. "Well, he's divorced, twice, and his son is older. He doesn't live at home, right?"

Sonia pressed. "I guess not, but somebody must have expected to see him."

Jet held up the piece of paper with the business manager's name on it. "You mean somebody like Missy Charles?"

"Yes." Sonia nodded in Jet's direction.

Brad put down his glass. "And that raises another question. How long has he been missing? How long was he marinating in that barrel?"

There was a moment of silence as all four of them thought about both questions. It was Jet who spoke first. "You know, Mason Holiday didn't say. Honestly, I don't think he knows." Her eyebrows went up. "I don't think anyone knows."

"If this was an official NCIS case, I could find out how long he was in the barrel by getting the body into the lab." Brad unconsciously pulled on his ear. "But that's not going to happen."

Sonia looked directly at Tee. "Brad still has connections at NCIS and can find out things most people never could. And he's got a Corvette that's loaded with cameras and other equipment that would blow your mind."

Jet gestured with her bourbon glass. "I'm guessing the best

one to ask is Missy Charles. She's his business manager. She must expect regular contact with him." Jet nodded, agreeing with herself. "She's the one to ask."

It appeared clear that everyone else agreed as well. Brad picked up his glass and toasted Jet. "Well, I guess we know who you're talking to first thing in the morning." He turned to Sonia and Tee. "Now, how are we going to split up the rest of the interviews?"

Sonia raised a finger. "First, though, don't we have to ask who benefits financially, I mean directly."

Brad was quick to respond. "Right, who inherits Victor's money."

Jet looked at Sonia. "You figured out the family relationships. Given he's divorced and only has the one son, wouldn't the boy inherit everything?"

"I guess." Sonia ran her fingers through her hair. "But we should probably try to find out if that's true. That is, if we can do that without raising a lot of suspicion."

There was a long moment of silence as everyone in the room seemed to be thinking about how they might pull that off. Finally, Sonia reached out and put her hand on Brad's knee. It just gave her a sense of comfort to be near him, to be working with him again. "Let's get back on track. I've got to say, I think the bourbon guys are the key to this. Someone in that group must know something. First thing in the morning I want to get in touch with Ed Rollins out at the James Bennington distillery. He's one of the real key players. If nothing else, I think he can give me some context for all of this stuff, send us in the right direction."

"Sounds good." Brad leaned forward. "I'm going to take a shot at the old man. If there's one thing experience has taught me, it's that if a man and his son are in business together, one of two things is true. Either the old man thinks the son hung the moon, no matter what the truth is, or the old man is pissed at the kid. If that's the case, it's either because the kid's no good at doing the old man's job, or because the kid's too good at doing the old man's job. I'd like to find out which of those it is."

A bit uncomfortable with Brad assigning his own task, Sonia hitched, unconsciously squeezing her fingers into a fist. Eventually, she let out a breath she didn't realize she'd been holding. "Okay, then. At least we know how we're starting tomorrow. As soon as we've spoken to that first layer of folks, we'll get in touch with each other and figure out where to go from there."

"Hey," Tee's voice had an edge to it. "What about me? What am I doing first thing tomorrow morning?"

Sonia gave her a motherly look. "Now, Tee. Remember, interviewing folks in a case like this isn't as easy as it looks on TV. You've got to know what to ask, how to read their faces, their body language. I don't think—"

Tee struggled to sit up taller on the soft, cushioned couch. "You don't think what? That I can ask a few simple questions. How the heck am I going to help you guys if all I do is wave goodbye as you go off to interview folks? Is my job simply going to be running downstairs to Magee's to get everyone fresh coffee?"

Sonia wanted to answer "Yes." She still wasn't comfortable with Tee getting involved, really involved, in a dangerous case.

"She's right," Jet interrupted. "Listen, Sonia, we need all the help we can get, and that means letting Tee talk to at least some of the more peripheral folks, you know, just to cross them off the list."

Sonia turned to Brad, looking for support. She was disappointed by the look on his face. "I'm afraid she's right, Babe. Lots of folks to talk to, leads to follow, and no guarantee people will be telling us the truth. For me, if Tee's in, she's in. Let's use her." His voice softened and his bright blue eyes smiled at Tee. "We need to use her."

There was silence in the room as everyone waited for Sonia's response. Finally, she spoke. "Okay. Why don't you go talk to his sister? Just ask her about background stuff, you know, maybe she'll shed some light on why he wanted to bring out Sultan's Choice in the first place. But remember, we don't know who does and who does not know that Rasmussen is dead. You'll have to have a good reason for asking any questions about him at all."

A smile crossed Tee's face. "Yes, ma'am. On it."

Brad lifted his glass high. "Okay, then. Here's to the BCI team. May we all have a productive morning tomorrow."

"Here, here," echoed Jet.

Tee lifted her empty glass as well. The smile on her face made it clear that she more than agreed. Sonia, on the other hand, tried to do her best to be positive. It was all she could do, given her fears for her little sister.

As Tee and Jet stood and headed for the door, Brad pulled Sonia aside, she assumed for a good-night kiss. He did hold her tenderly, stroking her hair and then kissing her lips gently. But when he released from the kiss, he pulled her close and whispered in her ear. "You know I love you, Babe, and I'm glad to be a part of this, but I'm not sure you should have signed that NDA."

Sonia pulled back, looking at him with a furrowed brow. "Why?"

He continued speaking softly, gently, carefully. "I'm just afraid that could come back to bite you in the butt if this whole thing goes south, legally I mean."

His admonition caught Sonia off guard. She respected his many years of experience and the fact that he was just looking after her best interests, but she had carefully considered signing the NDA and she was uncomfortable revisiting her decision. And besides, it was too late now. She reached up, touched his lips with her finger and smiled. "Don't you worry about it. It's all going to work out." She brushed a wisp of hair out of her face. *God, I hope it's going to work out.*

10

Joe Alexander took his normal seat at the bar in Willy B's, a watering hole inside the Riverwalk Plaza hotel in San Antonio. Though money wasn't an issue for the tall, attractive man, he liked this place more than the higher-end hotels like the Hiltons and Marriotts. It was a trendy, boutique hotel, with strong, modern décor and live plant installation filling a long wall.

Dressed in a dark gray, slim-cut suit with a white shirt and subtle French blue skinny tie, he felt comfortable surrounded by business types and well-dressed families. As he planned to tonight, he would often eat dinner sitting at the bar then lose the tie and walk through the hotel's little art museum. That would take him right out onto the famous Riverwalk itself. It made for a nice, professional, yet relaxed, evening for a man who was new in town and lived alone. It also created some nice possibilities for meeting women.

He had seen her two other evenings over the past week. Probably close to five-foot-ten and trim, he'd noticed that she was always dressed in nicely tailored suits. Clearly a professional woman of some sort, she had an attractive, full face, dark red lipstick, and shoulder-length blonde hair.

Like him, she ate dinner sitting at the bar, rather than alone at a table. And although he had seen several men make attempts to join her, she had always found a polite way of making it obvious that she was not interested. Joe was sure of one thing, she was no high-priced escort.

And yet, he was pretty confident that he had caught her scoping him out once on a previous evening and at least once again tonight. Already on his second bourbon, a taste he had picked up in a different part of his life, he was getting pretty close to thinking that he might just explore some possibilities. When she turned and gave him just a hint of a direct smile, a voting lever in his mind tripped—I'm going in.

He walked to her end of the bar. "Listen, I don't have any good pick-up lines, and I've noticed that you've made it clear to several other men that you weren't necessarily looking for company while you ate, but I was—"

"Sit down." Her voice was strong.

"Well," there was no hesitation in his voice, "I guess I was right."

The woman's eyes seemed focused on the bright blue mosaic wall tiles in front of them, just under the vast array of liquor bottles. "Now don't go ruining this by getting overly confident. It could be that the only reason I'm letting you sit here is to keep any of those salesmen from Podunkville in their seats so that they don't come up and embarrass themselves."

Reflexively, Joe moved back a half-step. A moment later he motioned for the bartender to bring him another bourbon. "Can I at least buy you a drink? You know, just to make the charade look a little more realistic."

"Merlot." It was the only word she spoke.

Joe slid his body onto the tall stool next to the woman, all the while wondering if this was a mistake.

Finally, she spoke. "Jane. You can call me Jane."

He nodded slowly then spoke cautiously. "Joe . . . but I would have expected a beautiful woman like you to have a more exotic name."

She turned and gave him a snarky smile and a wink. "I do, but you can call me Jane."

They sat in silence as the bartender brought Joe another James Bennington on the rocks and Jane a glass of merlot. As he waited, something tingled in his mind, something based on his past experiences.

Joe was usually pretty skilled at playing this game, but this woman had him off balance right from the start. He took another shot. "So, you're obviously in town on business."

Before he was able to get to his next sentence, she turned to him. "Are you" she dropped her chin, "in town on business?"

He stumbled over his words. "Well, actually, no. I just don't care much for my own cooking and I go out for dinner most nights. I like this place, the food, the people."

He expected a response from her but got none. Eventually, he felt the need to plow on. "So, am I way off base? You do work here in town, don't you?"

"I work where the work takes me. This week it takes me here. Now, are we going to continue the banal chatter all through dinner or are we going to get out of this place and go somewhere more comfortable."

Once again, Joe was knocked off stride. He recovered quickly. "Do you have a room here?"

She looked at him dismissively. "I may or I may not. Either way, we're not going to my place. I'm no fool. If you want to spend some time with me, we go to your place." Giving him no time to think about things, she put her hand on her purse. "Are we going or am I ordering dinner and sending you back to your end of the bar?"

Joe looked at the bartender, waving his hand over their

drinks. "How much do I owe you?" He threw some cash on the bar, the tab plus a generous tip, and took the woman's arm as she slipped off the tall bar stool.

They walked in silence through the lobby and out onto Villita Street. As they approached the parking lot, Joe asked, "So which car is yours?"

"The red Escalade at the end of the row." She was walking with him but falling just slightly behind. Offhandedly, she asked, "So what do you do for a living, Joe?"

As his mind filled with vague visions of what the evening might bring, he answered. "Oh, I guess you could say I'm in the import-export business. You know, bringing stuff in from other countries."

By the time she responded, the woman was standing a full four steps behind him. "Funny, Joe. I work for people who bring stuff in from other countries."

A flash of recognition tore through Joe's mind. Every hair on his body stood on end. He spun around, only to find the woman standing, legs spread, pointing a black handgun at him.

His training kicked in. Just as she fired, he leaped to his right, along the passenger's side of a parked, red Jeep Wrangler. His move was quick—but not quick enough. The bullet tore through his left side, scorching pain searing his mind. He couldn't help squeezing his eyes shut. Lying on the ground, he froze for an instant.

Within seconds, he heard the sound of her high heels clicking rapidly toward him. Pushing the pain out of his consciousness, Joe lunged to the front of the Jeep, slid around it and squatted as he moved down the driver's side. When he stood, he had his own Glock 19, a small 9mm semi-automatic, in his hand. Looking into and through the car, he saw the woman standing directly opposite him on the other side of the vehicle. Almost simultaneously, she sensed his presence and he fired his weapon. Glass shattered on both sides of the Jeep and a yelp flew out of her throat as she winced and fired at Joe through the same strange portal.

He, of course, had ducked down, certain that neither handgun could penetrate the body of the car. Slipping toward its rear, he was forced to make an instant decision—turn right behind the back of an adjacent Toyota, another SUV, or left behind the vehicle that had already been violated.

He did neither. Taking advantage of the Jeep's high ground clearance, Joe slid, face down, under the car. Looking along the ground, he could see the woman's legs and knees as she squatted at the front of the vehicle, clearly waiting for a sound that might help her locate her quarry. In a battle that would probably be over in less than forty-five seconds, the two were frozen in a stalemate that felt like it lasted an eternity.

Joe watched as the woman cautiously stood and began following his path down the driver's side of the Jeep. Certain that she would be wise enough to peek under the car, he slipped out from under the vehicle on the passenger's side. He moved quickly to a position next to the front tire, hopeful it would block her line of sight as he hid, waiting.

Taking a leap of faith, trusting that she had already peeked under the car, Joe moved. Crouching, he came around the front of the vehicle a second time. Holding his breath, he dared a look down the side of the Jeep. This time, he was rewarded with a view of the woman standing still, her back to him, her ears searching the night for his sounds.

Taking a kneeling position, Joe Alexander carefully aimed his weapon. Fully aware that leaving a dead body on the streets of San Antonio could lead to more trouble than he could handle, he responded according to his training. He placed the bullet squarely in her hip, shattering it and leaving her in such gruesome pain that she could never get off another round, one that might take him down. On the other hand, if it was important enough to her, she might be able to call for help and get picked up by some compatriot, avoiding difficult explanations to the local authorities. At minimum, he figured, she would do her best to concoct a tale of self-defense, blaming the attack on Joe—and that would be just fine with him.

By the time the first curious on-looker was cautiously poking his head around the corner of the Riverwalk Plaza, Joe had slipped out of the parking lot and across Dwyer Avenue, grateful that he had followed his instincts—the urging that always told him to park several blocks away from any building in which he planned to spend significant time.

Afraid to return to his apartment, and holding a blood-soaked handkerchief to his burning side, Joe drove his leased Dodge Charger to the long-term parking lot in which he kept his personal vehicle, a nondescript, relatively new Honda Accord. By morning, he would be hundreds of miles away and a simple phone call to the dealership would close out his lease—although with major penalties. He would be in the wind. For now, however, he had to find a busy Walmart and hope that, using his now stained suit jacket to hide his bloody shirt, he could purchase some sort of antiseptic, bandage, and painkiller without arousing too much suspicion. The wound hurt like hell.

DAY TWO

11

Sonia awoke on Saturday morning to the sound of rain. Her carriage apartment was over a garage on Central Avenue, and she often felt like there was very little between her and the shingles on the roof above her head. The apartment was a simple two-room affair, with a small bedroom and another space that served as kitchen, living room, dining area, and anything else she could imagine. Still, it was a pleasant place and just a short walk from Magee's and the BCI offices. The most frustrating part of her living situation was that the walk in either direction ended in some serious stairs, either up to the BCI offices or up to her apartment.

It wasn't long before Sonia heard Tee rattling around in the kitchen area, apparently dealing with breakfast. She slipped out of bed and stepped into the larger room. Tee was bent over. She spoke into the refrigerator. "You don't have much in the way of food here. Have you given up eating or something?"

Still sleepy in her cotton pajamas, Sonia stretched as she spoke. "I guess I mostly pick up something at Magee's in the morning. You know, almond croissants, the breakfast of champions?"

Tee stood up straight and gave her a look. "It wouldn't be because you don't sleep here very often anymore, would it?"

Sonia could feel a flush skitter across her face. She walked to the counter and turned her attention to her Cuisinart coffee maker, the same one that seemed to be on the set of every TV sitcom she'd seen recently. "I don't know what you mean."

Tee snorted. "Get off it, Sonia. You're engaged to Brad. He lives in that nice house." She cocked her head. "You know, the one with the big bed in the nice bedroom. I'm guessing you've moved in with him and the only reason I had to sleep on the fold-out couch last night was that you were trying to keep up appearances for your baby sister. Am I right?"

"Actually, Tee," Sonia let out a sigh, "you're not right. I know what you're thinking, and maybe I should just go live in that lovely house instead of this tiny apartment, but I just can't get the look on Mom's face out of my mind."

Tee scrunched her face. "What look?"

"The look she'd have if I told her that I'd moved in with Brad, with any man, before we got married."

Tee grabbed an empty bowl and a box of Honey Nut Cheerios. She took a seat at the tiny kitchen table. "How would she know?"

Sonia grabbed an empty bowl as well. "Oh, she'd know. Trust me, somehow, she'd know. Look, I like to think of myself as a modern woman. I'm independent. I have my own life. I have a good job, my own business. But that doesn't wash away all those years of Catholic upbringing, the years with the nuns in elementary and middle school, being dragged to confession once a month and church every Sunday." Tee quietly chomped on her Cheerios as Sonia continued. "And honestly, I'm not sure I want to leave all that behind. It's just who I am."

Tee swallowed and wiped the back of her hand across her mouth. "So, you're still going to mass every Sunday?"

Sonia stopped. "No. I guess I've let that slide for now. But still, there's a part of me that just balks at moving in with Brad before we're married." A memory raced across Sonia's mind, the memory of being left at the altar by the first man she'd been engaged to, John Eckel. She almost said something about that to Tee. Instead, she poured milk over the Cheerios in her own bowl. "And besides, with Brad out of town so much, I'm not sure it would be all that different."

Tee finished another bite and swallowed again. "So, you and Brad just—"

"Enough." Sonia held her hand up, rolling her eyes. "What Brad and I do is none of your business. Now finish your cereal and pour us some coffee. We're not going to Magee's this morning. You've got to get on the phone and track down Rasmussen's sister, and I've got a long drive out to see Ed Rollins. That assumes, of course, I can get Mason Holiday to set up a meeting with him on a Saturday."

TEE BEGAN her first day as a temporary professional private investigator by calling Brad and asking him to use his old NCIS connections to find out the name and location of Victor Rasmussen's sister. By eleven o'clock, she was in her Chevy Caprice, on her way to see Carla Lombardi in a bar on South Mill Street. Not knowing her way around Lexington, she had to use her GPS to locate it. She was pleased to find a parking spot right in front of the place.

The gray, rainy day matched the gloom inside McCullen's Irish Bar when Tee stepped inside just after eleven-fifteen. The green façade, set into a two-story, brick building, had made it obvious that the owners were serious about creating a true Gaelic setting. Lots of wood and brass, kegs mounted on the wall, and multiple dart boards, all played their part as well.

Tee took a moment to orient herself, then stepped to the bar and took a seat. The woman behind the bar—hefty, blonde, mid-fifties or older—walked up to her, wiping her hands on a bar towel. There was no smile on her face when she said, "You going to show me some proof you're old enough to sit at this bar at eleven in the morning?"

Tee was caught off guard. She'd been in plenty of bars before. She'd even played in bars with her old band, The Displaced Souls. But those were always hangouts for people just old enough to be there, or able to pass for being old enough. McCullen 's was not that kind of place.

"Well, you got proof of age or don't you girl? I ain't got all day to wait. Afternoon crowd comes in early on a Saturday. I got to be ready."

Tee reached in her back pocket and took out a small wallet. All it contained were her license, AAA card, insurance card, and about thirteen dollars. She showed the license to the bartender, who all but grabbed it out of her hand. The woman gave Tee and the license a good looking-over.

"Teresa Vitale. Italian, right?" She'd pronounced it Vy-tăl.

"Vi-tah-lay," Tee replied. "Not like the basketball announcer. The name has an accent on the "ah," ends in a long "a." She had the correction down to an art form.

"Yeah, yeah." The woman handed the license back to Tee. "I used to be married to one, you know. Anthony Lombardi. You know him?"

Tee was struggling to not back away from the woman and her harsh tone. She shook her head sharply and frowned. "Don't know him. I'm not from around here."

The bartender rubbed her nose with the back of her hand and twisted her lips. "What can I get you, girl?"

"Well, I was wondering—"

"I meant, what are you drinking? This ain't no library. You come in here, you drink. Now, what can I get you?"

Tee sat up straight. "A beer. Give me a Rhinegeist Cougar."

The bartender stepped back shaking her head. "You're not from around here is right. Listen, girl, that's a Cincinnati beer, local, actually a golden ale. I used to live up there. Now, does this look like some German beer garden?" She squinted her eyes and leaned over the edge of the bar. "No. It's an Irish bar. In Lexington, Kentucky." Her tone got even darker, as did the look on her face. "Oh, we've got Rhinegeist, boss man makes us carry it and we sell our share, but if you ask me, you walk into an Irish bar, you drink an Irish beer." Her hand slapped the bar, "Guinness, Killian's, Harp." She balled up her bar towel and threw it down onto one of the coolers below the bar.

Tee was tempted to simply ask for a Bud, but she was pretty certain that would only make things worse. She took a deep breath, hoping to start over. "Listen, I didn't really come in here for a drink. I'm looking for Carla Lombardi. I think I'm looking for you."

The bartender froze. Tee could see her mind racing. The woman rubbed her hands together as she eased into her next question. "And why would you think I'm Carla Lombardi?"

Tee was trying her best to get on a level emotional playing field with the aggressive woman. Her voice had its own edge. "Well, I know Carla Lombardi works here and that she probably doesn't look Italian. And didn't you just say you'd been married to Anthony Lombardi? Now, I need to speak with Carla Lombardi, and I'm guessing you and she just happen to be the same person."

Carla Lombardi seemed to lose a little steam. She stood silently for a moment then spoke in a softer tone. "Well, you're right about that. I'm not Italian, I just married that piece of garbage." She picked up a new bar towel and started wiping some glasses that were already dry. "And I'm not Irish. In fact, my grandfather came over from Denmark. We're Danish."

Tee lifted her eyebrows just a touch. "Rasmussen?"

Carla's head tipped sharply. "How did you know that?" Her

eyes locked with Tee's brown eyes, eyes darker even than her sister's.

Tee took a deep breath. "Actually, that's why I was looking for you. I'm from Bluegrass Confidential Investigations and I have some questions about Victor Rasmussen, the guy who said he's bringing out a new bourbon. I'm trying to find out something about his background with bourbon. You're his sister, aren't you?"

Carla let out a breath so heavy it was almost as if she had spit. "Half. I'm his half-sister."

Tee didn't say a word. Instead, she picked a red swizzle stick out of a small black, plastic holder and rolled it back and forth along the surface of the bar.

Carla must have sensed that Tee was waiting for more because she continued. "Our father, Carl Rasmussen, married my mother. They named me, their first child, after the bastard. And within two years he'd kicked her out and divorced her. Threw me out with her."

Tee stopped rolling the swizzle. "I'm so sorry, that sounds rough."

Carla's face reddened. She stopped wiping. "And I don't mean he just kicked me out of the house. What I mean is that he kicked me out of his life. I never saw the bastard again, except once, when I was around seven or so, my mom and I were walking around downtown and this fancy car happens to pull up right where we're standing." Carla's eyes rose to the metal, patterned ceiling. "Out steps my father from one side of the car and his new wife from the other. She's all dressed up real nice, so's the old man. And she's pregnant." Carla shrugged. "I guess with Victor." She leaned over the bar, speaking softly, almost conspiratorially. "And you know what. I don't even think he recognized my mother." She gave her head a nasty shake. "If he did, he just totally ignored her . . . and me. Wouldn't have even known it was him if my mother hadn't started cursing under her breath. I forced her to tell me why. The bastard just kicked us out of his life like we were last week's trash." She turned and took a few steps down the bar, apparently doing some busywork as she pulled herself together.

Tee sat silently for a few moments. Then she asked, as gently as she could, "So, you never had any kind of relationship with your brother, I mean your half-brother, Victor?"

Carla walked back to where Tee was seated. Her lips took on a pout. "Nah. Heard his name. Know about him. Heard he's been real successful in my father's business. That's about it." She paused. "Why are you asking, anyway?"

Tee sensed she should be on guard. She spoke very carefully though trying to sound nonchalant. "Well, we've heard he's going into the bourbon business and bringing out a real high-end product. We're trying to find out a little about his background with bourbon production. We thought his sister might be able to tell us something." She reached her hand behind her neck, through her thick black, shoulder-length hair, and scratched gently. "Looks like you really don't have much to say about that, right?"

Carla's left eye squinted. "Why don't you just ask him?"

"Makes sense, right?" Tee gave Carla her warmest smile. "But you don't ask the guy trying out for the basketball team if he's any good, now do you? You ask around. We'll be talking to him about everything as well, but we'd like to get some unbiased information from other folks who know him first. Now, that makes sense, too. Right?"

Carla paused before answering. "Look, I don't really know anything about my brother. Can't say I miss him. Can't say I've got anything against him. He's just not part of my life. Never has been." She shrugged. "Guess I wish him the best. Actually, I'd like to say we're both in the bourbon business." She looked behind her at the display of whisky bottles that ran from one end of the bar to the other, then smiled a yellow smile. "But I sell a hell of a lot more scotch whisky than bourbon, as you can tell." It was the first smile Tee had gotten out of her the whole time.

Tee tapped the bar twice with her knuckle. "Thanks for your time, Carla." She was at a loss for anything else to say. "Good luck with your afternoon crowd." She spun around on the barstool, slipped off and walked out the door. When she hit the damp but fresh air of South Upper Street, she took in a deep breath. It had been her first professional interview as a PI, and it had been a doozy.

12

Jet had gotten an earlier start than Tee. She'd called The Rasmussen Company, only to find out that her assumption was correct; Missy Charles didn't work on Saturdays. Making up some story about being from out of town and needing to talk to the business manager of the company about some on-site emergency, Jet had managed to wangle a phone number for Missy out of the young woman who was manning the phones. At eight forty-five, she'd called Missy's cellphone and asked for a meeting. Missy had told her that she was about to step onto the court at the Lexington Indoor Tennis Club and asked if the meeting could be put off until Monday. Without giving her much of an explanation, Jet had pressed and managed to get Missy to agree to meet at the club an hour and a half later.

Jet had never been to the club or even been much of a tennis player, but she wasn't intimidated by the setting. Given her experience as a girl's track star at Woodford County High School, she was comfortable around athletic venues. On the other hand, her tight jeans, bright yellow, sleeveless top, and red wedge sandals stood out amongst the white-over-white-over-white so many of the women were wearing for their weekend excursion into health and fitness.

Jet had looked on the company website and seen a picture of Missy Charles, so she had little trouble finding Missy as she walked off the court. Given the clothing Jet was wearing, Missy seemed to sense Jet's identity easily as well.

"Miss Jet, I assume?" Missy threw a white towel over her shoulder. She was clearly in her late forties or even early fifties, but her hair and face were well-conditioned and very pleasing. She looked trim and fit in her unofficial uniform. "Nice to meet you."

"Jet," she stuck out her hand. "It's just Jet. Thanks for taking the time."

Missy Charles looked Jet over somewhat cautiously. "So, you never did tell me what was so important that we had to meet on a Saturday morning."

Jet stuck with the style that suited her best—blunt. "Yeah, well if I had, I was pretty sure you would have put me off until Monday." She smiled.

Missy nodded gently, a form of tacit acceptance. "Well, there'll be a penalty for that deceit." She continued. "There's a coffee bar around the corner and down the hall. Decent lattes, but seriously over-priced. You're buying."

Jet hitched for a moment, then made a grand gesture with her arm. "Lead on."

When the women had gotten their lattes and taken their seats, Missy took the lead. "Okay. You've certainly gotten my attention. Now, what's this all about?"

Jet was tempted to spin a yarn about being a writer for some bourbon magazine, someone who was trying to get an exclusive story about the new bourbon Victor Rasmussen was promising. At the last minute, however, a close look at Missy Charles had given her pause. In Jet's mind, there was every reason to believe that the attractive, well-kept, clearly successful woman she was sitting with was exactly the kind of woman who might read bourbon magazines; it was possible she could sniff Jet out as an impostor with just a few simple questions. Jet decided to go in a different direction. "I'm not sure I'm at liberty to say."

That response set Missy back for the briefest moment, but she was quick to recover. "Very interesting. Go on."

The thought flashed through Jet's mind that this woman might well be quite good at playing chess. She hoped she could pull this off. "Well, let's just say that I represent a small group of investors who are always interested in finding, how would you say it, unusual opportunities."

Missy's face lost a little luster. "Listen . . . ah, Jet. The Rasmussen Company has all the capital it needs to continue being very successful, in fact, to continue to grow. I'm not sure what your," she used her fingers to create air quotes, "*group* is thinking, but I'm pretty certain we're not interested."

Jet felt the chill coming off Missy Charles and knew she had to work quickly. She smiled broadly. "Oh, Ms. Charles. The people I represent have no interest in your employer's roofing business." She looked at Missy over the glasses she never wore. "I'm sure you know what I mean."

Jet could see that she had scored a point with that answer. Missy seemed just a bit flustered. "Honestly, I don't think I do."

Jet took a slow, deliberate sip of her latte, her eyes on Missy the whole time. Then she looked down at her cup. "Interesting how important the taste of a fine beverage can become to some folks," she looked up, "isn't it?"

Missy Charles sat silently for a moment, the subtle look on her face making it obvious that her mind was running a mile a minute. Finally, a spark of recognition crossed her face. "Are you talking about a certain beverage that might be said to have historical importance in our fine commonwealth?" Her eyes searched Jet's face for a response.

"Let's just say that the finer things in life often require a process of aging. Wouldn't you agree?"

A tiny smile touched the corners of Missy's lips. "I do believe I understand what you're saying."

Jet could sense Missy playing things as close to the vest as she was herself. "I'm glad." She leaned in, her voice becoming softer, more discreet. "And would you agree that if someone had found a way to bypass part of that aging process and still wind up with a beverage of the highest quality, that person would be on the path to a special sort of success?" She smiled ever so slightly. "One might say a level of success almost hard to believe?"

Missy took a long sip of her own. "Listen, Jet." She spoke softly and had no problem with the name this time. "I think I understand completely the type of circumstance to which you are referring. Unfortunately, I'm afraid I have very little information to share with you about that situation." She picked up a small, square napkin and blotted her lips. "And even if I did, I would not be at liberty to share it."

Jet took a moment to look around the coffee bar, taking in the small tables, the two-some of women in white-on-white-on-white, the bored-looking young girl with the perfectly cut hair behind the counter. She was hoping to give the impression that she was about to say something of great import. She leaned back in her chair. "Okay then, Ms. Charles. I guess I'll have to take my questions directly to Mr. Rasmussen."

"Good luck with that," Missy almost snorted. She gave Jet a snarky smile. "He's in Europe."

Jet was truly taken aback. She used a sip of her latte to help hide her surprise. "Oh, is he? And how long will he be there?"

The tone of the conversation had shifted from conspiratorial to quietly confrontational. Missy shrugged. "Actually, I don't know. He's off galivanting around Europe, supposedly learning about the history of . . ." She stopped herself. The next words out of her mouth were slow and almost sensual. "The history of creating finer things." She ended with slightly pouted lips.

Jet knew she had to stay with this line of questioning—without being obvious. "And how long has he been in Europe, if you don't mind me asking?"

Missy took a final sip of her latte. There was nothing dramatic in her motions or speech. "He left about ten days ago." She didn't elaborate.

"And he left you in charge?"

The look on Missy's face instantly told Jet that she had pushed the wrong button. "Yes, he left me in charge." Missy's tone was sharp, defensive. "I've been his right-hand for almost twenty years. If something happened to him, I wouldn't have the slightest problem keeping that business running."

Unconsciously, Jet's hand flew up in surrender. "I'm sorry, Missy. I didn't mean anything like that." She shrugged. "I was just wondering if you were able to stay in touch with him, you know, about day-to-day issues."

Missy backed down a bit, fiddling with the napkin. "Yes, we talk every day."

Jet struggled to keep her face blank. "Every day?"

"Sure, via email. Each night I send him any questions that arose during the day. Given the different time zones, by the time I get to work the next morning, I've got my answers . . . for what they've been worth lately."

"Oh." Jet wasn't quite sure what to say. Finally, she looked down at her watch and tried to rev herself up one last time. "Look, it's getting late, and I've taken up a lot of your Saturday. Just do me a favor, if you don't mind."

Missy's eyes crinkled just a bit as she spoke. "What?"

Jet jotted her name and phone number on a napkin, hoping to solidify the impression that she couldn't reveal her employer's identity. She pushed it across the table to Missy as she spoke.

"When next you speak to Mr. Rasmussen, ask him if he has any areas in which his attempts to create finer things might use a little support." She stood up. "Thank you for your time, Missy." She slipped out of her chair, turned sharply, and got herself out of the tennis club as quickly as she could.

13

A person's address was one of the kinds of information Brad could easily get from his former colleagues at NCIS. That morning he had gotten Carla Lombardi's address for Tee and an address for Rasmussen's father as well.

Around ten o'clock, Brad pulled up to the metal bars that led to a gated community off Tates Creek Road, not far from his own home. The door of the guard booth slid open, revealing a man in khaki slacks and a sharply pressed white shirt, an epaulet on each shoulder. A dark blue ball cap with the logo of a security company completed the image. The crisp uniform gave the impression of professional protection. The gray hair, bent shoulders, and slack skin of the body within created a significant dissonance with that allusion.

"I'm here to see Mr. Rasmussen," Brad answered to the guard's unspoken question.

"Do you have an appointment?" His voice was more robust than his body would have implied.

Brad smiled comfortably. "No, but I'm sure he'll want to see me, it's about his son." He gave the guard a friendly smile and waited patiently while the man phoned the Rasmussen residence, his Corvette purring quietly, a powerful wildcat lying at rest.

"He said he'll see you right now." The guard pointed as he bent toward the car. "It's 7722, just around the bend on the right."

Brad knocked on the door. He was surprised when it was answered by a middle-aged woman in a pink dress that gave the impression of being some sort of uniform. "Za mister is expecting you." The Germanic flavor of her speech was hard to miss. "Right this way, *bitte*." She stopped, turned back to Brad and spoke softly. "Be kind, he can't be upset, *ja*? He is not well."

Brad followed her clicking heels through the marble hallway, past the piano room, and into the den. He took in the sophisticated surroundings. Dark green walls, dark walnut furniture, touches of brass throughout. The smell of Lemon Pledge was pervasive in the room. He chuckled silently. I guess if you make a ton of money putting roofs on houses for a living you get to build a heck of a nice one for yourself. A moment later he looked up to see the father entering the room from the other end. "Mr. Rasmussen. Thank you for taking the time to see me."

In his eighties, Carl Rasmussen, Victor's father, was a visual dichotomy, much like the guard at the gate. Dressed in dark brown slacks, cordovan penny loafers, and a white, expensive-looking polo shirt, the gray-haired man appeared ready to head out for a successful day's work, the owner of a large and successful local roofing company. Conversely, the tubes running around his head and to his nose came off a tall, thin tank he pulled along with him as he entered the room. His face was sunken, sallow. He gave Brad a fragile wave, then headed directly for a leather recliner, an obvious favorite, and much more well-worn than any other piece of furniture in the room. "Have a seat Mr. . . ." His voice was as thin as he was. Raspy, airy.

"Dunham, sir, Brad Dunham." Brad took a seat in a leather chair opposite the old man. He nodded and spoke softly, "Very nice," indicating his appreciation of the room itself.

Carl Rasmussen sat silently, clearly waiting for Brad to begin. "Mr. Rasmussen, I'm here to ask a few questions about your son." His voice was gentle. "Would that be alright?"

Rasmussen focused his blue eyes, much paler than Brad's, directly on his visitor. "Well, I guess that would depend on exactly what those questions were about and who you are."

Brad smiled, hoping to appear as unthreatening as possible. "Oh, these are just a few simple questions about his new business ventures. I'm a potential business partner of Victor's. Honestly, I would have asked him the questions in person if I had the opportunity. It just seems like I'm having a little trouble connecting with him."

Brad was hoping for some sort of response from Rasmussen but got none. He decided to jump right in. "I understand your son has worked with you for quite a while."

The old man nodded. His eyes became just a bit watery. "You know, he was quite the football player. Tight end for Henry Clay High School when they won the state championship."

He stopped there, leaving Brad waiting for more. "I see."

Rasmussen bobbed a little as he spoke. "Went on to play for the University of Kentucky for two years, well, almost two years, 'til they treated him badly. He had to leave the team. Couldn't take it anymore. They accused him of selling drugs to his teammates." He shook his frail head. "It was all bullshit." He stopped, taking a deeper, labored breath. "Finally dropped out of school altogether and came to work with me in the company."

Brad smiled politely. Here we go. The kid hung the moon. "Can you tell me a little more about the family?"

"Got married in '55 I think; I know I was twenty. Married a girl I met in a bar." He gave Brad a look that was just a touch salacious. "She was crazy, but boy she was something else. Hot to trot if you know what I mean."

He reached over, taking a sip of water from the glass the woman in the pink dress had left for him as if it were part of a special routine. "Hell, we were only married two years and I had to get rid of her." He waved a frail hand back and forth. "Crazy. Sexy. I always thought she might be running around on me."

Brad was working hard to stay patient. "And the business? When did that start?"

The old man paused and took another labored breath. "Well, I guess it was right after I booted her. I wanted to get started, you know, really started, getting somewhere. I'd been putting roofs on for other guys and had learned a lot. So, when she was gone, I took every penny I had and started a roofing business under my own company name, The Rasmussen Company."

He swallowed awkwardly. "And I wasn't putting on anything but the best. Not super fancy, you know, but high-quality. I watched over every guy that worked for me. I bought the best materials I could get my hands on." He pointed a crooked finger at Brad. "No one put on higher quality roofs or put them on any better than Carl Rasmussen. You can count on that."

Brad was listening patiently. "And your son, Victor? When did he come along?"

Rasmussen let out a little chuckle. "Yeah, my son. Wasn't too long after the first wife was gone that I married again. Harriet. Just the opposite of the first one. Nice, easy to deal with, compliant." He winked at Brad. "But no slouch in bed, if you know what I mean."

Brad smiled passively. Damn, this guy's a real son-of-a-bitch.

The old man reached for the glass of water. Misjudging its location, he knocked it off the table, making a wet mess on an obviously expensive rug. Brad rose up in his chair, but Rasmussen raised his shaking hand and stopped him. "Don't worry. The woman will get it later." He shook his head, looking at the glass on the floor. "Damn glasses. Bottoms are so small they're always falling over on me." Rasmussen looked back at Brad, seemingly confused, having lost his train of thought.

Brad helped him out. "You married Harriet . . . ."

"Yes, yes, Harriet. Nice lady, but boring. Couldn't stand her after a while. Divorced her too, but not before she gave me Victor. She's dead now, for years." He seemed to mentally drift away for a moment.

Brad had spent hours patiently waiting for victims or suspects to tell their stories. He was having no problem waiting for the old man to get to important things. "And the business?"

Rasmussen smiled. "Yes, the business. It became very successful." He grinned at Brad. "You can make a hell of a lot of money putting quality roofs on expensive houses . . . if they're worth it. And mine were. Top quality."

"And when did Victor join the business?"

Rasmussen closed his eyes for a moment. "After that thing at UK, the drugs and everything." He shook his head again. "Sad, sad."

Brad couldn't quite tell whether the father felt his son was guilty or wrongly accused. He just nodded, hoping the old man would continue.

"Anyway, Victor dropped out of school and came to work for me. At first, he just helped me put roofs on those high-end houses." The old man took a deep, shaky breath. "But one day he comes to me and tells me we should get into commercial roofing as well. I didn't really agree with him, it's a whole different animal, but I wanted to let him feel like he really was part of the business, not just an employee." He looked closely at Brad, "You know how that is." Brad nodded again, staying silent.

"Anyway, those first commercial roofs were pretty nice. Not the highest quality, but still good roofs. Nice. People liked them. We got a lot more contracts." The white-haired head wobbled slightly. "But that got Victor going. Next thing you know we were doing more and more projects." His chin dropped a little. "More commercial buildings and more homes, less and less quality."

Brad saw what appeared to be remorse creeping across the old man's face. "I see."

By then, Rasmussen's face was actually looking downward. "Strange. You develop a reputation by doing good work, high-quality work, then the company makes a fortune churning out job after job that . . ." He stopped, seemingly unable or unwilling to finish the sentence.

After a long moment, Brad asked, "And Victor? He was okay with that arrangement—lower quality, more profit?"

The old man sat silently.

"And he's running things now?"

Rasmussen looked up, pale blue eyes imploring bright blue eyes for understanding. "It's all his now. I'm too old. The only part of me that's still in the business is my name. He runs it the way he wants." Brad could feel the old man's energy rising. "In fact, he's not even really running it anymore." The crooked finger came up again, pointing at Brad. "It's that Missy Charles, his assistant manager. If it weren't for her the whole damn thing would go to hell." His eyes squinted. "But it's not her fault. He's the boss. He's just left a vacuum. She had to fill it." He leaned toward Brad. "And she's damn good at it."

Brad waited another moment to see if anything else would come out of Rasmussen's mouth. Nothing came. Brad pressed. "So, what's Victor up to these days? I heard he bought a race-horse, and now he's talking about bringing out a high-end line of bourbon."

The old man reached for the water glass that was no longer there then pulled his hand back. He gave Brad a sly look. "You know, it's women. They're the source of all our trouble." He chuckled, "And sometimes one man's trouble is another man's fortune. Seems like some poor fellow over in Arabia or some such had this great racehorse and thought he was going to get richer than he already was. But then he gets himself all tangled up with the daughter of the head guy over there and next thing you know he's running for his life. Got to sell the horse." Rasmussen's finger wagged again. "And who do you think managed to steal that horse away for a song?" A big smile crossed his face. "My boy, Victor. Next thing you know Victor's got himself a big-time winner. And do you know what comes with that, Mr. Dunlop?"

Brad let the mistake go by. "What?"

"Money. Money and prestige, just the things that Victor has been chasing all his life." His eyes squinted, his voice got smaller. "Not quality, not reputation, money and prestige." His lips curled, almost in disgust.

Brad sat silently, patiently listening. Hung the moon? Maybe not so much. "And do you know anything about the bourbon he's planning on marketing? Do you know where he's going to distill it? Distill it, or maybe purchase it?"

Carl Rasmussen waved his hand. "Bullshit. Probably just more of his bullshit." He snorted. "I been drinking fine bourbon all my life, and one thing I can tell you for sure, you can't come up with that stuff in a few months. He's either buying it, stealing it, or this is just more of his bullshit." He licked his lips. "I wouldn't spend a lot of time worrying about it if I were you."

Brad looked at Rasmussen. He could tell the conversation had taken a lot out of the old man. He didn't want to press things further. Besides, he'd gotten plenty of information out of him, more, in fact, than he had expected. "One last question, if you don't mind, sir."

Rasmussen looked up at him. Brad couldn't tell which looked more worn out, the old man or the leather chair. "Do you know where your son is now?"

He shrugged. "Who knows. Sometimes I don't talk to him for a week or two."

Brad pressed. "But you don't know where he is right now? Maybe out of town or something?"

Rasmussen seemed to take offense. "I told you. Sometimes the bastard doesn't call me for weeks. What's it to you?"

Brad wanted to ask about the last time Rasmussen had heard

from Victor but he felt like that window had already closed. He took a breath and spoke calmly. "And you don't know if there are people he's having any problems with?"

The old man dismissed the question with the wave of a frail hand and a sneer on his face. "No more than I can count on two hands." He finished with a snort.

Brad sat up taller in the leather chair. "Well, I want to thank you for your time, sir. I appreciate your talking to me." Brad stood and began walking toward the door.

Rasmussen surprised him. "I know where he is."

Brad turned, totally off guard. "You do?"

"Out screwing. Screwing some woman, or screwing some family, or screwing any fool who'd go into business with him." He looked Brad in the eye. "And you, Mr. Dunlop? Are you a fool?"

Brad walked over to the man. He reached out and took a frail hand in his own and shook it gently. "I hope not, Mr. Rasmussen. I truly hope not."

14

Sonia had made an early call to Ed Rollins, the Master Distiller at the James Bennington distillery in Clearview, Kentucky. Rollins' secretary had said that he wouldn't be in, but when Sonia mentioned Mason Holiday, she was put on hold. A few minutes later Sonia was told to be there at eleven o'clock. As she hung up the phone, her eyes rested on the Smith & Wesson *Airweight* sitting on her nightstand in its holster. She felt uncomfortable about arming herself as she went to have a conversation with one of the leaders of the bourbon industry, right at his company's main facility. Still, she put her left foot on a small stool near her bed, grabbed the holster, and brought it to her ankle. I'm either committed to being armed at work or not.

The drive from Lexington to Clearview took a little less than an hour and a half, a pleasant ride through rural Kentucky. Sonia left her car in the parking lot in front of an odd-looking, brown and brick, two-story structure. The logo of the James Bennington company was emblazoned across its face. She walked around the campus a bit before heading for the main office and was impressed with its size; building after building, including the actual distillery and rackhouses nine stories tall, were spread out across the property.

Sonia walked into the main office and asked for Ed Rollins. She was disappointed when she was told that he wasn't on the property but that she was expected and would be meeting with Oscar Branch, a man who had a long history with the company.

Sonia was escorted into a small, private conference room. Sitting before her, in a dark brown, leather, wingback chair, was a man who appeared to be in his mid-to-late eighties. There was a glass tumbler holding a half-inch of amber liquid sitting on a small round table next to him. Gray-haired and dressed in a flannel shirt and blue jeans that were by no means of the hip designer variety, he wore a brimmed, felt hat. Though he was indoors; round, dark-lensed sunglasses sat on his weathered face.

He smiled at Sonia warmly and gestured for her to take a seat. "Being a gentleman," his voice was strong, but edged with the rasp of time, "I would normally stand for a young woman like yourself. But these bones and joints are a mite tired, and if you don't mind, I'll just tip my hat." His hand touched the felt brim for the briefest moment.

"Certainly, sir." Sonia smiled warmly. "Not a problem." She took a seat in a matching chair, noticing how beautifully the room all came together—leather chairs, hardwood flooring, rustic paneled walls, and a fireplace stacked with wood that wouldn't be lit until next fall. "Thank you so much, Mr. Branch, for taking the time to meet with me. Unfortunately, I'm not sure that you're the one who can help me with my questions."

A smile crept across Oscar's face, showing his yellowed teeth, probably from a lifetime of smoking or chewing. "Darlin'," he shook his head gently, "there's nothing that goes on around here that I don't know about. The first thing Rollie did when he came back from that meeting with John O'Neal was tell me all about it." He smacked his lips, leaving Sonia wondering if there was a pinch of tobacco between his cheeks and gums at that very moment. "In fact, if there's anyone here can tell you about how things go on in the world of bourbon, it's me. Been part of the brotherhood since I was fifteen. Worked for almost every distiller what is or was. You got a question about bourbon and its people, nobody more likely to give you the answer than me."

Sonia ran her fingers through her hair and dove in. "Well, it seems we both know what happened to Mr. Rasmussen; and it's become my job, or my firm's, to figure out two things, who and why. Obviously, Mason Holiday thought that talking to the leading people in the industry would help me accomplish that. So, I guess I'm here to ask if you can shed any light on either of those questions."

Oscar gave her an almost fatherly smile. "All I can say is this, I got no idea of the who, and to understand the why you got to understand bourbon, what it is, where it comes from," his palms opened and traced a circle in the air, "the whole big picture."

Sonia got the immediate sense that she wasn't about to get any quick answers here, but she knew a man like Oscar Branch needed to be given time to answer questions in his own way, that there might be some nuggets in his answer that even he wasn't aware of. She put on a patient smile. "Well, I do know it's considered the all-American drink."

"Hmph. You would think so. Wasn't always the case." Sonia sensed that behind those dark glasses his eyes were taking on a wistful look. "Listen," he started, "America's first drink was rum, even before there were Americans." His face twitched into a wink. "See, the British grew sugar cane in the Caribbean, turned it into molasses, sent that to New England to be turned into rum." His head tipped downward as he took a deep breath. "Sent that rum to Africa and traded it for slaves, then sent them slaves back to the Caribbean." He ran his curved index finger along the top of his chin as if it was a habit grown out of years of chewing tobacco. "Dark times."

There was silence in the room for a moment, then Oscar

brightened. "Anyway, rum was the American drink for a long time."

Sonia was hoping to get on with things. "So, after independence, we shifted to corn liquor?"

She watched a playful smile cross his lips. "Darlin', drinking habits die hard. Rum was still the main American drink until well after Daniel Boone and those boys opened up the Cumberland Gap and folks poured in through those mountains to Appalachia, into what's now Kentucky." He stopped, reached out, and took hold of his glass of amber liquid. He held it out to Sonia as if in a toast, and took a sip. "Would you like a little something, darlin'? You look a bit parched."

It being just past eleven in the morning, Sonia decided to decline, though the thought of taking a break from Oscar's instruction had its appeal. "No thank you. Can we go on?"

"Sure, sure." Oscar put down his glass. "So, after Daniel Boone opens up this part of the country, the Scots-Irish start pouring in." His face twitched into a wink again. "Now, those people, they knew how to distill liquor. They also knew that it didn't make a lick of sense trying to transport molasses over those mountain roads. But there was something else, something better. They were surrounded by beautiful, sweet corn. Corn that grew so easy that even on their tiny parcels of land, up in the hollers of the mountains, they could produce more than they ever could use."

Sonia interrupted confidently. "Or get to market easily."

Oscar smiled broadly. "Exactly. Next thing you know, on this side of the mountains, corn is the way to make liquor." He plucked his chin with his thumb in such a way as to put an exclamation point on his thought.

Sonia was hoping to wrap this portion of the lecture up. "So, as long as it's made from corn, liquor is considered bourbon, right?"

Oscar shook his head. "Darlin', I could go on for hours telling you the history of bourbon, but let's just say it's got to be made from a mash bill that's fifty-one percent corn and there's a whole bunch more rules and regulations you got to follow if you're gonna call it bourbon."

Sonia slowly rubbed her hands together as she tried to get back on track. "Now that we've got that settled, let's get back, if not to the who, to the why."

15

Oscar Branch reached down to the floor and picked up the cane Sonia had failed to notice as she sat talking to him. With effort, he rose up out of his chair. "Come with me, darlin'."

Sonia rose as well, waited for him to walk past her, then followed the octogenarian through the room and out of the building. They walked together toward the main distilling plant. As she walked next to him in the warmth of the day, Sonia could almost feel the sense of pride that swelled in the old man.

Oscar coughed quietly and looked out over the different buildings. "You know why Kentucky is the heartland of bourbon?" He never looked down at her.

Sonia answered as her eyes tried to follow his. "Actually, no. I really don't."

"Three reasons." He stopped walking. "First, it's the water. You see, so much of Kentucky rests on a bed of limestone. When the rains come, that limestone acts as a filter that takes iron out of the water." He turned and looked down at her. "That iron would make the mash dark and the bourbon would have rough flavor." He grinned. "You know, it's that iron-free water which is rich in calcium that makes the bluegrass so good for horses, too." He started walking again. "The water we all use, all the brotherhood, comes from springs full of clean, limestone water."

He took a deep, slow breath. "Now, the second thing is the climate. We've got the perfect climate for making bourbon."

Sonia felt like she should comment or ask a question, but she was pretty certain Oscar would go on without her doing either.

Oscar pointed with his cane. "You see, we store the barrels in these here rackhouses, tall wooden buildings with no temperature control and dirt floors. We have hot summers here and mild winters. When the heat comes on good and fierce in the summer it forces the liquid to expand, pushing it into the wood of the charred barrels. In the winter, the liquid cools and contracts, drawing it back out. In and out, year after year." He ran his finger along his chin again. "When they finally pour it out, what went in as a clear liquid comes out with a beautiful amber color and all the rich, vanilla and caramel taste that nature stored in those oak staves of the barrel." He looked down at Sonia with a mischievous grin on his face. "It's as if God, himself, wanted us to be the ones who would help Him bring this beautiful nectar to His people."

Oscar was quiet then. Finally, Sonia nudged him. "And the third reason?"

"Oh. Some folks say it's the oak for the barrels, but that wood grows all over the country. No, it's the abundance of good sweet corn. Most of the distilleries here have special relationships with local growers, people who will actually grow their corn with bourbon in mind. Just the right sweetness and flavor for our needs."

As they walked on, Oscar lifted his cane again to point to a set of barrels that indicated the several major bourbons, James Bennington, Bartholomew Hughes, Kendall Run, that were produced at the facility. "You know how it is that we make all these different bourbons here?"

"Different ways of making it?" Sonia ran her fingers through her hair, a little uncomfortable about her lack of knowledge.

"Well yes, in a sense. The process is the same. It's the ingredients that change."

Sonia looked at him. "I thought it was always corn, right?"

He shook his head slowly, "Yes, darlin', it's all about the corn. But there's so much more. The corn got to be fifty-one percent of the mash bill, though it's usually between sixty and eighty percent. The other grains are barley and rye, though some folks, like Settler's Pride, use wheat to make the bourbon a little smoother on the tongue. These different mash bills are pretty common knowledge. But it's the yeast, that's where it gets personal."

Sonia's head turned quickly around. She hadn't expected the word, "personal."

"That's right, darlin'," Oscar grinned at her as he kept walking. "Each company produces its own. In fact, the reason we can make so many different bourbons at the same facility is that each one uses a different mash bill and a unique yeast recipe." He stopped, leaning on his cane and looking off into the sky. "And if you want to hear about one reason why somebody might have popped ol' Victor Rasmussen into that barrel, there's one right there. If somebody thought Victor had stolen, or was trying to steal, their yeast recipe, or worse yet some actual yeast, some bad things could happen."

Sonia reached out and grabbed his arm instinctively. "Aren't there legal protections? Wouldn't someone just go to the authorities about it?" She wished he didn't have those dark sunglasses on so she could read his eyes when he looked at her.

"Darlin', that may be true. But I told you, this is personal. This is family history, family tradition, family reputations." He started walking again. "Sure, there are legal remedies and all that, but if you're looking for a reason someone might take things into their own hands," he spit some tobacco juice into a nearby planter, "that might be one. Yes, ma'am, that might be one."

Finally, Sonia was getting to the kind of information she

wanted. Her eyes widened as she asked the next question. "And is that possible? Could Victor or someone who worked for him have stolen the yeast recipe of one of the other distillers?"

Oscar stopped again and turned to her. As he started to speak, his face twitched into that wink again. "That I don't know, darlin'. It would sure take some doing. Each distiller got their recipes and their yeasts under lock and key. No question, it would have to be some kind of inside job."

Sonia paused for a moment, then took a seat on a park-like bench, tacitly inviting Oscar to join her. "So, what you're saying is that the notion of Victor Rasmussen somehow stealing the yeast recipe, or even some actual yeast, from one of the distillers is hard to imagine but certainly not out of the realm of possibility?"

Though Oscar was sitting next to Sonia, his eyes roamed the vast campus as he spoke, seemingly taking great pleasure in it. "Not out of the realm of possibility."

Sonia ran her fingers through her hair again as she tumbled ideas through her mind. Finally, she asked, "What about this notion of him bringing high-end bourbon to the market without the years it takes to create it? Without twelve, fifteen, twenty years to age it? What about that?"

Oscar ran his finger along his chin again. "Darlin', that's a tough one. Time. It takes time to make bourbon. The law says it takes a minimum of two years, but no distiller worth his salt is selling anything less than four years old." He pulled a red handkerchief out of his baggy pocket and wiped his chin, returning it without comment. "And if it doesn't say anything about age on the label you can be pretty sure it spent about four years in the barrel, not much more."

Sonia's foot was tapping. She needed to get an answer here and Oscar wasn't being much help. "And?"

"And there's no way a man makes a *good* bourbon right out of the chute. Takes years to refine the process, to develop the yeast recipe, to experiment with the mash bill, to tweak the cooking and cooling processes. And that's only half of what it takes." Oscar stood up without explanation and started to walk away.

Sonia stood up quickly but sensed she wasn't supposed to follow. "Oscar?"

He spoke without stopping or turning to face her. "Nope. That's a tough one. A real tough one."

Sonia soon found herself standing alone, watching the old man shuffle back toward the building from which they had come. Whether she liked it or not, she knew their time together was over.

16

Brad's conversation with Carl Rasmussen had finished around ten forty-five. It being early in the day, and the clock ticking on the investigation, he decided to move directly to his next interview, Sherry Rasmussen, one of bourbon-soaked Victor's wives, his second. Brad hoped to find out more about the man who wound up floating in a barrel of bourbon, more about who he was, who he was associated with. Sherry Rasmussen lived down in London, Kentucky, about an hour and twenty minutes south on Interstate 75. The trip would cost him several hours.

Brad found Sherry at her workplace, a local eatery just off the interstate, Bob's Pitstop. He was glad for the opportunity to grab a little lunch in the simple brick building with battleship gray walls. Sitting alone at the faux marble counter, he briefly glanced at two truckers stretched out in one of the four red-leather booths, probably tired of being cramped up in their big-rigs' cabs. He ordered his lunch and casually observed the middle-aged woman behind the counter as she went about her business.

Her auburn hair color had clearly come out of a bottle, as was evidenced by the gray roots showing in the part at the top of her head. He wondered what her natural hair color had been. With a pert nose, cute smile, and still-relatively-trim figure, Sherry was quite attractive.

She held out his plate. "Tuna on rye toast, chips, extra pickle. Can I freshen that coffee for you?" Her voice was smooth, gentle. She seemed eager to please.

"Yes, thank you." Brad pushed his hefty, white, classic-food-joint mug forward just an inch or two.

"That do it for you? Can I get you anything else?"

Brad noticed her quick glance at his left hand. "No, thanks. Looks great." He sat quietly on his stool at the counter, eating his sandwich and trying to get a sense of the woman and the best way to approach her. When he finished eating, he crumpled his napkin and tossed it on the empty plate, then leaned his elbows on the counter.

Sherry approached. "Piece of apple pie and another cup of coffee?"

Brad couldn't help but remind himself that pie and keeping his body trim and muscular didn't go together. "Sure. What's your specialty?" He smiled. The more I eat the more likely you are to talk to me.

"Well, sir," her eyes sparkled, "whatever kind of pie you like, that's our specialty. And if you have a real sweet tooth, I'll just stick my little finger-tip in the middle to sweeten it up. Besides, all we've got left is apple." She gave him a wink and an even bigger smile.

Brad was well-aware that women often found his manly personae and bright blue eyes appealing. He wasn't above using those tools to move an investigation along. He was also aware that the more information he could get from Sherry before she knew what he was doing, the more likely he was to get something important out of the conversation. He started gently. "Now, ma'am. I'm sure you've sweetened many a pie in your time." He winked at her. "And many a man's disposition as well."

Brad watched a tiny blush scoot across her face. She tugged

on the ends of the denim shirt she was wearing over her T-shirt and jeans and smoothed it with both her hands. "Oh, I might have given a man something to smile about a time or two." She seemed at least ten years older than Brad, but in the world of roadside café relationships, a few years one way or the other were often dismissed, no matter which side of the equation one was on. She lingered for just the briefest moment as she handed Brad his pie.

Brad didn't rush. He took a bite of pie, then a sip of coffee. He looked up at her and smiled his approval toward her expectant look. As he lifted his fork for a second taste, he used it to point at her hand. "I notice you're not wearing any particular jewelry on that left hand of yours. You're not hiding something from us, are you?" His eyes were on "full bright."

Sherry's gaze went unconsciously to her hand. "Oh. No." She let out a sigh. "It's been a while." Her smile remained in place, but Brad could see a tiny frown touch the corner of each eye.

He took his time with his next bite. "So, you're telling me some man was lucky enough to have you and then foolish enough to let you go?"

Sherry picked up a cleaning rag and began wiping down the counter to the left of Brad. "You know how it is," the smile remained steadfast, "sometimes things just don't work out." She stepped back from the counter.

Brad's head was bent over his last morsel of pie. "Some men just don't know how good they've got it." He looked up at her with kindness in his eyes.

"Gave it my best, you know," she had moved to the counter on Brad's right, "tried to keep him happy. But," she shrugged, "a girl's best isn't always good enough."

Brad looked down again. Dang, I feel like I'm talking to *Carl's* second wife, not Victor's. He shook his head then looked up. "Or sometimes," Brad pointed with his fork again, "a man just can't be pleased."

There was silence for a moment as Sherry turned her back on Brad and headed back to the coffee maker to pick up the carafe. She came back to him and topped off his cup without saying a word.

"Any kids?" Brad tossed off the question as if it had no real importance.

A smile crossed Sherry's face. "Yes. A boy. Well, he's a man now."

"Oh, yeah?"

"Yeah. His name's Carl David, we call him Davey." Her smile warmed significantly.

Brad took a sip of coffee and put his cup down slowly. Take your time now. Don't rush this. "He live here in London?"

"No, up in Lexington." She let out the tiniest sigh. "But he stays in touch. We talk all the time."

"Nice." Brad let a few moments pass. "Good-looking boy, I'll bet," he gave her his best grin, "based on his mother's looks."

The blush came back to Sherry's face. "Well, I don't know about that." She began straightening the already neat condiment basket.

Brad pushed, just a little. "Come on now. Don't be coy with me. I'll bet he's a good-looking boy and I'll prove it to you."

Sherry pulled back and furrowed her brows. "How?"

"I'll bet you've got a picture of him somewhere right here in this café." She didn't respond. "Well, you do, now, don't you?"

Sherry waggled, the universal sign for, "*Well, you've got me.*"

"Come on now. You go get that picture and show it to me, Sherry."

It was the first time he had used her name, though it was clearly displayed on her name-tag. The sudden shift in intimacy sent a rose-colored flush across her face. She took a deep breath. "Okay. Give me just a second. I've got to get it out of my purse. It's in the back."

Sherry was gone for a few moments. Brad sat pondering. He

knew he had opened up lines of communication. He just wasn't quite sure how to proceed, or for that matter, what he was trying to get.

"Here you go." Sherry's smile was in full bloom. She handed him a wallet-sized picture of her son, one that had clearly been in her wallet for several years.

Brad took it and inspected it closely, but just for a moment. "So, your boy's in high school?"

Sherry chuckled, "Oh, no. He's twenty-four already. All grown up. He is handsome, isn't he?"

"He certainly is." Brad winked at her. "See, I told you I could prove he was good-looking." He smiled and raised his chin. "And there's no question he gets those looks from his mom." Brad paused again. "So, what's his name again?"

"Carl." She sighed. "Named after his grandfather. We really didn't have much choice in that one." Her smile brightened. "Like I said, we call him Davey."

"And what's he do?"

There was another shift in her countenance. Again, the smile stayed steadfast, but the light behind it went out quickly. "He works for his father. They're in the roofing business, up in Lexington."

Brad gave her a big smile, hoping to not lose momentum. "Oh, yeah? I'm from Lexington. Maybe I know him. What's his father's name?"

"Victor. Victor Rasmussen." Sherry was clearly doing her best to not seem negative about the man. She was mildly successful.

Brad finished the coffee in his mug. "And that's the guy that let you slip away." He made a big show of nodding his head back and forth.

Sherry was quick to go for the coffee carafe. "I guess so." She gave him a warm smile as she held the carafe up in invitation. "Who knows." She let out another small sigh. "Things work out for the best."

Brad took a final sip of his coffee, impressed with the woman's integrity, especially when he already knew what a low-life Victor was. "Sometimes." He put his hand over his cup, indicating he was done. "You ever talk to the old man?"

"Once in a rare while." She put the carafe back on the burner. "Haven't spoken to him in quite a while."

"But your son must talk to him almost daily, right? I mean, they work together."

Sherry turned back to him, smoothing her shirt again, the smile returning to her face. "Not lately. He's been in the UAE, you know, the United Arab Emirates. He'll be flying back home Tuesday. Gets in around seven or so, I think."

Brad cocked his head. "Your son Davey is in the UAE? What's he doing there?"

Sherry finally leaned against the workstation behind her and crossed her arms. "He's in Dubai. I guess they're all about horse racing there. That's where his dad bought that racehorse that's done so well for him."

"His dad has a racehorse, too?"

Sherry's lips pursed as she tried to smile. "Yes, he's a very lucky man."

Brad nodded several times, forcing himself to continue moving slowly. "Wow," his voice was gentle, "that must be pretty cool for your son. How long has he been over there?"

"I guess it's almost a month now." Sherry pushed herself off the counter and started busying herself with cleaning the faucet area under the counter.

"So, I take it he's over there looking for another horse while your ex stays home working the company?"

Sherry nodded. "Oh, sure. If anything, Victor is always out there trying to make a buck." She gave Brad a weak smile. "One way or the other."

Brad began unconsciously tapping the rim of his empty coffee cup with his index finger, thinking that Victor wasn't always out there trying to make a buck, not anymore. “That doesn’t sound very positive. He wouldn’t get involved in anything illegal, would he?” He got no response. “I mean, he’s not the kind of guy who has to look over his shoulder is he?” He knew he was pressing.

Sherry looked at him as if she were about to say something important. Then, “Are you sure you don’t want any more coffee?”

Brad knew he had pressed too far. He held up his hand. “Oh, no. Probably had too much already.” He gave her a warm smile. “Just hard to pass on such pleasant conversation.” Brad stood up and gave Sherry one last wink. He had a tug in his heart for this warm-hearted woman who had been tossed aside by Victor Rasmussen and had no one to go home to that evening. “No question I’ll remember that this is the right place to stop for lunch next time I make this trip. You have a nice day, Ms. Sherry.” He nodded at her, threw a twenty on the counter, turned and walked out the door. He could feel Sherry’s eyes follow him out into the parking lot.

17

Joe Alexander had driven all through the night—I-35 from San Antonio through Austin and on to Dallas—I-30 from Dallas to Little Rock—ten hours. At five o'clock in the morning, Little Rock was just waking up. Not so for Joe Alexander. Exhausted after ten hours of driving, the wound in his side screaming at him each time he sat up—and each time he didn't—he knew he needed sleep.

Joe also knew that it was too early to check into a motel room. Too early, that is, for the average traveler. But for him, the timing might be perfect, or so he hoped. Pulling into a Motel Six on West Markham Street, one that described itself on the web as "unpretentious" and cost only forty bucks a night, Joe had a plan that might get him some sleep and at the same time keep him safe.

A voice called out to him the moment he walked into the lobby. "Can I help you, sir?" It had come from a brown-haired young man, rather tall, with a name tag that said, "Bobby," a shiny smile on his face, and a shiny cross hanging around his neck. The last item did not bode well for Joe.

"Yeah." Joe realized his voice was scratchy after his long, difficult night. "Ah, I need a room." He gave the boy a weak smile.

"Been driving all night. I know it's not check-in time yet," his eyebrows went up, "but maybe you have a room that didn't get rented last night?"

"Yes, sir. In fact, we do." Bobby was eager to please. "We can set you up right now. Give you a room for tonight, but let you get an early start, if you know what I mean."

"Yeah, yeah. That'll work. Yeah, great." Joe was exhausted. His mind was scrambled but he still had to try to figure out how to pull this off.

The shiny smile looked up from his computer. "That's forty dollars, forty-four eighty with tax. We can put that right on your credit card."

"Uh, yeah. Listen, how 'bout I just pay in cash." He slipped a fifty across the desk. "You just keep the change."

Bobby hesitated, a sad frown crossing his face. "I'm sorry sir. You can pay in cash, but I still have to run your card. In fact, we'll be putting an additional twenty-five dollars on it to cover incidentals." The smile came back. "But don't worry. That will all come off within twenty-four hours after you check out."

Joe took a deep breath. "Yeah, sure. Okay. But," he slipped another fifty across the desk, "what if I promise to be out by check-out time. Eleven, right? Could we just keep this between ourselves?"

The look on Bobby's face told him all he needed to know. This young man, with his shiny face and his shiny cross, wasn't going to give up his eternal salvation for fifty bucks. "You know what? Never mind." Joe pulled out his wallet and his Visa card. "Just put it all on this." He didn't ask for his money back, but he wasn't surprised when Bobby slid the two fifties across the desk using his fingertips as if the bills were somehow radioactive.

Three minutes later Joe was opening the door to a motel room that looked exactly like every other budget motel room he'd ever seen. Several moments later he'd taken off his suit jacket and flopped, exhausted, onto the not-so-fresh bedspread and slipped immediately into a restless sleep.

~

A LITTLE AFTER three that afternoon, Joe woke up, his mouth dry, his stomach roiling. He hadn't put anything into it but black coffee since the bourbon he drank with Jane back in San Antonio.

He went to the sink—back of the room, just outside the toilet/shower—next to the open closet space—where it always was—and washed his face. He couldn't brush his teeth or even run a comb through his hair since he hadn't brought any luggage into the room. Of course, there was no luggage in his car either. He was on the run.

Looking at himself in the mirror, trying to smooth the wrinkles out of his clothing with nothing but his hands, Joe slipped his now distressed jacket back on. He just had to get something to eat. After that, maybe he'd find some place to buy some new clothing, come back to the room to change the makeshift dressing on his wound, and take off again.

As he stepped out of his room and walked to his car, Joe could see into the main office. What he saw there sent an icy chill down his back. Two men, large, dark clothing, were talking to the middle-aged woman who had taken Bobby's place. She was gesturing in the general direction of Joe's room—or maybe she wasn't. It didn't matter. Whoever those men were, whatever they were talking to the woman about, the fear that wracked Joe's body pushed him forward. Head down, he walked directly to the Honda. Slipping behind the wheel, he started the car and pulled out of the parking lot, his face turned away from the office. He was on the move. No food, no new clothing, no new dressing. "Damn it to hell."

18

It was nearly four o'clock on Saturday afternoon before the team gathered in the BCI offices. Sonia could see from their faces that it had been a stressful day for each of them. Brad was the last one to arrive. His smile seemed to warm the room, if not for the others, certainly for her. "I tried to stop downstairs and pick something up for you all," he opened his empty hands, "but it appears Magee's closes early on Saturdays."

Sonia popped out of one of the folding chairs she had set up around their temporary conference table in the center of the waiting room. "Don't you worry about that, sweets. Ms. Jet, here," she turned and smiled at Jet, "was knowledgeable enough to know that," she turned back to Brad, "and kind enough to stop in and get us a four-pack of Kentucky Bourbon Barrel Ale." Stepping over to him, she poured the golden-brown liquid into one of their two clear glass beer mugs as she walked.

Brad looked down at the tall, tan head the ale created. He smiled at her but waved her off. "You and Jet take the glasses, babe. Tee and I can drink right out of the bottle." He turned to Tee. "Right, hotshot?"

Tee returned the smile. "Won't be the first time today I've been asked to have a drink."

Sonia took Brad by the hand and led him over to the white, plastic table, directing him to the seat next to hers. She was all for professionalism in their relationship, but they didn't have to act like they weren't engaged.

"Alrighty, then. Let's call this thing to order." It was Jet's voice taking control, at least temporarily. "I've had a long enough day for a Saturday, and I'd like to get on with my own life if that's okay with the rest of you." There was a playful smile on her face.

"Sounds like someone's got plans for the evening." Sonia smiled and ran her fingers through her hair. "Am I right?"

All eyes turned toward Jet. She cocked her head. "Well," her voice slipped into that southern belle accent that sometimes drove Sonia crazy, "does it surprise you that a certain gentleman might have asked me to meet him for drinks before dinner tonight?"

"Oh, brother." Tee was not as accustomed to Jet's shifting speech patterns as the others.

Jet lifted her eyes to the ceiling and huffed. "Well, I've *nevah*."

"Okay, ladies." It was Brad's rich voice. "I think we've probably all got plans for this evening," he glanced at Sonia, "if work allows, that is. So, let's get this report over with and see where we stand. Anyone want to go first?"

"Yes," Sonia sat up and brushed a wisp of hair out of her face, "who would like to go first?" Her chocolate brown eyes caught Brad's with a silent message. Okay *Captain Dunham*, let's remember this is a *BCI investigation*. Brad gave Sonia a slightly perplexed look. He took a long swig of his drink.

One by one, everyone around the table shared what they had learned. Tee made it clear that Carla Lombardi, Carl Rasmussen's daughter, had been kicked out of her father's life along with her mother. She'd had no relationship with her half-brother, Victor

Rasmussen, and was probably a dead end in terms of the investigation.

Brad followed, describing Victor's elderly father, Carl, and the relationship between the two men. He verified Tee's information about how Carl had treated his first wife and daughter and that Carl hadn't even mentioned the first wife's name. He noted that Carl's second wife, Harriet, had also been sent packing, but not before she gave him the son he wanted, Victor. She was now deceased.

Finally, he shifted gears and spoke about his visit with Victor's second wife, Sherry, the sweet lady working at the roadside diner. He was convinced that she wasn't the type to have been involved. In addition, it turned out that their son, Carl David, or Davey as they called him, had been out of the country for almost a month. It was certain that he hadn't done the deed, at least not personally.

Jet had asked to go last, so Sonia told the group that she had learned little at the James Bennington facility, other than the fact that no one really knew, or wanted to talk about, how Victor Rasmussen was going to bring out a twenty-year-old bourbon on his own, especially when Mason Holliday had made it very clear no one was going to be willing to sell him any aged bourbon to work with. She continued. "The one thing that caught my attention was that Oscar told me how important the yeast is in the process, that they make their own and keep it under lock and key. He told me that if Victor had tried to get his hands on some of that, or even just the recipe, it would have taken an insider's help."

Sonia let the group ruminate on those thoughts then turned back to her partner. "Okay, Jet. You're the only one left. Let's hear it."

Jet let a Cheshire-cat grin cross her face. "I've only got one thing to say. " She paused. "Victor Rasmussen is alive."

A shocked silence filled the room. It was obvious by the look on her face that Jet had gotten the response she expected. "Well, let's put it this way. The only person who has regular contact with Victor, his business manager, Missy Charles, *thinks* he's alive."

Sonia sat up taller in her chair, as did the others. "Go on."

Jet's eyes were sparkling, and it was clear to Sonia that Jet enjoyed being the center of attention. "Okay. So, I really didn't get much from Missy Charles about reasons why Victor might have been killed," she gave Sonia a quick look, "or about the twenty-year-old bourbon." She turned her attention back to Brad and Tee. "But I did find out she thinks he's," she made air quotes with her fingers, " 'gallivanting around Europe'. I asked her about how the business ran with Victor away, and she said two interesting things. First, she said that she sends him an email every day with questions or information about the business and that he responds by the next morning."

Tee leaned forward, her forearms on the table. "So, clearly, someone is receiving and answering those emails. How is that possible?" Sonia was glad to see her little sister handling herself so well at the meeting.

"Well." Brad's voice was enthusiastic. "Looks like whoever did Rasmussen in was able to hack his email account as well."

"Or . . ." every head turned toward Sonia. "Maybe something much simpler than that. Maybe they just stole his laptop."

"I agree." Tee leaned back in her chair and crossed her arms. "Most people don't bother to keep their email accounts protected. It's too much of a pain in the butt. I'll bet if I stole twenty laptops, I could get into fifteen of the owner's email accounts by simply opening Gmail."

Jet's expression made it clear that she was very pleased with herself. "So, this really gives us something to work with, right?"

"Maaaybe." Brad rubbed his chin between his thumb and his forefinger. "This would be huge if we could track it down to a desktop computer. But if Sonia's correct and this is coming from his laptop, then the question is whether or not we can tell where a laptop computer is when it sends an email, a real geo-location."

"Can we?" Tee asked.

"Honestly, I don't know. I'll check with my NCIS guys and see what they have to say."

There was silence around the table for a moment as all four pondered the new information. Then Sonia looked back at Jet. "So, what was the other thing you were going to tell us."

"What?"

"You said you had two things you wanted to share."

Jet took a sip of ale out of her glass mug, the large foamy head having long dissipated. "Yeah, Missy said something like, 'I've been his right hand for twenty years. If something happened to him, I could run the whole thing.' She even implied she might be able to run it better than him."

"Now that's interesting." Brad leaned forward. "Old man Rasmussen made a similar comment as well. He said something that implied *she* was really running the company now, not Victor."

Tee furrowed her brows. "You don't think . . ."

"Now let's not jump to any conclusions." Jet looked at Tee over her imaginary glasses. "You're going to hear a lot of things that sound important as we go along. We just have to be careful before we go chasing our tails on every little tidbit that comes past us."

"Still . . ." Tee's voice was almost plaintive.

"She's right, Tee." Sonia sounded a bit motherly. "We have to be careful. But you're right, too. This could be important."

Sonia knew how critical it was for the team to work quickly. She could see, however, that the long day had taken a lot out of each of them. She stood, indicating that the meeting was over. "Look. We're all beat. Let's get some rest and get right on it again in the morning." She smiled at Jet. "My partner and I thank you for your efforts today, right, Jet?"

Jet grinned, clearly enjoying the explicit reminder that this was a BCI case. “Absolutely.”

Sonia pushed her chair in. “And now, apparently, my partner seems to have plans for the evening.” She turned to Tee. “And what about you, employee number zero-zero-three?”

Tee was already out of her seat and picking up the notepad she’d carried with her all day. “I, boss, or should I say, *mother*, am going out to explore the Saturday night-life in this one-horse town.”

Jet jumped in, her southern accent soaking her words. “Now look here, missy. Never cast aspersions on horses, not while you’re standing in Lexington, Kentucky—unless, of course,” she winked, “you just lost a bunch of money on some nag at the race-track.” Smiles went around the table again.

“And you, Mr. Hunky,” Sonia’s chocolate-brown eyes locked with Brad’s bright blue orbs, “what are your plans for the evening?”

Brad stood, the last one to do so. He put his thumbs inside the top of his pants, tugged, and puffed out his chest. “I plan on going home, having a nice dinner and a good glass of bourbon, and then starting a fire.”

Sonia cocked her head, a curious smile on her face. “In May? Isn’t it too warm?”

Brad smiled right back. “I don’t recall saying anything about a fireplace, now did I?”

19

Tee stood in front of the mirror in Sonia's tiny bathroom, freshening up her makeup. She was glad to be in the apartment alone, Sonia being off with Brad for the evening. She didn't have a lot of clothing with her, and she had enjoyed taking advantage of Sonia's absence by roaming freely through her sister's closet.

Tee checked her hair in the mirror one last time and headed out the door and down the steps to Central Avenue. She was wearing a sleeveless, coral-colored knit top, with a cream lightweight jacket over it. She had a silk scarf with swirls of coral, royal blue, and greens tied closely off the side of her neck. The seemingly mandatory blue jeans and sandals were in place, and the finishing touches were dangly green earrings. She didn't normally dress so nicely for a night at a club, but then again, she didn't own the kind of clothing Sonia could afford. She was certain that Sonia wouldn't mind her borrowing her clothing. The earrings were another matter altogether.

Tee had texted a few friends up in Cincinnati, girls who also knew their way around Lexington. She'd found out that there were a number of new bars that featured young crowds and good music out on Manchester Street. She headed for one called The Burl. When she got there, she was glad that she actually was twenty-two, since the bouncer at the door gave her and her ID a pretty close inspection. *Wow, that's the second time today.*

Tee paid her seven-dollar cover charge and stepped into the darkened and extremely loud bar, fully aware that she only had enough money left to buy herself one beer. She worked her way to the bar and was lucky enough to commandeer a seat on a stool that had just been vacated. She ordered a Bud, not wanting to get into the same hassle she'd faced that afternoon with Carla Lombardi.

As was often the case in bars like this, there were three bands on the bill that evening. The first, an indie-pop band with a country flavor, was just finishing when she arrived. Given her experience as a singer herself, she couldn't help but listen to them pretty discerningly, if only momentarily. Half-way through the first song to which she paid attention, she had made her evaluation. *Not terrible. Not good. Too loud for the room. Excellent drummer. Bass player over-plays. Guitar player would be better off behind the bar slinging beers.* Having been surrounded on stage by puffed up male egos a few times herself, she was a little more accepting of the female singer—*adequate but not very dynamic.* She was relieved when they finished and began moving their equipment off stage.

During the lull between bands, Tee sat quietly, checking out the other "talent" in the room. She wasn't exactly at The Burl trying to pick up a guy, but a girl never knew when something might just happen to pop up. She slowly nursed her beer, knowing full well that it wouldn't be long before some guy would be leaning over her, using some lame pick-up line. It happened three short minutes after the first band wrapped up.

"Hey, how're you doing?" he yelled at her over the sound of the piped-in music. "Haven't seen you here before. My name's Bud."

"That's funny." Tee raised her beer to her lips but was careful not to drink too much of it. That one beer had to last a long time, and this first suitor wasn't likely to be around long enough to buy her another.

"What's funny?"

"Bud, that's the name of my beer, too." She kept her eyes on the large mirror and display of hard-liquor bottles behind the bar.

He was brown-haired, stocky, broad-faced and not particularly attractive. She figured his faded *Grateful Dead* T-shirt had fit better when he'd first purchased it and it certainly wasn't enhanced by the ketchup that must have been captured by way of his protruding belly. In addition, he had either fallen in a bottle of Polo cologne or thought the instructions for its application were the same as for his shampoo—lather, rinse, repeat. "Yeah, cool." There was a long, deadly silence before he tried again. "So, really. You go to UK?"

Tee gave him a snarky look. "Already graduated." The "*almost two weeks ago*," went unspoken.

There was another deadly silence and then he gave it another try. "So, how'd you like that band?"

"Not much." She knew he was hoping for more, but her eyes were already roaming the room, hoping this guy would finally get the message.

"So, my buddies and I have a table closer to the band. You want to come join us?"

Tee finally turned and looked at him. She was struck by the fact that as clumsy as Bud was, he was trying, and she knew that was hard on a guy. She leaned over toward him and gave him the tiniest smile. "Listen, I think my cop boyfriend just got me pregnant, and I'm nursing this one beer because I think it may be the last one I'll be able to have for the next nine months. Maybe you'd better find someone else."

His eyes opened a little wider. "Yeah, sure." He turned to walk away, then stopped and turned back to her. "Good luck with all that." He said it nicely.

"Well, look at that," Tee spoke into the top of her bottle, "ol' Bud has a heart." She knew she'd been hard on him. She shrugged and touched the bottle to her lips. Better to let him down fast and save us both a lot of trouble.

As the next band came on, Tee noticed that one of the guitar players, she was pretty sure that's what he played, seemed quiet and polite as he dealt with the others on stage. He was also darn attractive—certainly dressed a notch higher than any other male in the room. She was pretty certain it was worth sitting there waiting to watch him play. As she waited, however, she noticed a guy standing near one of the exposed poles, not too far from her. He stuck out. He didn't fit the rest of the crowd. Tall and thin, his comb-over barely managed to succeed in its mission, and the scraggly goatee he sported was so thin you could see right through it. The sloppy dark blue T-shirt and poorly fitting jeans didn't help. Tee was drawn to looking at him, but when she did, he ducked behind the pole.

When the second band came on, the guitar player who had caught Tee's attention stepped to the mic. "Evening. We're Sundown Service." He quickly stepped back from the mic, confident, but clearly not interested in drawing attention to himself. The drummer clicked off the first tune and they dove into a strong version of *Tennessee Jed* by *The Grateful Dead.*

It didn't take long for Tee to get a sense of the group. Tight. Clean. Not overly loud, Good vocals. Excellent guitar work. And that guy is hot. "Hmm. This could be interesting." She was speaking, again, into the top of her bottle almost as if it was a microphone.

Tee leaned back and hitched her elbows on the back of the bar stool. She turned to face the band directly, in order to get a better look at the "show." When she did, however, she noticed that the guy she had seen before had moved to the bar and was standing just a few feet away from her. As she turned back to the stage, she could feel his eyes on the back of her head. It creeped her out.

As *Tennessee Jed* bled into an Allman Brothers tune, Tee was torn. She enjoyed the music. She was particularly enjoying watching, or was it simply looking at, the guitar player. On the other hand, she could feel the presence of *Creepy Guy* watching her. It pissed her off.

The cute guy on stage turned toward the bass player while he played a soaring guitar solo. Tee got goosebumps listening to his playing, but the images in her mind crashed when the stage lights glistened off the simple ring he was wearing on the fourth finger of his left hand.

Her empty beer bottle thumped onto the bar. "Damn." Oh well, so much for that. I'll bet he's married to one hot and lucky lady. She could feel her enthusiasm for the evening, at least for this part of it, slipping away very quickly. Between that and the way Creepy Guy was making her feel, she decided it was time to move on. She opened her purse and put her last dollar on the bar for a tip, then spun the bar stool around and slipped off. She was relieved that Creepy Guy was nowhere in sight.

Tee worked her way toward the front door. She was disappointed but had to admit that she'd heard some good music and enjoyed the little fantasy she'd had about meeting the guitar player. As she stepped outside, she took out her car keys, automatically grasping the attached black, plastic container of pepper spray her sister had given her last Christmas for protection. She always had it in her hand when she walked to her car or her apartment, especially at night.

Tee took only a few steps toward her car when a chill ran through her body. It was as if she knew something was there in the dark parking lot, something that was waiting for her. She took a deep breath, put her thumb on the trigger of her pepper spray, and walked as quickly as she could to her car.

When she got there, she opened the door, fully aware that at the moment she was using her keys to do so, she was "unarmed." She tried to do it as quickly as possible but that only led to her fumbling with the keys, missing the hole, taking what seemed like forever to get the f'ing door open. When she finally did, she all but jumped into the front seat and locked the door, holding her breath the whole time.

Finally. Finally. She took a deep breath and let it out slowly. It pissed her off that her hand was shaking when she put the key in the ignition and turned it; she was relieved when the Chevy came immediately to life. She put the car in gear and lifted her right arm onto the top of her seat, looking over her shoulder as she palmed the steering wheel and backed out of her parking space. When she turned around and faced forward, her heart stopped. Standing in front of her, fully illuminated by her headlights, was Creepy Guy. He was looking right at her, his eyes wide and boring through the windshield, right into her being. He had something long and dark in his hand.

Tee was stunned. She knew she had to get out of there, but he was almost directly in front of her, just standing there, staring. Her eyes darted to her rearview mirror. She realized there were only thirty or forty feet behind her before the parking lot ended in a line of trees. She looked back and forth, left and right. Back up all the way and jump out of the car? No. He'll come right after me. He'll catch me. She froze.

A world of terrible images shot across Tee's mind as if she was watching some terrible movie—abducted women, assaulted women, murdered women. Her eyes flew open as Creepy Guy took a step toward her. His motion shook her out of her stupor. She slammed her foot to the floor, driving the accelerator pedal as far as it would go, almost further. She didn't worry about hitting him, not if it meant getting away from those eyes. The front wheels of the car spun wildly, kicking up huge clouds of gravel and dust. She could hear rocks clanging off the bottom of her car, off the sides of some of the cars near her. She didn't care.

The car leaped forward, headed directly for Creepy Guy. Tee pulled the wheel to the right just barely enough to get past without hitting him. He spun away from the blue bullet that was coming at him full force, a look of panic distorting his face. He stumbled backward, out of the beam of the headlights and into the darkness.

Tee was past him and took only the briefest peek in the rearview mirror. There was little to see, other than a cloud of dust. She spilled the car out onto Manchester Street without observing proper driving etiquette. She didn't give a crap. She drove like a bat out of hell for a good thirty seconds.

As she approached the lights of a more populated part of town, Tee brought the Chevy to a more normal speed and finally to a full stop at a traffic light. The car was still, but her heart was thumping like the kick drum in one of the bands she'd seen that night. Her hand was shaking as she ran it through her hair, glad to be leaving the bastard in the dust.

DAY THREE

20

Sunday morning, Sonia woke with a smile on her face. She'd had a nice evening with Brad, some dinner, some teasing, just the tiniest bit of wedding discussions, and then some intimate time together. When she'd come home, however, she'd unexpectedly found Tee already sprawled out on the couch and rather uncommunicative. Not wanting to ruin her own good mood, Sonia had let it slide, said goodnight and gone on to bed.

Sonia slipped on her jeans and faded blue Kentucky Wildcats T-shirt. When she stepped into her living room, Sonia found Tee still asleep on the couch, twisted in rumpled sheets. Remembering that young people can sleep pretty late, and cognizant of that fact that Tee might not have had a great evening, Sonia decided to walk down to Magee's, it was only a few blocks each way, and pick up some bagels that would go with eggs and coffee for breakfast. She slipped on her blue and white running shoes and stepped out onto the small landing outside her front door. Taking in the sun and warmth, she stretched her arms above her head. *It's a beautiful day. Why waste it? Let Sleeping Beauty in there get some rest. It's going to be a long day.*

Sonia returned from Magee's to find Tee stirring, but still

lying on the couch. The sound of Sonia making coffee and starting the eggs, however, was enough to bring Tee fully awake. She popped her head up over the back of the couch, sleepy-eyed, her hair reminiscent of a scarecrow that had lost a battle with a tornado. "Morning." Her voice was croaky.

"Good morning, Teresa." Sonia was in too good a mood to notice that the pleasantness in her voice didn't exactly match Tee's state of mind.

"Do you have to sound like Little Miss Sunshine so early in the morning?" Tee plopped her head back down on her crumpled pillow.

"I'm sorry. Did you have a rough night last night?" Sonia's voice was still light and airy.

"Not bad," Tee mumbled into the sheets.

As Sonia stepped from the kitchen to the living room, about three steps, she noticed the coffee table in front of the couch for the first time. There were two empty beer bottles on the dark walnut table. She paused for a moment, absorbing the sight. "You have somebody over last night?"

"No, why?" Tee's eyes were still closed. She was lying on her side, facing away from Sonia.

"Nothing. Never mind." Sonia's voice shifted back to sunshine. "C'mon, sleepy head. I've got some nice fresh bagels, eggs, and coffee for us."

Sonia sat down at her tiny kitchen table and started to eat, waiting patiently for Tee to join her. When she did, Sonia gently pushed a plate full of eggs over to her. "You okay?"

Tee silently began buttering her bagel.

Sonia wanted to press harder, but she knew she needed to be patient. Finally, she asked. "So, tell me about your evening. Have fun?"

Tee spoke with a bite of bagel in her mouth. "It was okay." Silence.

"Where'd you go?"

Tee took a sip of the coffee Sonia had brought to the table. "The Burl."

Sonia knew that she was displaying her lack of knowledge about hip places in town, but she didn't feel like she could fake her way through the conversation. "The what?"

"The Burl. It's a new joint out on Manchester Street." Tee shoveled some eggs into her mouth and followed that with a big bite of bagel.

Sonia knew that Manchester Street was the new hot spot in town. Several bars, eating places, and other businesses had opened in the last year or so and were popular with young adults and, given the type of music being played, some older folks. The area drew steady crowds, especially when the weather was nice. For all that she'd heard, Sonia had never actually done more than drive through the area and stop for a slice of pizza and some ice cream once or twice. "I'm afraid I don't know it. Nice place?"

"Yeah, it's okay. Big mural on the outside and a stained-glass window with a cool tree in it. I heard there was a big arcade with a wall full of old TVs on the other side of the street, but I didn't go over."

"And you had a good time?"

Tee was beginning to lighten up. "Yeah, it was alright. Heard a couple of bands. One kind of sucked, but the other one, a psychedelic rock band, they were pretty good."

"And everything worked out okay?"

Tee simply nodded, her mouth full of food again.

"You meet anybody nice?"

Tee let out a big sigh. "No, Mom. I didn't meet anybody nice. I didn't go home to any guy's place and—"

"Sorry." Sonia raised her hand like a guard at a school crossing. "Just wanted to know if everything worked out for you last night."

Tee had finished her food, while Sonia still had half-a-plate-full. Taking a long sip of her coffee, Tee relented. "Everything was fine. I came home, grabbed a couple of beers out of your fridge, and then you came in." She gave a Sonia a mildly dismissive look. "End of story."

"Good." Sonia turned her attention to her eggs. She was certain that she wasn't getting the whole story, that Tee wasn't the kind of girl who regularly came home from a decent evening and had several beers before going to sleep. She also knew better than to keep pressing. "Well, lady, Sunday or not, it's Day Three out of five. Now that you're finished with breakfast, why don't you jump in the shower while I try to make arrangements for you to meet with Clay Baratin.

MOST DISTILLERIES DO NOT RUN their normal tours on Sundays, so it took a little doing for Sonia to make arrangements for Tee to meet that day with Clay Baratin of Elk Horn Distilling, the company that produces Isaiah Adams bourbon. Unlike some distillers, who do most of their actual distilling in small towns but have a presence in downtown Louisville, Elk Horn was solely located in Bardstown, Kentucky, a picturesque burg known as, "The Bourbon Capital of the World."

When she finally sat down with Baratin, a surprisingly young man in almost preppy clothing, it was in the visitor's center at the distillery, empty of course, because it was Sunday. The room looked like part of a working distillery, but that was mostly for show. Everything was clean and shiny, dark-wooded and polished-brassy.

They sat on stools next to an informational display on the wall. "Thanks for seeing me on a Sunday," she started.

"Of course." He smiled broadly, but then his countenance shifted, darkening quickly. "Given the circumstances, I really had no choice. How can I help you, Ms. Vitale?"

Tee's conversation with Baratin lasted almost an hour. He told her about bourbon—his family's years of experience making it; the difference between his sweeter, "wheat forward" varieties and spicier, "rye forward" recipes; everything else he could possibly think to tell her about the production of the amber-colored elixir. Unfortunately, when she tried to get information about why anyone would have killed Victor Rasmussen, Baratin shrugged his shoulders. "He wasn't one of us. None of us really knew him, nor cared much about him." She got even less of a response about her questions regarding Rasmussen suddenly bringing out a twenty-year-old bourbon. She stood and extended her hand. "I really want to thank you for time, Mr. Baratin. I hope it wasn't too much of an imposition." The words, *"Thanks for nothing,"* stayed in her mouth.

As Tee got into her car to drive home, she couldn't help but question the allure of being a private investigator. She had driven all the way to Bardstown, had a lengthy interview, and had to do two more interviews—at Bald Knob Trace and Johnston Springs, makers of Andersen's—on the way home. It was likely that all she would have to show for her efforts was more information about the history and production of bourbon than she ever, *ever*, wanted to know, and a screaming headache. To add insult to injury, it had rained like crazy the whole way home.

21

Brad had gotten up early on Sunday morning and hit the pavement for three miles of good road work before breakfast. Running was especially nice on such a pleasant spring morning in Lexington. After a shower and a quick breakfast, Brad had made a few calls and set up an appointment with Victor Rasmussen's first wife, Patricia Huntington-Jones. He had decided, if it was possible, to put off telling her the reason for the meeting and been successful in that endeavor.

In order to meet with the woman, Brad had to drive out to Woodford County on Route 60, past Blue Grass Airport and beautiful Keeneland Race Track, into real horse farm country. He turned right at the famous Lexington Castle, onto Pisgah Pike. He drove past Dahlia Farm, the small farm that had played a central role in the first case Brad and Sonia had ever worked together. Approximately four miles later, he came to Stove Pipe Farm, a small working broodmare farm owned by Patricia's husband, Jackson Huntington-Jones.

Driving up the long driveway, Brad was taken by how classic the antebellum house was. Two-stories high, it appeared to him to have been built in the late 1800s. Tall windows peered out toward the road from the dark brown, brick frontage. The peaked roof gave the building even more height, and the fact that it was more slender than modern designs gave the impression that the building had somehow been squeezed after being built. The lack of a covered porch on the front of the building only heightened the impression.

Brad was greeted at the front door by a woman dressed rather formally for a Sunday afternoon. He smiled. Maybe she's just gotten home from church.

"Mr. Dunham, I assume?" The voice was almost syrupy and came from a woman in her late forties. Blonde, trim, more cute than pretty, she was well-manicured and wearing tight jeans, a white top, and red high heels.

"Yes, ma'am." Brad touched his finger to his forehead, tipping the hat he wasn't wearing. "Ms.," he tripped over how to deal with her hyphenated last name, "Jones?"

Her eyes had taken a long drink of the muscular man with the rugged face and intensely bright blue eyes who stood before her. Her reddened lips formed a coy smile. "Yes, yes. Do come in. I've been expecting you."

Patricia Huntington-Jones led him into a wide entrance way—wood floors, ten-foot ceilings, white plaster walls, a tall staircase directly in front of them—and into a parlor on the right. The room was large, its tall windows allowing lots of light, the walls covered in floral wallpaper so bold Brad found it disconcerting. The furniture was gilded and ostentatiously expensive.

She reclined on a velvet divan, slipping off her shoes and curling her legs onto the sofa while she rested her arm over its rounded end. Brad could almost imagine her purring as she extended her arm, directing him to a matching couch that barely responded to his body as he sat on it. Brad's eyes roamed around the room. "Lovely."

"Thank you." Patricia was still all smiles. "Now, Mr. Dunham, what can I do for you?"

Brad decided that, unlike Sherry Rasmussen, this woman would best be handled directly. "Well, Mrs., ah Huntington-Jones—"

She waved her hand at him coyly, a hint of southern belle in her voice. "You can call me Patricia."

"Thank you." He let out a small sigh of relief. "I'm here to talk to you about Victor Rasmussen."

The look on Patricia's face shifted, the same way a beautiful summer afternoon can suddenly turn black and explode into a thunderstorm. Her brows furrowed. The smile became tight, the corners of her lips curling only slightly upward. "Oh, really." Gone was the syrup from her voice.

Brad's face became earnest. "Believe me, Patricia," using her first name felt suddenly uncomfortable for him, "I'm not here to bring you any problems or bad news. It's just that I've been hired by a private investigation firm to do a little background checking on Mr. Rasmussen. It seems their client is considering going into business with him and they'd like to know what kind of man he is."

Brad could almost see the battle brewing in Patricia Huntington-Jones' mind. Clearly, raw emotions were erupting deep within her, yet her sense of personal decorum seemed to demand that she remain calm and discreet, if not polite and ladylike. "Well, Mr. Dunham, all I can say is that Victor has his good points and his not-so-good points." She turned her head up to the side. "I'm not certain I'd like to say anything more than that."

Brad had faced this type of interviewee before. He knew that all it would take was patience on his part for everything to come flowing out. "Can I simply ask how long you were married?"

Silence. Brad could almost sense the bile bubbling up inside her. "Mrs. Huntington-Jones?"

She took a gigantic breath, then began. The tone of her voice surprised him. She had suddenly become more historian than participant. "Well. You should know that Victor Rasmussen and I met when I was a cheerleader at Henry Clay High School and he played on the football team." She couldn't help but sound proud when she slipped in, "We won the state championship that year you know. Victor caught the winning touchdown."

She caught herself and shifted quickly back into her didactic tone. "We'd had an on-again-off-again romance, as many high schoolers do." She nodded demurely. "Actually, most of our problems grew out of the fact that whereas Carl Rasmussen was a relatively successful businessman at the time, my family was, how would you say it, well-established—doctors and lawyers who became owners of large tracts of land that made them wealthy over many generations. They were never very pleased with my being associated with the son of a," she hitched, "construction person." She paused. Some thought must have flashed across her mind. Brad could almost see it on her face. "Oh, dear. I haven't offered you anything to drink. Would you like some iced tea or something, Mr. Dunham?"

Brad just waved his hand gently and responded, "No, thank you. Please go on."

Patricia gathered up her thoughts and began again, trying to be upbeat. "Anyway, after high school, Victor went off to UK and I went to a small school up in Louisville, Bellarmine College. One weekend, when I was home from school, I attended the homecoming game and saw Victor play. It was all very exciting." Her voice, her energy, and her eyes all began trailing downward. She took in a deep breath. "And we got together after the game at one of those frat parties."

The energy fell away again. "Anyway, I'm afraid we celebrated a bit too much and got carried away." Her eyes drifted around the room as she spoke. After another pause, she turned to Brad. "Is this all that important? Do I really need to go on?"

Brad knew that what he was about to hear was not going to be pleasant for her, and honestly, he was pretty sure he could fill in the blanks, but it was what might come after that that he was looking for. "I'm sorry, ma'am. You don't really need to go into specifics."

Patricia gave Brad one of the tightest, quickest smiles he'd ever seen. "Okay, then. Let's just say that it wasn't too long before it became obvious that we should get married." She shook her head and curled her lips. "It was an awful affair."

Abruptly, she stopped, tossed her hand in the air and laughed. "Oh, screw it." She looked right into Brad's blue eyes and smiled broadly, surprising him. Her voice took on new life. "Look, everyone knew he'd knocked me up. His dad was pissed because his son had to marry someone he thought was a bimbo." She held the back of her hand up to her mouth and spoke out the side, "and let me tell you, that Carl Rasmussen is one piece of work." She dropped her hand, "And everyone on my side was making believe I was the lovely princess marrying the commoner who had won my heart." She chuckled and looked around at the tables near her.

Brad guessed she was looking for a drink, and probably not sweet tea, but was afraid that if he offered to get her one, he might be there much longer than he cared to. "So, the two of you had a child together?"

Sadness seemed to drop over Patricia like a parachute floating down into a field. "No. I'm afraid I lost the child pretty soon after the wedding." She sighed. "Very sad, very, very sad." Her voice was almost inaudible.

Brad waited patiently for her to speak again. Finally, she gave him a weak smile. "I guess the only thing good about it was that I no longer felt like I had to be tied to Victor for the rest of my life." She stopped there.

"So, the marriage didn't last long?"

Another weak smile. "Actually, we gave it the old college try." She shrugged. "I mean, we'd liked each other in high school. We'd dated for a while. It wasn't like either of us hated the other. Why not give it a go?"

"But it didn't work out?" Brad was trying to get to anything that might actually be helpful.

"No." She shook her head. "I could take the coarse joking. I could even take the womanizing," she gave Brad a telling look, "if it didn't get out of hand." She pursed her lips. "It was the gambling. That I couldn't take."

Brad tried not to show any reaction, but this was clearly new information.

She continued. "That son-of-a-bitch just couldn't resist a bet." She took a deep breath. "I'm telling you, if we were out to dinner with only twenty dollars between us and some guy looked up at a basketball game on the TV behind the bar, Victor would poke him in the arm. 'Twenty bucks says he makes the next shot.' Sometimes that meant we ate really well that night." A sad smile crossed her lips. "Sometimes it meant we were going home to see if there was enough peanut butter and jelly to put on crackers for dinner."

Brad sat silent for a moment. "Always little bets?" He knew what the answer would be.

She laughed. "Let's just say this. One year we went six months without a car," she turned her head and spoke to the wall, "when we had just bought a brand new one earlier that year."

This was new information, but Brad was able to keep his questioning calm, level. "So, would you say he had a gambling problem?"

Patricia gave him a snarky smile. "What would you say?"

Brad's mind ran through a number of responses. None came out of his mouth. Finally, he said, "And later you married Mr. Huntington-Jones?"

Patricia smiled and once again waved her hand gently. "Oh, that's another story completely." She slid off the divan, her body, Brad noticed, moving gracefully, almost seductively. It reminded him of how she had moved and spoken when he had first gotten there.

"Well Mr. Dunham," there was no missing the allure in the smile she gave him, "I've got some Settler's 38 behind the bar and I'm about to pour myself some. Can I interest you in a glass?"

Brad stood almost suddenly, aware that the conversation might be taking a potentially dangerous turn. "No, thank you, ma'am. I'm afraid I've got to get going."

Her eyes and lips became a blend of pouty and mildly seductive, her voice more southern than before, almost Jet-like he thought. She was already behind the bar pouring the drink out of a small bottle and into a crystal tumbler. "You know, they finish it in old wine barrels."

"Again, ma'am," Brad could almost hear a hint of southern gentleman in his own voice, reflecting hers, "I've taken up enough of your time. I'll be glad to let myself out."

She stood behind the bar, hips racked, holding the crystal tumbler and amber liquid in her hand in the way only self-assured women do. "I appreciate that Mr. Dunham. I believe this 38 is going to keep me quite busy for the next few minutes."

Just before Brad turned to leave, he took one last look. Patricia Huntington-Jones was an attractive woman, the kind that knew how to use that attribute to get what she wanted. But he didn't really believe that Patricia was offering him anything more than a fine glass of bourbon. He chalked her behavior up to her need to try to regain some sense of control, to get beyond the memories and feelings she had just dredged up. When he stepped out of the front door, he was surprised to find it raining heavily.

22

Jet had started her day quite early and in the sunshine of a pleasant Sunday morning. It was a good thing since she had a lot of driving to do. First, she headed off to Rosland, Kentucky. Driving out of town on Versailles Road, a few miles beyond Blue Grass Airport, she turned onto the Bluegrass Parkway. Driving through Woodford County, in a direction opposite to the one Brad was taking, an uncomfortable feeling began to creep its way into Jet's body, her mind. It was a feeling that came over her almost every time she drove down this highway.

Knowing that the small town of Versailles was off to her right, though she couldn't see it, old tapes began to play in Jet's mind, tapes of a childhood growing up near the edge of that town. The open spaces of the parkway, along with its rolling hills and relatively straight path, created an almost dreamlike atmosphere of serene calm, one that allowed the mind to wander. For Jet, that often meant traveling back over twenty-five years, back to a time when the term, "home," meant a small, two-bedroom house at the end of a not-so-pleasant street.

"Look, Mama. I'm a southern belle, aren't I? I'm going to make all my workers come and have tea with me every afternoon."

"Well, Lordy, Lordy, Joyce Ellen, aren't you just the prettiest six-year-old belle ever. Your daddy, the Colonel, would be ever so proud of you, don't you think?"

"Yes, Mama. That's because I have golden hair, isn't it?"

"Oh, sweet little girl. It's more than that. Don't you know you have Mama's pretty blue eyes and the cutest little smile as well?"

An eighteen-wheeler pulled in front of Jet, close, startling her. She checked her mirrors and reminded herself to focus on the road. She drifted on toward Rosland. Within a few moments, the road sang its mesmerizing song to her again.

"Mama, why don't I have four grandparents like everyone else? Everyone in Ms. Jackson's class has two grandmas and two grandpas. It's like I'm the only girl in second grade that only has one grandma and one grandpa."

"Oh, sweetness. Of course you have two grandmas and two grandpas. You know Papaw and Mamaw. They're your daddy's parents, right? They come up to visit us from Georgia once a year, don't they? And we talk to them on the phone. And we send them pictures of you."

"Uh huh."

"And didn't they send you a nice dress for your birthday last year?"

"Yes, ma'am. But what about your parents? Didn't you have a mommy and a daddy?"

"Well, sugar. Of course I did. It's just that I was born right outside of Savanah and my parents still live there. That's a long way away. But I'm sure they love you very much."

"Why don't they come to see us like Papaw and Mamaw? Are they too old?"

"Well . . . maybe. Maybe that's it. Maybe they're just too old to make that long trip in a car."

A car horn jolted Jet back into her lane. Damn, I've just got to stay focused here. Maybe I should have had more coffee before I left. Jet kept on driving, knowing that it would still be a while before she saw the signs for Bardstown, where she would leave the parkway. The rhythm of the road rose again in her ears.

"Joyce Ellen, sweetie, what's wrong? Why do you look so glum? Did something happen at school today?"

"No, Mama."

"Don't you say that, Joyce Ellen. I can see it on your face. Did those boys bother you in class again?"

"They made fun of my dress, Mama, and on third grade picture day. All the girls wore dresses, but the boys made fun of mine. They said it was too small for me, that I looked like a bean pole that had grown up through the dress."

"Those boys. I've got a good mind to go right up to the school and box their ears. That's what I should do."

"No, Mama, please don't. If you do, then they'll just make more fun of me. That's what they always do."

"Now, Joyce Ellen, you come right over here and let Mama hold you. Let me make it all better."

"I'm okay, Mama, really it's okay."

"Joyce Ellen. You come over here right now. You let me hold you, hear?"

"Yes, Mama."

"Now, doesn't that feel better?"

"Yes, Mama."

"And now, I've got an idea. Let's me and you put on our best dresses and then we can make believe that we've gone over to those boys' houses and tricked them into coming to a party, a party with all our friends. And then all the nice people at the party can make fun of the silly old clothes they're wearing when they should have come all dressed up to the party. That would show them, wouldn't it, Sugar?"

"It's okay, Mama. We don't have to do that."

"Joyce Ellen, you go right into your room and put on that pink dress of yours, the one with the big flowers. Go ahead. You go put that dress on right now, hear?"

"Yes, Mama."

Jet may have been lost in her thoughts, but when she passed a Kentucky State Trooper parked on the side of the road her attention shifted quickly. She slowed down, though it was too late. Damn. Her eyes remained glued to her rearview mirror, hoping to see if the trooper had pulled out behind her, lights flashing. She was relieved when there was no sign of him as she rounded a large bend in the road. She set her cruise control five miles over the speed limit and reminded herself, again, about staying focused on her driving; but by then the voices in her mind were having their way, no matter how hard she tried to shake them.

"Mama! Mama! Guess what, Mama!"

"Joyce Ellen, you lower your voice. Ladies don't shout when they come into a house. You just settle down and act like a lady, and close the door behind you."

"But, Mama, guess what?"

"Okay, Joyce Ellen, you go ahead. You tell me."

"Mama, the gym coach, he saw me running today. He said I was fast as greased lightning. He said he wants me to be on the track team, Mama. I'm going to be on the high school track team. Varsity, too. I'll be the first ninth-grader ever to be on the varsity team, Mama, for a girl that is."

Miles passed. Jet was still lost in thought.

"Joyce Ellen! You get in here right now and wipe that lipstick off your face. No fourteen-year-old lady walks around with bright red lipstick, looking like one of those nasty ladies. You know what I mean. And don't you slam that screen door at me!"

"Ugh, Mama. Why do we have to live in this tiny house anyway? It's so small and dark. And why doesn't Daddy paint it nice like Mr. Joseph's? I feel like we're the poorest folks on the street."

"Now you mind your tongue. Your daddy brought us up here from Savanah so he could learn to work with the horses. Someday he'll be a trainer, maybe even an owner."

"Then why does he keep changing jobs, one farm after the next? Why doesn't he stay at one job?"

"Never you mind. You go clean yourself up before he sees what you look like. You know how he can be."

The voices took on a darker tone. One tore at her heart with an old, not-so-faded pain.

"Mama? Mama? Are you okay? Wake up, Mama. It's almost five o'clock. I'm home from practice. Mama, wake up. Daddy will be home soon. You know how he can be if we don't have dinner on the table. Come on, Mama. I'll put the bottle back in the cupboard. You don't want him to know you've been drinking his bourbon again."

Finally, sounds came to her that were not quite so dark, though not pleasant—not pleasant at all.

"Joyce Ellen?"

"Yes, Mama."

"You got a phone call today while you were at the grocery."

"Who was it?"

"That's not the question. The question is why did that boy call for someone named Jet?"

"I don't know."

"Don't you go lying to me, Joyce Ellen. You know that boy was calling for you. Now you tell me right now why he asked for Jet. Go on. You tell me."

"It's no big deal, Mama. It's just a nickname."

"What kind of nickname is Jet? Makes you sound like some silly airplane or something."

"It's just my initials, Mama. It's just J.E.T. Everyone on the team just thinks it's cool to turn my initials into the word Jet, because I'm the fastest girl on the team, the fastest girl ever at Woodford County High School."

"Well, you tell them to stop calling you that. No southern lady allows herself to be called by any nickname, especially one that makes you sound like some sort of machine."

"But, Mama, I like it. I like that they have a cool name for me. It makes me feel—"

"I'll have none of it, Joyce Ellen. You tell them to stop calling you Jet and refer to you by your name, your given name, Joyce Ellen."

"Yes, Mama."

Jet saw the sign, *Bardstown 10 Miles.* She was relieved. The miles were going quickly, but she couldn't shake her uncomfortable feelings. Fight as she may to change the locus of her thoughts, words and phrases that pained her kept coming back to her.

"Joyce Ellen, is that you?"

"Yes, Mama, it's me."

"Well, look at you girl. What's that in your hand?"

"Nothin'."

"Don't nothin' me. What is that, another trophy?"

"Yes, Mama. It's another trophy. I took first place in the 5K."

"Well, isn't that nice Joyce Ellen. Come here and let me give you a kiss."

"Please, Mama."

"Joyce Ellen. You come here now."

"Yes, Mama."

"And don't you think we should dress up in our Sunday best and play like you're at some big event with the governor and a thousand people? I could play like I was his wife and I could be the one who has to give the trophies out."

"Mama, please. Let's not do that again. I just want to go to my room. Please, Mama. Here, you take the trophy. You put it anywhere you want. You make believe it's a big ceremony and you place it on the table over there if you'd like."

"Joyce Ellen, don't you want to be part of the ceremony? It's no fun without you."

"No, thank you, Mama. Really, I have lots of homework and I need to get it done before Daddy gets home, while it's still quiet."

"Joyce Ellen? Joyce Ellen?"

The sign for US 150 and Bardstown came up, along with a sign about it being the site of *My Old Kentucky Home*, the antebellum home that Stephen Foster had written about in his famous song—the official state song of Kentucky. Just two more miles to go. Just . . .

"Elsa! Elsa! Where the hell are you? Where the hell's my dinner? Elsa, you been drinkin' again?"

"Huh? Chuck?"

"There you are. You have been drinkin' again, haven't you? No wonder I keep losin' my job. Everyone at the farm keeps talking 'bout you stayin' home makin' believe you're some kind of southern belle, dressin' up all fancy in a dress and phony pearls and sittin' around doin' nothin' but drinkin' all day."

"Now that ain't fair, Chuck."

"Not fair, nothin'. I work my ass off all day and you sit home doin' nothin'."

"You knew when you married me that I was a lady of breeding, that I wasn't meant to be working in some factory."

"Oh, you're a lady of somethin' alright. Home all day drunk, and me losin' one job after the next because of your reputation."

"Oh yeah! Because of me! What about you going out every Friday, drinking with the boys. What about that? And sometimes not a damn penny left from your paycheck when you get home. And don't you think for a minute that I don't know where you go on Saturday nights. You're not with the boys. You're out with that red-headed whore from the diner. You son-of-a-bitch, you're a drunk and a shitty father, that's what you are. My parents were right. They said I shouldn't marry you, that you were no good, and they were right. I should have listened to them when they said I had to choose between you and them. I should never have left Georgia and come up here to this God-forsaken place with you. Now I haven't seen my own parents in almost twenty damn years."

"You get over here woman! You quit that bawlin' and get over here so I can teach you a good lesson with this belt. Elsa, you get over here!

At last, the exit appeared. Fully-formed tears sat in Jet's eyes, not willing to slide down her face. As she drove down the exit ramp, Jet was glad that the smaller road ahead would demand her full attention, attention that would finally allow her to silence the voices screaming at each other in her head.

23

About fifteen minutes after Jet came down the exit ramp onto US 150, she turned on to KY 635. Forty minutes later, she arrived in Rosland, a town with an estimated population of just over nine hundred people. The town was dominated by one thing, the Settler's Pride facility.

It being Sunday, she walked around the neatly kept property by herself. Each of the bright white, wooden buildings was set off by dark blue trim, the same blue that appeared on the label of each and every bottle of Settler's Pride Bourbon. After getting a sense of the property, Jet walked into the main office and told the only person there, a woman in her late fifties or early sixties, quite thin, glasses, dressed in blue jeans and Settler's Pride-blue T-shirt, that she had an appointment with Gary Dumas, the Master Distiller.

Jet found Dumas a pleasant man in his late forties, slightly balding and very gregarious. He was, of course, eager to say that Settler's Pride was probably best known for its double-oaked variety. In that process, bourbon is matured in a second charred oak barrel, one which has been deeply toasted before being lightly charred. The process creates an even sweeter oak character.

When she finally got around to asking Dumas about Victor Rasmussen's death and his purported twenty-year-old bourbon, Jet was disappointed to find that she got the same kind of information she and her colleagues had gotten the other day, *no* useful information. She said her polite goodbyes and stepped out into a day that had turned dark and threatening.

After a relatively short drive, about a half hour on Rosland Road, Jet was at the Woodland Acres distillery, a huge property with a full distillery, eighteen seven-story tall rack houses, and a beautiful modern heritage center. She was there to speak with Avery Hobart, the Master Distiller, and a true Kentucky legend.

She found Hobart an attractive, articulate man in his mid-seventies, standing behind his desk as she entered his office in a secluded section of the heritage center. "It's an honor to meet you, Mr. Hobart."

"A pleasure to meet you as well, Ms. . . ."

"Jet. Everyone just calls me Jet.

"Certainly." He took a seat behind the generous, finely carved mahogany desk and motioned to her to take a seat in the dark red leather chair opposite him. "I know that Mr. Holiday asked you to speak to me." He grinned. "That's why I'm here on a Sunday afternoon and not at home with my family. How can I help you?"

Jet smiled, glad for the opportunity to get right to the business at hand and avoid hearing more about different bourbons. As she well knew, the Woodland Acres distillery produced more than its share—Jeremiah Clark and Edward Willard, along with the Woodland Acres products, among them. "Sir, I don't mean to use up any more of your time than absolutely necessary." She waited for a response.

"That's fine. Whatever it takes." His expression darkened. "This is a nasty bit of business we're involved with. Isn't it?"

She opened with the most straightforward question she could think of. "What I'd like to know is if you can think of anyone or any reason someone might want to hurt Victor Rasmussen." The word "hurt" seemed a little overly polite to her.

Hobart sighed. "Honestly, he wasn't very well known in the bourbon brotherhood," his eyes widened, "if it all. He was not one of us. I certainly know I never met the man. And trust me, I've been at this a while. I know pretty much everyone in the family."

Jet was taken by his use of the word, "family." "I just have to ask, sir, and I apologize for my ignorance about this, but I heard you are a cousin of the Bennington family. Shouldn't you be working at the James Bennington distillery?"

Avery Hobart let out a solid chuckle. "One thousand, five hundred and ninety-six."

Jet cocked her head. "Excuse me?"

He smiled broadly. "That's the number of times I've been asked that question." He took a quick breath. "Let me explain. My family, the Rheums, came to America and started making whiskey in 1795. Since then almost every male in my family has been in the business. But people in all the bourbon families moved back and forth from one distillery to the next, crossing bloodlines, so to speak, over and over again. In fact, Ed Rollins and his brother, over at James Bennington, are our cousins. It's almost like we're all one extended family."

Jet smiled politely. "Interesting." She took a deep breath. "Now, if we could get down to brass tacks. Is there any way you can help me understand what happened to Victor Rasmussen?"

Avery Hobart rocked back in his upholstered leather chair, the wood-paneled walls in his office reflecting the last remaining rays of sun as the sky continued to darken. "I think I just did."

Jet cocked her head sharply. "Excuse me?"

"You want to know if I can help you understand what

happened to Mr. Rasmussen. I just told you that we're family in the bourbon business. That's who we are. That's how we operate."

"Oh." The sound of Jet's voice made it clear that she didn't really understand.

Hobart leaned forward, his arms resting against the edge of his desk. "Look, I'm sure you've heard about the fire they had over at the Heaven Hill distillery in 1996. It started in an old warehouse. Before they knew it, it had spread to other buildings, even to their vehicles. It was a river of fire flowing downhill. They lost almost one hundred thousand barrels of bourbon that day, seven rackhouses, the distillery, almost every vehicle." He shook his head sadly. "There was simply no way to stop that fire." He shrugged. "Heck, six percent of the world's bourbon went up in flames that day."

Jet nodded. "I certainly had heard about that. Anyone who's lived in Kentucky long enough knows that story."

Hobart smiled. "So, how do you think those folks survived over the next few years? Ever wonder about that?"

"I guess," Jet shrugged, "I never thought about it."

"Well let me tell you." His voice was resolute. "The other members of the bourbon brotherhood. We all helped them survive. For a short time, Heaven Hill products were actually made in the distilleries of other companies."

Jet's eyebrows raised. "Really?"

Hobart nodded. "Really. And to this day, if one distillery is short a piece of equipment, they know they can call down to someone else and they'll have it as long as they need it." He stopped and looked right into Jet's eyes. "You know of any other business in which that would happen?"

Jet was actually in awe. "Really, I don't."

Avery Hobart winked at her. "We may be competitors in the marketplace, but we're family down here in the world of bourbon."

After a pause, Jet squinted. "Sooo, that helps me understand how?"

"Family," Hobart stated proudly, "doesn't treat family that way. Even if it's new family."

A flash of pain pricked Jet's consciousness. Well, maybe some families don't.

Hobart shook his head again. "No. I just find it hard to believe that anyone in our community would respond that way to another man planning on making bourbon," he paused, "even if he didn't seem to have the slightest idea about what he was getting into."

"Oh." Jet's voice conveyed her disappointment. Then she brightened up. "I mean, that's wonderful, about the community and all. It just doesn't help me with my Victor Rasmussen problem."

Hobart looked at her and spoke softly. "Sorry."

After a moment, Jet ratcheted up her energy one last time. "And about the twenty-year-old bourbon that Rasmussen was going to bring out. Any ideas?"

Hobart shrugged. "That would be a tough one. Takes time to make bourbon." He shook his head. "Can't see how he could do it. That would be a tough one."

Somehow, those words sounded awfully familiar to Jet. She tried to hide her surprise, but inside her mind, bells were going off. She stood and extended her hand over Hobart's ample desk. "Mr. Hobart, sir, it's been an honor meeting you and I thank you ever so much for taking the time to speak with me. I'll let you go." She shook his hand, gave him a big smile and headed for the door.

"Ms. Jet," he called out.

She turned back to him. "Yes?"

"You all will let me know what you find out, now, won't you?"

She gave him a pleasant smile. "You can count on it, sir."

When Jet reached the exit door of the Woodland Acres

Bourbon Heritage Center she stepped into a teeming rainstorm. The first part of the trip back to Lexington, on small country roads, was going to be challenging.

24

After breakfast with Tee on Sunday morning, Sonia found herself sitting at her kitchen table, writing out Roman numerals—a nervous habit she had developed during her years in a Catholic elementary school. She was starting to become even more nervous about the fact that they had been given only five days to solve the murder of Victor Rasmussen, and it was already the morning of Day Three. To make matters worse, she wasn't at all certain that they had found any information that they could count on to lead them to his murderer.

She took a little inventory. Tee and Jet were off doing the last interviews with the significant leaders of the bourbon industry that Mason Holiday had identified as important. The only exception was John O'Neal at Horatio Blevins. He was out of town and wouldn't be back until Tuesday. Sonia wanted to speak to him herself, face to face. Rasmussen had been found, after all, on O'Neal's property, and was in fact, being "stored" on O'Neal's farm.

Brad was off talking to Patricia Huntington-Jones, Rasmussen's first wife. The only family member left to speak to was Victor's son, Davey. He had been in the United Arab Emirates for at least a month and wouldn't be back until seven o'clock Tuesday evening, the very end of Day Five. There just didn't seem to be much in the way of promising leads in terms of family connections.

And that was what was making Sonia so nervous. Conversations with the people in the bourbon industry had turned up nothing. Conversations with family members had turned up nothing. Talking to other business associates was another possibility, but the Rasmussen Company was no small affair. They had business arrangements with tons of other businesses, and for that matter, other individuals as well. Sonia was fully aware that with Tee joining the firm, albeit temporarily, and with Brad offering help, BCI was more fully staffed than it had ever been. Yet, together, they would barely be able to make a dent in the list of Rasmussen Company business connections in the next three days. She brushed a wisp of hair out of her face. Damn it, we need more help.

Sonia had slipped off her blue and white running shoes and was sitting, barefoot on her couch. As she sipped her coffee, it suddenly struck her that there just might be one other person to whom she could turn for help, someone who understood investigations and yet wasn't a police officer—well, not anymore.

Lifting her phone off the end table next to her, Sonia began scrolling quickly. It was only a half-second before she was into the J's. James Harris, Jessica Strong, John Aaronson . . . . There it was, Johnny Adams. It had been several months since Johnny Adams had pursued her romantically and then, in an incredible moment, saved her life. It had been so very difficult for her, only moments later, to tell him that as much as she cared for him, she was choosing to be with Brad Dunham. Shortly thereafter, Johnny had resigned from the Lexington Police Department and left town. Sonia had heard, through Jet's friend on the force, Malcolm Withers, that losing Sonia to Brad had been part of the reason for his leaving.

And now, here she sat, her phone in her hand, ready to call this really nice guy and ask him to come help—with almost no notice. She took a deep breath and touched his name on the screen.

"The number you have reached is no longer in service."

Sonia was confused. Nobody changed their phone numbers when they moved anymore. Too much of a hassle letting everyone know your new number. She tried again.

"The number you have . . . ."

Sonia sat almost motionless, her fingers drumming out a rhythmic pattern on the screen of the phone. Finally, another thought crossed her mind. Tapping on the phone's home screen, she came to another phone number and pressed CALL.

"Hello?" The voice was quiet, guarded.

"Johnny?"

There was a pause before he answered, even more hesitant. *"Who is this?"*

"Johnny. It's me, Sonia Vitale."

There was another pause, but when he answered, Johnny Adams' voice was distinctly different, upbeat. *"Hey. How are you? Wow, how good to hear your voice."*

"Yeah." The smile in her voice came through. "Good to hear yours as well. How are you, Johnny?"

"Great. I'm doing just great. But what about you? Everything going okay for the ladies of BCI?"

"Yes, actually, things are great. So, where are you these days?"

The answer came quickly. *"Colorado. Denver, Colorado, and having a great time. You should see how beautiful it is out here in the spring, Sonia. You really should."*

"Well, I'd love to sometime. Truly, I would." Recalling some of the more intense moments of their romantic relationship, she was careful not to go any further.

"So, wow, I'm surprised you were able to track me down."

"Well, I tried your old number but, as I'm sure you know, it's out of service. And I remembered you had told me that, as a detective, there was always the possibility that you might find yourself in a sticky situation and need a phone you could use for, how do we say it, discrete conversations?"

"Yeah, well, after what happened in Lexington, I just wanted to leave a whole lot of things behind. So, I moved out here to Denver, started doing some private security work, and got a new phone number. You know, a fresh start. I'm glad you remembered this other number, though. It might have been tough to find me without it. Now, why did you say you were calling?"

Sonia took a deep breath. She was heartened by the fact that she had received such a warm reception from Johnny, but she wasn't sure he was going to be amenable to dropping everything and coming to help her, especially once she made it clear that Brad was still a big part of her life. That, in fact, they were now engaged.

Sonia spent the next few minutes laying things out to Johnny. She told him what she could without exceeding the limits of her NDA with Mason Holiday. She figured that if Johnny actually came to help for the next few days, she would sign him to some short-term contract, making it possible for her to share all the pertinent information. When she finished sharing what she could, she held her breath. She was rewarded with the words she wanted desperately to hear.

"Sonia. I would do anything to help you. There's nothing going on here that I can't get away from for a couple of days. You just hang on. As soon as I can, I'll text you about when I'm getting into town. I'll be there sometime tomorrow, maybe even later today."

"Oh, Johnny, that would be so wonderful. It'll be great to see you, great to work with you again. Just let me know when to pick you up at the airport."

There was a moment's silence, then Johnny responded. *"Oh, no need for that. I'll just rent a car. I'm sure I'll need wheels if I'm going to do any real investigating. You just hang out at that crazy office of yours, and before you know it, I'll be there with bells on."*

"Really?"

"Well, okay. I'll wear clothing if you'd rather, but trust me, the bell thing looks great on me."

Sonia couldn't help but laugh out loud. "Oh, Johnny. There's that dad humor I've missed so much. Just let me know when you'll be getting in. The least I can do is have a nice hot cup of coffee and one of Magee's famous pastries waiting for you."

"You've got it. See you soon. Say, "Hi," to, ah, Brad for me. Bye." The last few words had not come out of his mouth as smoothly as he had hoped.

25

As the phone call ended, Sonia stood and began walking around her tiny apartment. She was thrilled that she was going to get more help with the case. She also had to admit that there was a part of her that was eager to see the handsome man who had tried so hard to be with her—and had succeeded in winning at least a tiny part of her heart.

After calming herself a bit by making yet another cup of coffee, Sonia sat back down on the couch and tried to get back to the matter at hand—solving the murder of Victor Rasmussen.

Eventually, something came to her. It appeared that the one lead they still hadn't tracked down was the mention, by two different people, that Missy Charles might be more than Victor Rasmussen's right hand. She might possibly be the one person who could take over The Rasmussen Company if something happened to Victor. Sure, Sonia thought, Victor's son might be the heir-apparent, legally speaking, but did he have the know-how to run the company? Sonia ran her fingers through her hair and spoke into her cup of coffee. "I wonder if she thinks she could take on Victor's son, Davey, fight him for control of the company." She knew that it was conceivable that Missy could try to get rid of him by paying him off, or worse, and therefore wind up with the company in her own hands.

Sonia reached down and lifted her computer into her lap. Her fingers tapping on its sides, she watched the screen come alive. "Let's see who you really are, Ms. Charles."

Sonia had been a computer science major at The Ohio State University, but all of the things she had learned in college paled when compared to what she had learned since she'd hooked up with Brad Dunham and his old NCIS colleagues. What she was about to attempt certainly wasn't listed on the syllabus of any of the classes she'd taken in college.

Sonia had hacked into two computer systems in the last year, one with access through a public website, the other by physically placing a keystroke monitoring device on the computer. This time would be different. With no physical access to the computer and a truly stand-alone company website, she was left using the most rudimentary form of hacking, sending a trojan file. She would send it as an attachment to an email and hope the recipient would open it, thereby allowing the virus to infiltrate the system. It was an approach that didn't always work, and even if it did, it wasn't likely to produce any results very quickly.

Sonia created the virus, sent the email off to Missy, and sat back on her couch. She took a long, slow breath. Now what? Heading to her coffee maker to drain the last quarter inch of coffee into her cup, she turned the case over and over in her mind. The pressure of the five-day time constraint was starting to become an impediment in and of itself. She felt like it was keeping her from really concentrating on the facts and their implications. She gave her head one quick shake. I've got to go do something, *something* that will move this thing forward.

It struck her that Carl Rasmussen might just have more insight into Missy Charles and what she was capable of than Brad had surmised. After all, when Brad had spoken with Victor's father, he hadn't yet heard about Missy's own words implying she could handle the company with or without Victor. After a final sip, Sonia turned and rinsed her coffee cup in the sink, leaving the carafe and the machine for later. Time to go see Mr. Rasmussen myself. Let's see what the old man has to say.

SONIA GOT HERSELF TOGETHER. Hair, make-up, white pants—heck, it's almost Memorial Day—pink oxford shirt, blue flats, Smith & Wesson .38 special. She walked down the wooden stairs outside her apartment, climbed into her old Subaru, and headed off to see Carl Rasmussen.

After using her dark brown eyes and big smile to get past the security guard at the entrance, she pulled up to 7722 Bellevie Road. Unfortunately, it had begun pouring rain. She'd have to use her umbrella. With a determined sigh, she peeked the door open, slid the umbrella out, and of course, struggled to get it to open all the way as she stepped out of the car. By the time she reached the front door, her feet and the bottoms of her white pants were already soaked.

Sonia knocked and the door was opened—same sturdy woman, same German accent. "Come in, come in, *ja*?" She motioned Sonia to an indoor floor mat in the vestibule. Sonia wondered if she needed to remove her shoes.

Sonia wiped the moisture off her face and shuddered. "Oh, it's terrible out there. Thank you for letting me in."

"*Ja*, sure. No need for you to stand out in za rain." She gave Sonia a weak smile with a hint of warmth in it. "How can I help you?"

"Well, Ms.—" Sonia was stuck.

"Frieda. Frieda Schiessl."

Sonia's eyes darted to the woman's left hand. "Yes. Mrs. Schiessl. I'm here to see Mr. Rasmussen if that's possible."

Frieda shook her head. "It's not." Both the answer and the sound of her voice were clipped.

Sonia put on her best pouty face. "Oh, I know I don't have an appointment. It's just that—"

Frieda raised her left hand. "It's not possible because za mister is not here." The answer was followed by silence rather than an explanation.

"Ohhh." Sonia's mind was scrambling for a way forward. "Do you know when he'll return?"

"He's in hospital. Maybe he's not coming back at all." Sonia was having trouble reading Frieda as she responded. The first part of her statement had been pure employee reporting. The second part actually held some warmth, almost compassion.

Sonia gave the woman a weak smile of her own. "Oh, I'm so sorry to hear that." She looked around the vestibule—simple walls, wood flooring, some odd-looking sculpture of couples entwined. "I guess I'll leave then. I'm sorry to have bothered you."

"Do you want to look at his computer?"

Sonia was taken aback. She cocked her head. "Excuse me?"

Frieda puffed up, apparently a little put out by having to explain herself. "Do you want to see his computer?" she repeated firmly. "Za others wanted to look at his computer."

"Oh." Sonia feigned understanding. "Right. The computer. So, some of our folks were already here?"

Frieda's impatience showed through her huff. "*Ja*, za last time he was in hospital."

Sonia tried her best to look both comfortable with the information and impatient. "Of course." She shook her head. "Which ones came?"

"Za man and za woman. They said they were from za company and they needed to see his computer. I let zem see it." There was no ambivalence in her words.

"Sure, sure." Sonia nodded her approval. "Right, they needed to look at the computer. Of course." She paused, uncertain how to pose her next question. "So, where is it? I don't want to track rain all over the floor."

Frieda spun and took off walking. “Follow me. You take your shoes off, *ja*?”

Sonia couldn’t believe it. She slipped her shoes off and followed the woman in the pink uniformish dress down the marble-floored hallway and toward the same room in which Brad had met Carl Rasmussen, though she didn’t know it. She was on her way to Rasmussen’s computer. That had never even been her goal for the day, she’d only come to speak to the old man. As she entered the den, she coughed gently, “So, you said Mr. Rasmussen might not be able to return?”

“Cancer.” There was just the slightest nod in her head. “He’s had it a long time. Ve vas surprised when he came home za last time.”

“Sure, sure.” Sonia sounded saddened. She actually was. She sat down at the computer and turned it on. She spoke while her eyes watched the computer screen come alive. “Thank you for your time, Mrs. Schiessl. I’ll let you know when I’m finished. This won’t take very long.”

“*Ja,* sure. I’ll be in za front room. Call if you need something.”

Sonia began working her way through the computer, her foot tapping the expensive-looking wood flooring. It was easy since the computer wasn’t password protected in any way. She didn’t immediately see anything that seemed to pertain to the business, no folder marked Rasmussen Company or anything like that. She opened his email. AOL. Wow, that’s old-school. Has this guy never heard of Gmail? There was little there, and it all seemed to pertain to personal correspondence. She took a very close look at the names attached to the incoming emails in both his inbox and deleted items. The only name she recognized was Victor’s, and those messages held nothing that seemed particularly important. She checked his internet history as well, but it appeared the old man took little advantage of his connection to the worldwide web.

Frustrated, Sonia decided to try one last thing before shutting the computer down and leaving. She clicked on the list of recently opened files. There was little there of interest as well, except a folder marked WOCR. When she clicked on that file, she realized the letters stood for Will of Carl Rasmussen. She wondered if there would be some bombshell information in the document. As she skimmed through the document, however, she noted that it was pretty much what one would expect. She ran her fingers through her damp hair. Poor old guy. Knows this is probably it. Just wanted to make certain everything was in place before he . . . .

Sonia manipulated the mouse, turning off the computer, then headed for the front door. She found Frieda waiting for her. She wondered if the woman had been standing there watching and waiting the whole time. "Thank you again, Mrs. Schiessl. I told you it wouldn't take very long."

Frieda nodded silently.

"One last thing. I saw that the last two who were here had been working on a particular file. I was wondering if they'd finished and I'm not sure which two came that day. What were their names again?"

Frieda shook her head. "I don't know. Zey didn't say. Zey just said they were from za company."

Sonia waved her hand nonchalantly. "I'll find them. There are only two teams that do that kind of work. You just describe them and I'll know who they are."

Frieda squinted her eyes. Sonia couldn't tell if she was trying to remember what those people looked like or wondering whether or not she should say. "I don't remember much. Tall man, thin, beard. Blonde voman."

"How old?"

Frieda looked a little perturbed. "Ach," she shrugged. "Forties, fifties?"

"Uh huh." Sonia nodded knowingly. She could feel the clock running out. "Anything special about them."

Frieda thought for a moment. “Ze woman. She was za boss.”

“Ohhh.”

Sonia reached out tentatively and touched Frieda on the forearm, so tentatively she wasn’t even sure she’d made contact. “Thank you again, Mrs. Schiessl.” She turned, opened the door, stuck her umbrella out, and opened it. She turned back, gave Frieda one last smile, and took off running for her car. As she sat in the Subaru, the sound of rain pelting the roof, a thought crystallized for Sonia. No question. Missy Charles is making her move and she wanted to make certain that there’s nothing on Carl Rasmussen’s computer that could incriminate her. In fact, maybe there had been something there and Missy had removed it.

Sonia started the car and headed for her office. As she drove, she pushed several wet strands of hair out of her face. Dang, I wish I’d figured this out before I left that computer. I’d love to get back in there and go through all the erased files. She huffed out a tiny breath and a snarky little smile crossed her lips. She knew better than most that nothing ever really gets erased from a computer.

26

By three thirty, Sonia was back in Magee's parking lot. When she reached the bottom of those wooden steps, she wished she could just pop into the bakery to pick up a hot cup of coffee and an afternoon treat. It being Sunday afternoon, that was just not in the cards. She looked at the rain-slicked steps. And up we go.

Once inside the office, Sonia put on a pot of coffee and checked some phone and email messages. Nothing of great importance. One by one, the BCI team arrived as well. Eventually, three of them were seated around the white table in the waiting room while Sonia brought out a cup of coffee for each. That accomplished, she sat down next to Brad. "Okay, ladies and gentlemen. Let's see what we've all been up to this lovely, rainy Sunday. But listen, let's cut to the chase. The clock is running and it's time we get something going here. Who wants to start? Tee?"

Tee sat up straighter, her voice filled with obvious frustration. "Well, I met with Clay Baratin at the Elk Horn Distillery down in Bardstown and learned nothing except what a rye forward bourbon is. I got nothing special at Bald Knob Trace and Johnston Springs. Oh," she twisted her lips while squinting one eye, "and the trip back in the rain was great."

Sonia tried to hide a sigh by scratching her nose. I wonder if I should remind her that no one told her this was going to be easy. "Jet?"

Brad interrupted. "Wait. Before you hear from Jet, I've got something important to share." Every head at the table turned toward him. "I met with Patricia Huntington-Jones this afternoon, Victor's first wife. I won't go into a lot of detail, but here's the main thing I learned." He let a half-moment go by. "Victor Rasmussen was a constant and reckless gambler."

"Whoa. Now ain't that interestin'." Jet's southern belle was back momentarily.

"Interesting and then some," said Brad. He took a sip from the cup he was holding. "The question is: 'How does that play into what was going on?' I mean, did he take on some big bet and lose? Was he simply killed over a gambling debt?"

Silence filled the room as all four of them wondered about the implications of Brad's information. Finally, Sonia tried to get things going again. "Let's move on. What do you have for us, Jet?"

Jet sat up taller and put her coffee down. "Well, I spent the day with the folks at Settler's Pride and Woodland Acres. I know they're just vague, but I got two things I think could be important from Avery Hobart at Woodland." She held up one finger. "First, I asked him about being related to the Benningtons and working at Woodland Acres instead of the James Bennington distillery. He told me all about the bourbon families moving around and working in all the different bourbon organizations. He used the word, 'family.' When I asked him specifically about someone hurting Victor Rasmussen his answer was all about family again. I think the message he was trying to send me was to stop looking in that direction, that he didn't think someone in the bourbon brotherhood would hurt Victor, even if nobody liked him or respected him."

Sonia pursed her lips. "Okay. What's the second thing?"

Jet leaned in toward Sonia, tipping her head and squinting just a bit. "Do you remember telling us that when you asked Oscar Branch about Victor coming up with twenty-year-old bourbon, his response was, 'That would be a tough one?' "

Sonia nodded again. "Uh, huh."

Jet banged her fist gently on the plastic table and pointed right at Sonia. "Well, those were the exact same words that Avery Hobart used, 'That would be a tough one.'"

Tee shrugged. "So?"

Brad leaned in immediately and turned to his left. "Wait a minute, Tee. There could be something there." He turned back to Jet. "What are you thinking?"

Jet shrugged. "I don't know, but I got the feeling that these guys have gotten together and talked this through long before they called us in. It's almost as if they came up with some planned response to questions about that bourbon."

Sonia brushed a wisp of hair out of her face. "Planned, or maybe inadvertent. Maybe that phrase got used a lot during their conversation and it just stuck?" She turned to Brad. "How does it strike you?"

Brad put his coffee down and rocked back in his chair. "Look. I've done a lot of investigations," he pinched his thumb and fore-finger almost together, "where one little thing catches your atten-tion. You can ignore it, write it off as insignificant, or you can track it down." He smiled at Jet. "For some reason, I'm getting the same vibe Jet got." He turned back to Sonia. "It may well be that the fine folks of the bourbon brotherhood are sandbagging us. And if that's true, we need to find out right away. Day Five is coming—fast."

There was a moment's silence before Tee spoke. "So, what do we do now?"

"I'll tell you what we do now." Sonia's tone had turned from frustrated to determined. "We call Mason Holiday and tell him to get his Sunday afternoon you-know-what over here to explain what the heck is going on."

Brad leaned forward. "Agreed. The clock is ticking and we've got nothing but vague notions. We've got to try to get our hands on something concrete."

Sonia smiled a Cheshire-cat grin. "Will this do?" Like Brad, she let her question hang in the air for the briefest moment. "What if I tell you that I just found out that Carl Rasmussen is dying of cancer, and that Missy Charles and some man were at his home just after he went into the hospital?"

The expressions on the faces of the other three brought an even bigger smile to Sonia's face. "Yup. I went over there to ask him a few more questions about Missy Charles, and his housekeeper told me all about it. In fact," she took a dramatic pause, "she asked me if I wanted to see his computer."

"Seriously?" Tee's dark brown eyes were opened wide.

Sonia let out a deep breath. "Seriously."

"Yeah," Brad nodded, "I sensed the old guy wasn't doing well. Sorry to hear about the dying part, though."

Jet ran her ponytail through her fingers. "I agree, but did you get to the computer or not?"

"I got to the computer." Sonia teepeed her fingers. "Unfortunately, I didn't find anything there about Missy or the business. That's probably because Missy got there before me. I'm guessing she's already deleted anything that would implicate her in this mess. The only thing that I really got to look over was his will, and there was nothing there that you wouldn't expect."

"So," Tee's voice was tentative, "it's Missy Charles that we're after?"

"We're not sure," said Sonia. "It just seems—

CRACK! CRACK!

"GUN!" Brad's booming voice filled the room. "HIT THE FLOOR!"

27

Brad was on his feet in an instant, pushing Sonia to the floor and waving Jet and Tee out of their seats and down. "Get down! Stay down!" Squatting, he pushed Sonia along the floor and under the table, then waved his arms at Jet and Tee. "Under here, both of you!"

The room was silent for a long moment.

"Anyone armed?" It was the voice of Captain Brad Dunham, U.S. Marine Corps, strong, yet quiet—totally under control.

It took a moment, but Sonia finally responded. "Me. I am."

Brad looked at her curiously. "Okay." There was an unspoken question in his tone. "Anyone else?" He saw a blank look on Tee's face.

Jet's response was different. "Damn, mine's at home, locked up for safety." A disgusted look crossed her face. "Lot of good it does me there."

Brad pulled a Glock G43 from the holster at his back, a slightly thinner version of the Sig Sauer Jet had left at home, and significantly smaller than the .45 caliber Colt 1911 he carried when he felt he might be going into a dangerous situation. "All I've got is this little nine." He turned his attention back to Sonia and asked a question with his eyes.

"I've got my .38." Sonia reached down, tugged up her white pant leg, still damp from her run in the rain, and pulled the Smith & Wesson out of its holster.

"Okay. Stay here." Again, his voice was without hesitation.

"No." Sonia's voice was equally strong, and equally without hesitation.

"Sonia, stay here." There was no question it was a command.

One she didn't plan on following. "I'm coming with you."

Brad huffed. "Okay, but stay down."

Sonia brushed a wisp of hair out of her face and nodded. Yes, sir. Right.

Brad crept out from below the table, Sonia following behind. They crawled along the floor toward Sonia's office. As Sonia followed Brad across the room, her eyes were drawn to two small holes in the glass that separated her office from the waiting area. Things started to come into focus. Someone had fired two rounds into the BCI offices while the team was sitting at the table.

Brad made it through the door into Sonia's space and then to the outer wall, the one that looked over East Main. Sonia followed, scooting around Brad and placing her back against the wall to his right, the way she'd seen so many actors position themselves in movies and TV shows. Gingerly poking his head up, Brad scanned the rain-soaked area across the street.

At the same time, Sonia's eyes searched their office space, examining the damage the rounds had done. Within moments she focused on two marks in the ceiling over the waiting area. Glancing back to the holes in the glass between her office and the waiting area, Sonia made a quick calculation. The holes in the glass were near the top of the pane. She could imagine a straight line from them to the marks in the ceiling, the places where she imagined the lead projectiles were currently lodged.

Brad was still scanning the area, hoping to see something,

anything that would give him a clue as to where the shooter was. Still holding her .38 in her right hand, Sonia reached across her body with her left and squeezed Brad's arm. He turned to her. Using her small, two-inch-barreled gun as a pointer, Sonia drew Brad's eyes along the trajectory she was convinced the bullets had traveled. He turned to her and nodded. Then he leaned back and looked more closely at the window through which he had been peering. Without saying a word, he pointed to the two holes in that window, holes near the bottom of the pane.

Brad slouched down and turned his back to the wall, leaning against it just as Sonia had. "Low entry through this window," he said softly while he pointed with his empty hand, "high exit on that one, impact in the ceiling." He turned to her and smiled.

Sonia was way ahead of him. "The shooter was lower than us, probably on the ground." Her voice was soft as well.

"And," Brad let out a breath of relief and spoke a little more loudly, "probably long gone. I'm pretty sure."

"Right." Sonia began to relax as well. "He probably fired then ran." She began to stand.

Brad reached out and grabbed her arm, pulling her back down. "*Probably*. Stay low and let's move back to the girls. Make sure they're okay."

Brad swung around and crept back to the table, hunched over to keep the lowest profile possible. Sonia did the same.

When they got back to the table, Brad asked, "Everyone okay?" His tone of voice indicated he was pretty certain about the answer.

Sonia bent down and put her arm around Tee, her eyes locking with Jet's. "Really. Are either of you hurt?"

Tee answered first. "Son-of-a-bitch didn't get us. But holy crap, I got to tell you, I almost peed my pants."

"Now, now, little girl." Jet's southern belle was back and full-throated. "Looks like we ladies are going to have to do some serious thinking about this. Lordy, if they're gonna start shootin' at us we're gonna have to be a whole lot more careful . . . and a whole lot more certain to be carryin', if you know what I mean."

Brad looked at Jet and rolled his eyes, but Sonia knew better. She was certain that Jet's theatrics were meant to calm Tee and, in fact, Jet herself. She gave Tee another squeeze. "Don't worry, honey, we're going to be alright."

Jet reached into her back pocket and took out her phone. "Let me get the police over here, just in case Brad's wrong and that guy," she hitched, "or girl, is still out there."

"No, wait." Sonia reached out and grabbed Jet's arm. "You'd better not do that."

Jet's eye's squinted. "Why?"

Sonia let out a sigh. "It's that non-disclosure agreement we signed. I was afraid something like this might happen." She looked at Brad, then back to Jet. "What are we going to do, tell them someone shot at us because we're investigating a murder they don't even know about?" She shook her head. "Agreement or not, I'm pretty sure the police would say we've been impeding an investigation, or at a minimum withholding pertinent information. I'm thinking that if you make that call, we might be spending the night in jail for obstruction of justice."

Brad gave Sonia a small "*I told you so*" look, one she wasn't particularly pleased to see. After a moment, he stood up, tentatively. "Okay, I'm going outside to take a look around. See if I can find anything."

"Like shell casings?" Tee asked, a lift in her voice.

Brad turned to her and smiled. "Like shell casings."

"And I," said Sonia. "am going to get Mason Holiday on the phone and tell him to get his ass down here right now. It's time we find out exactly what he's gotten us into."

28

Sonia made her phone call to Mason Holiday from her office, trying her best to indicate her frustration while not letting her emotional state get the best of her professional demeanor. As she spoke, her eyes couldn't resist the urge to keep tracking the trajectory of the deadly projectiles that had blown through their offices, lodging in their ceiling. She was pretty certain that whoever was shooting at them wasn't really trying to hurt them. She ran her fingers through her hair. Better in the ceiling than in one of the people I love.

When she had finished her call, Sonia stepped back into the waiting area and over to the white, plastic table at which the team was sitting. Brad had just returned from looking around. She let out a quick huff. "He's on his way." Sonia took her seat next to Brad. "He said he'd be here a little before six."

"And when he gets here," Jet's southern accent was in full bloom, "he's gonna feel like Paula Dean, herself, slathered his whole body in butter. 'Cause I'm gonna fry his ass."

Sonia could tell from the look on Tee's face that she was mildly amused by Jet's outburst. "Whatever," slipped out of her mouth. Meanwhile, Brad sat silently, apparently mulling over possibilities.

Sonia put her hand on Brad's leg as she spoke. "Well, I'll tell you one thing. With how things are progressing, I'm glad we've got a little more help on the way."

Jet gave her a look. "You mean Mason Holiday?"

"No. I mean Detective Sergeant Johnny Adams."

Jet's eyes popped open, but it was Brad's response that got Sonia's attention. He sat suddenly taller in his chair, his body noticeably stiffer. Aware of his reaction, Sonia continued. "Yeah, I was sitting there thinking about it this morning. There are so many Rasmussen Company business contacts we need to question that we're never going to come close to completing the task by the end of the fifth day. I just became convinced we needed more help."

Brad's voice seemed to have dropped half an octave. "So, you called Johnny Adams?"

Sonia could feel the chill coming off his presence. She removed her hand but she didn't allow herself to flinch. "Yes. He's a skilled investigator and someone we can trust. I called him, and he said he would be glad to assist, especially since it was only for a few days. He said he'd be here by the end of the day or early in the morning."

Brad said nothing. His body spoke volumes.

When Sonia turned to look at Jet, she could see that Jet's antennae had clearly picked up on the tension between Sonia and Brad. The look on Tee's face indicated she had no idea what was going on—but she was pretty sure it was darn juicy.

Silence lingered at the table for a long moment. Finally, Brad stood, "Sonia, can we talk?"

Sonia rose and began following him into her office. The thoughts that were flying around in her mind had her spinning. On the one hand, her mind flashed back to her very first meeting with Brad. He had been sitting behind his big desk playing mind games with her as she tried to establish herself as a professional, while at the same time asking for help in investigating a suicide she was almost certain was a murder. On the other hand, they were now walking into *her* domain, *her* space, inside the *BCI* offices, the place where she and Jet were in charge. She brushed that stubborn wisp of hair out of her face. Why do I feel like I'm the teacher, yet *I'm* the one being sent to the principal's office?

As soon as Sonia had entered the office, Brad turned. "You called Johnny Adams?"

Sonia stopped short. She braced herself. "That's what I said. I called him this morning. Do you have a problem with that?"

"Yes, I have a problem with that. Why him? Why didn't you ask me if I had someone else, someone right here in town who could help?"

"Is there something wrong with Johnny? Some reason why I shouldn't have called him?"

Brad took a beat before he answered. "Look, I know he's an ex-cop and all but . . . but, well I don't know."

Sonia leaned in. "Well, maybe I do know. Maybe you're upset because I dated Johnny before you and I . . . well, before we became us. Is that the problem?"

"No, of course not. It's just that I don't have a good feeling about the guy."

Sonia's answer shot out of her mouth. "Well, I do. He's a good man. A good cop and a good man. A real professional." Sonia was quite certain Brad's reaction had more to do with romantic rivalry than any gut feeling.

Brad bristled. "More of a professional than me?" He glared at Sonia.

"No. Not *more* of a professional. Just a professional. And someone I know will keep our work confidential." She turned away from Brad, unclear if she was mad or hurt. Doesn't he get this? There's nothing between Johnny and me. He's just a solid guy I know I can trust.

One more thought smoldered in Sonia's mind, became red hot, then finally burst out of her mouth. "And isn't it *my* call, *our* call, Jet's and mine, who we bring into this investigation?" She took a step toward Brad, now quite certain it was anger she was feeling—anger driven by hurt. "Is it because you think that you're in charge of any investigation we work on together, whether it's yours or ours? Is that it?" Another step closer, her finger now wagging in Brad's face. "Listen. Get this straight. This is our investigation, BCI's, and we appreciate your help, but don't you think for a moment that we can't pull this thing together without it. Don't you think for an instant that in some perverse way Jet and I work for you, that we're under your command, *Captain* Dunham. And don't you think for one minute that when we're married, you're going to be the big, strong, boss man and I'm going to be barefoot and pregnant."

Sonia stopped, still. Suddenly realizing that there were tears running down her face—coming to grips with the fact that this whole deal was about more than their professional relationship. Deep down, she wasn't entirely sure that Brad would ever be able to truly respect her—as an equal—as a person.

Brad didn't say a word. The frustration and anger that had been etched so deeply on his face just moments before were gone. His bright blue eyes moved to the floor and back, silently changing their message from one of contrition to one of supplication—wordlessly saying, "*I'm so sorry for hurting you*," then "*Please forgive me, please don't reject me.*" Finally, his voice joined in, "Sonia, I'm . . ."

She turned and walked out of the room.

29

It was a little after six before the door opened and Mason Holiday walked into the BCI offices, tiny droplets of water glistening on the light jacket he wore over his khakis and blue, Ralph Lauren sport shirt. The looks on the faces of the four people sitting around the plastic table waiting for him were less than welcoming.

"Mason." It was the only greeting he got from Sonia—from any of them.

"Ladies." He looked over the table at Brad. "Sir."

"Welcome, again, to our humble abode." The sarcasm dripped off Jet's voice. "Do you happen to notice any changes we've made lately?"

It was obvious that Holiday's focus was on the people in the room as he answered, "I see we've added two new folks to our discussions. I hope they are all well aware of our agreements."

"Completely aware, Mason." Sonia's voice was terse. "This is Brad Dunham and my . . . and Teresa Vitale. They are both working with BCI at the moment." She opened her hands, making a show of the next statement. "They are fully aware of our agreements and, I should say, in full compliance."

Holiday scratched his forehead unconsciously, clearly uncomfortable with the greeting he was receiving. "Is there something I can do for you all?"

Jet waved her arm in the direction of the table in front of him. "Oh, please have a seat, Mason. But before you do, why don't you take a closer look around the room. Can you see some of the other changes we've made?"

Before moving to a chair at the table, Holiday stood in place and turned slowly around, his eyes searching for the answer to the riddle. He stopped, turning quickly back toward the four of them. "Are those bullet holes in that glass?"

Tee banged her fist on the table. "Yes, they're damn bullet holes." It was obvious she was not going to be able to play nice.

Holiday recoiled from her comments and turned his attention back to Sonia and Jet. "I'm so sorry. I mean it. I'm so, so sorry. What happened?"

Sonia was determined to turn the scene into a useful dialogue. She spoke in more measured tones. "Have a seat, Mason, and we'll explain."

While Holiday sat down at the end of the table, Sonia took a few moments to explain what had happened and how frustrated she and her team were about getting the run-around from the bourbon distillers.

Holiday seemed truly rattled and not at all cavalier about the shooting. "Again, I'm so sorry. Have you called the police?" He took a moment to look across the table at Brad, who had not yet said a word.

Sonia stayed calm, though she brushed a wisp of hair out of her face and her foot was tapping a mile a minute. "No, Mason, we'll not be calling the police." She leaned toward him. "You see, when you got us to sign that non-disclosure agreement you sucked us into this mess. Of course," she leaned half way across the table, anger in her voice, "we had no idea that this case was going to devolve into people shooting at us." She waited a moment, then started again, more calmly. "Now, Mason, we think it's time you tell us everything you know about what's going on." She gave him a snarky smile. "Wouldn't you agree?"

Holiday put his elbows on the table and his hands together in front of his face as if he were praying. "Yes, you're right. But you've got to know, we never expected it to come to this, never."

Sonia, Jet, Tee, and Brad all sat wordlessly, watching and listening.

The room was silent for a long moment while Mason closed his eyes, silently thinking. Finally, he opened his eyes and spoke. "Look, you've got to understand. Like I said when we first met, this whole episode has the potential to absolutely kill the momentum the bourbon industry has built up over the last few years, especially for Horatio Blevins." He looked at them, his eyes almost pleading. "Remember? An urban myth about the entire output of a distillery being tainted by a corpse rotting in one of the barrels? It doesn't matter that it's not true. It would kill John O'Neal and his crew over there. It would hurt all of us."

"Yes," Sonia remained calm as she watched frustration, maybe even anger, growing on Jet's face. "We remember. We understand. But . . . ."

"Okay." Holiday let out a breath and held up one hand. "I know." His gaze moved to Jet. "Listen. It's like what Avery Hobart said to Ms. Jet—"

"Excuse me?" Jet all but popped out of her chair. "You know what Avery Hobart said to me?"

Holiday sat silent for a moment, his eyes searching for a place to settle.

Jet leaned forward, her hands on the table, her eyes glaring. "You talked to him after I left, didn't you?"

"Well," Holiday's voice was quiet, contrite, "yes, I did."

"Hold on." Sonia sat taller as well. "Have you been getting reports on all of our interviews?"

Holiday didn't answer.

"Dang it, Mason." Sonia's brown eyes held none of the inviting warmth Brad had often perceived in them. "What the hell's going on?"

Holiday looked first at Sonia, then Jet, then Tee. Sonia could tell that the look he got from Brad prompted him to speak. "Yes." He dropped his head. "Everyone's been reporting to me." He looked up again, his gaze passing all four faces. "Look, like I said, Avery Hobart tried to explain to Jet that all the people in the bourbon community, we're family. We've worked together for generations. We've helped each other when times were bad." He looked at Jet as if reminding her of her conversation with the man. "Even when we don't much care for somebody or respect them." He looked back at Sonia. "You make bourbon in this part of the world, you're family."

Sonia took a deep breath, trying to control her frustration. "Yes, Mason. Jet got the message. In fact, she's already shared it with us. But I still don't understand. Why were you all not fully transparent with us? What were you hiding? You hired us, remember?"

Again, there was silence before Holiday began. "Look, you've been asking who in the bourbon brotherhood might have killed Victor Rasmussen, and we, all of us, don't believe anyone in the brotherhood did." His eyes searched the faces across from him plaintively. "We really don't." He took a deep breath. "You've also been asking about the twenty-year-old bourbon that Rasmussen said he was going to bring to market, bourbon he couldn't just pull out of thin air." He shrugged. "You had no idea how he could pull that off." He paused, took a deep breath, and spoke softly. "We did."

Sonia could see Jet about to go off. She waved a calming hand at her partner and took a deep breath herself. "Go on, Mason."

He nodded. "Okay, I'm going to tell you something, something I'm pretty certain none of you know. But please believe me. The only reason we didn't tell you before was that we were hoping you would be able to solve the case without knowing, without getting other people involved." He turned to Brad, looking for support. He got none.

It was obvious to Sonia that the silence coming from Brad, a large and clearly powerful man, was beginning to make Holiday nervous and more likely to be honest with them. "Well, Mason, it appears we're beyond that point."

"Yes, I know that now." Holiday's eyes drifted to the bullet holes in the office glass. "Believe me, we never thought things would go this far. We never would have put you in danger on purpose. But now, I'm going to tell you the truth, the whole truth. I promise."

"No time like the present." Jet's voice had more than a little edge to it.

Holiday sat up taller, folding his hands on the table in front of him. "So, you all know that for almost a hundred years coal has been the backbone of the Kentucky economy." He waved his hand. "Oh, sure, the horse industry is important, flashy, world-renowned. And, I'm proud to say, there have been times, like now, when the bourbon industry has been important. But the real backbone of the state has always been coal. In fact, in 2010 there were something like four hundred and fifty active coal mines in the state."

He pointed at Sonia, then Jet. "And twenty years ago, things were still good for coal, especially out in Eastern Kentucky." Pausing, Holiday rubbed his chin between the thumb and forefinger of his right hand. "So, back then, two brothers, Ephraim and Ezekiel Bartley, they were making lots of money mining coal out in Knott County," he pointed absently with his thumb, "down 64, past Hazard? Anyway, they decided that they were going to get into the bourbon business, but not like everyone else."

Sonia and the rest of the team sat quietly, fully engaged.

"Now, what they were thinking was that the real money in bourbon was not in cranking out a lot of it, but rather, in turning out only the very best," a small smile crossed his face, "twenty years in the barrel or more." He stopped, almost as if he was thinking about the virtues of twenty-year-old bourbon on a cold winter's night.

"You going to finish the story, or what?" Jet's impatience was clear in her every word.

Holiday pulled himself out of his momentary revelry. "Sure. Sorry." He rubbed his nose with a crooked finger. "Anyway, they found themselves a place just south of the Woodland Acres distillery and built a small production facility, I mean, almost tiny. They were able to use the same water, and they kept it real low-profile. Then they got one of the Bennington clan to put together their yeast recipe and figure out their mash bill." He pursed his lips. "Now some folks say that yeast, or at least the recipe, was stolen, but I honestly don't know the truth about that. So," he took a short breath, "they produced a small batch of the best bourbon they could come up with without years of tinkering. But, given it was one of the Bennington boys, it was probably pretty decent stuff. Then they put it in a small, six-story-high rackhouse. They had to hire a few different folks over the twenty-year period to keep producing small batches and to keep track of things, rotate the barrels and such. They even had to build a second rackhouse." He gave them an almost sly look. "But they never let the world know what they were up to, never." He stopped and smiled. "The one thing they did allow themselves, after the first four years, was to go up there yearly, check on things, and bring back a small portion for their own personal use. Of course, they always took it from the original distilling, meaning they were sampling the beautiful stuff each year, smelling, tasting, absorbing its development and growing complexity." He stopped again, nodding silently as if reveling in the beauty of the brothers' plan.

"Yeah, yeah." Jet's voice was still edgy. "Listen, I'm as big a fan of fine bourbon as anyone else, but what does that have to do with us and this case?"

"I think," said Sonia, "that Mason is about to connect those two brothers to Victor Rasmussen somehow. Is that true, Mason?"

Holiday became serious again. "Look. I don't want to tell stories out of school, and I don't know if there are any connections or not, no one in the brotherhood does. Let me say, though, that if I was suddenly in need of some twenty-year-old bourbon and hadn't made or purchased any myself, the first people who would cross my mind would be Ephraim and Ezekiel Bartley."

Sonia tipped her head. "And the reason you never mentioned these two before is . . ."

"Think about it. If it turns out that anyone associated with the making of bourbon is involved in this, the whole industry is going to get hurt."

Jet sat up in her chair. "So, you wanted us to solve this as long as it didn't turn out to be someone who makes bourbon?"

Holiday looked at her for a moment then dropped his eyes to his lap. "Well, maybe yes."

Sonia pressed. "And the bullet holes in our office?"

Holiday shook his head. "I haven't the slightest idea about that."

30

After Mason Holiday left the BCI offices, Jet and Tee began sweeping up the little bits of broken glass they had left on the ground for Holiday to see. They had wanted him to get the full effect of the incident.

Meanwhile, Brad climbed up on a small stepstool Sonia and Jet kept in the office, neither one of them being tall enough to reach the stationery materials they kept on shelves above their armoires. Even at six-foot-four, Brad could just barely get the tip of the knife he always carried into the ceiling. Finally, he was able to pry out the two slugs that had whizzed through the room several hours earlier.

"Nine millimeters." He held out his hand, showing the three women. "Almost certainly from a handgun."

"You think?" Tee asked the question while she bent down again to sweep tiny glass shards into a dustpan.

Brad stepped down from the stool. "Oh, there are lots of nine-millimeter carbines out there, long rifles, but given the trajectory those bullets followed, I don't believe anyone was really trying to hit us."

Sonia nodded. "I agree. This guy shot from the street into

these offices. If he really wanted to hit us, he would have climbed up on one of the surrounding buildings."

Brad held the slugs out again. "And used a long gun with a much larger caliber, something that would be heavy enough to stay true over a long distance and through two panes of glass."

Jet walked over to Brad and Sonia. "So?"

"So," Brad smiled as he rolled the slugs around in his hand, "whoever took that potshot was not trying to kill one of us. They were just sending a message."

Sonia sat down at the table and reached for her coffee. "Message received." One sip told her it had long since passed its "best by" moment.

Jet took a seat as well. "So, now what?"

Brad sat down and motioned to Tee to join them at the table. "So, now we figure out where we go from here. Any suggestions?"

Sonia swirled the coffee cup in her hand. "First thing in the morning Brad and I are off to Eastern Kentucky. We've got to find out if anything Mason Holiday just told us makes a bit of difference in this case. There's got to be some reason Victor wound up in a barrel of bourbon." She looked around the table. "Right?"

Brad gave her a tiny, one-fingered salute. "Right." He put the slugs down in front of him. "We've got to know how that twenty-year-old bourbon plays into this . . . if it does at all."

Jet jumped in. "And how the hell he got in there, too."

There was a moment of silence, then Sonia put her coffee cup down. "On the other hand, I'm definitely interested in getting back to see if there's something on Carl Rasmussen's computer, something Missy Charles saw or copied and then erased."

Brad turned to Sonia. "Right, I'm still thinking that Missy Charles is our strongest suspect so far, unless there's something cooking with those brothers." He glanced back at Jet and Tee. "And when Sonia gets to go after that computer, I'm going to make a little unannounced visit to Missy Charles, right at the Rasmussen Company offices."

Sonia gave him a tiny wink and a smile. She turned. "Jet, what about you?"

Jet shrugged. "I'm not sure. Do Tee and I start checking out Rasmussen Company clients?"

"Wait." Tee tipped her chin down. There was uncertainty in her voice. "So, we're not going to talk about the fact that someone," she swallowed, "sent us a message today?"

Sonia looked at her sister. What have I gotten her into? Here we are getting shot at and we've become so numb to it that we haven't even talked it through. She took a deep breath and spoke softly, slowly. "You're right, Tee." She reached out and put her hand on Tee's arm. "Things have gotten way too dangerous. It's time you stepped aside. We can do this without you."

Tee slammed her fist down on the table, shaking it on its flimsy legs. "Like hell, you will." Her olive skin took on a hint of pink. "Did you think I was asking about that because I'm afraid? No f'ing way. I was just asking if we were going to talk more about who did it and why?" She shot a look at Brad and Jet. "I'm in this to the end, dammit." She turned back to Sonia. "You're not sending me away, *mother*. I'm here to stay."

Sonia started to respond, then thought better of it. Tee was, after all, a Vitale through and through, just as strong at her core, Sonia realized, as her big sister.

It was Brad who spoke next. "Listen, Tee. If we knew who had fired those shots, this investigation would be over. And we already know why, sort of. Somebody out there wants us to drop the investigation."

Sonia picked up the thread. "And again, if we knew who that was or why they wanted it to stop, we'd know who the killer is." She shrugged. "But we don't." Her voice dropped off as she gently shook her head. "We simply don't."

There was a moment of silence before Jet began again. "So, like I said before, do Tee and I begin working—" She was interrupted by the sound of the outer door opening.

"Greetings." Johnny Adams' voice was bright and cheery, if not powerful.

"Johnny." Sonia rose quickly to her feet. "How great to see you. Come on in." She turned to Tee. "Go get another chair for us, would you?"

Johnny walked across the room, directly to Sonia. As he did, her eyes took in the tall, attractive man with the quiet demeanor. His gray eyes and short brown hair, slightly damp from the misty evening, brought back memories of their brief time together—times when Sonia's heart was torn between him and Brad. She ran her fingers through her hair. Hmm, still good-looking, but not looking entirely well. Has he been ill?

Jet interrupted Sonia's thought. "Well, well, well," her voice was only lightly covered with peach marmalade, "if it isn't Detective Sergeant Johnny Adams, pride of the Lexington Police Department."

Johnny just smiled and shrugged, just as Sonia would have expected.

As he reached her, Sonia gave Johnny a quick hug, then turned her attention toward Tee. "Johnny, this is my sister, Tee. She's working with us now."

Tee set the extra chair next to the table then walked over to Johnny, her hand extended. "Nice to meet you, Detective."

"No, no. Not detective anymore. Just plain old Johnny." He looked her over quickly. "Very nice to meet you as well."

Sonia took a quick breath then turned to Brad. "And you remember Brad Dunham, don't you?"

"Sure. Nice to see you again, Brad."

Brad nodded solemnly.

"Have a seat." Sonia directed him toward a chair on the opposite side of the table from where she and Brad had been sitting, forcing Tee to move into the newly placed seat at its end, next to Sonia. "We were just dividing up our tasks for tomorrow's work."

Sonia spent the next few minutes filling Johnny in on the case as a whole, the limitations put on them by the NDA the firm was working under, and what they had learned thus far. The last thing she spoke about was the message that had been sent to them via two nine-millimeter bullets.

"Whoa." Johnny's eyes opened wide. "I had no idea this was so serious. What are you thinking, Brad?"

Sonia was a little perplexed that Johnny had directed the question to Brad but hoped that it was his way of building a bridge to his former romantic rival.

Brad scratched his nose. "Somebody out there is trying to get us to drop this investigation. Don't know who it is, but there's no question they're serious about it."

"And," Sonia interjected, "I'm darn curious about how they even know we're involved."

"You know," Jet was quick to speak, "I hadn't thought about that, but you're right. Somehow, somebody knows what we're up to. Good chance it's someone we've already spoken to."

"Not necessarily." There was no hesitation in Tee's voice. After having been shot at, she was all in and ready to share anything she was thinking. "It could be that one of those brotherhood guys is telling somebody about everything we do—either on purpose or without realizing what they're doing to us."

Brad shuffled in his seat. His voice seemed lower than usual. "Hard to tell. But Sonia raises a good point. From now on, we need to start isolating the different parts of our investigation. That way, when we get a hint of someone knowing what we're doing we may be able to track it back to the person or persons we've spoken to."

After waiting a moment to see if anyone else had anything to contribute, Sonia pressed on. "Okay, we know that Brad and I are going to Eastern Kentucky tomorrow. I'll do some research on the brothers from home tonight." Still rattled by the notion of having put her sister in danger, she reached out to Tee's hand. "Why don't you work with Johnny and start going through as many

Rasmussen Company clients as you can, just asking them if they are aware of any problems the company had, anyone who might be holding a grudge against Victor." She turned to her partner. "Jet, there's something else that's bothering me, something maybe you could check out tomorrow."

31

As everyone was preparing to leave, Sonia picked up a few notes and headed for her office. Once inside, she dropped them on her desk before turning to retrieve her coat from the rack next to her armoire. When she did turn, she was surprised to find Johnny standing close behind her.

"Oh, Johnny." She took a step back. "Do you need something?"

"Yeah, well," his voice was soft, almost tentative, "I just wanted to thank you for inviting me back to help with the case. Sounds like it's pretty heavy duty."

As she spoke, Sonia was more and more aware of the fact that Johnny just didn't look at all well. "Sure, Johnny. Look, it's you who are helping us. There are so many leads we have to track down and so little time. I don't know how we'd be able to do it without you." She paused. "In fact, I'm not sure how we're going to be able to do it *with* you." She gave him a gentle smile.

"Don't you worry." His voice strengthened. "Detective Sergeant Johnny Adams, retired, is on the case. Your sister and I will work our way through that list of contacts you gave us in no time."

Sonia's concern came through in her voice. "But not before you get some rest." She reached out, placing her hand on his arm. "You really look like you need a good night's sleep."

"Yeah," his gaze dropped to the ground, "about that." His head rose and his eye's looked deeply into Sonia's. "Listen, I won't be here in town more than a night or two. I was wondering if maybe I could just crash on your couch or something."

Sonia withdrew her hand, the request having caught her off guard. "Well . . . ."

Johnny leaned in, his eyebrows rising plaintively. "It would just feel more comfortable than being in a strange motel room."

"Well . . . I'm so sorry, Johnny," Sonia took a small step backward, regretting that she had reached out to him physically and quite certain she felt sexual heat standing so close to him, "It's just that Tee is already crashing on the couch and there's no other place to sleep in my apartment. You understand, don't you?"

There was silence as Johnny stood speechless, still imploring her with his eyes—so much so that Sonia could feel the heat rising in her face. After a long moment, Johnny broke the tension. "Yeah, sure. I understand. I'll just get a room at that Holiday Inn off Virginia Ave. There's a couple of places around there where I can get something to eat. Jalapeños was always a favorite of mine when I lived here."

"Sure, sure. That would be great. You'll get a much better night's sleep that way." Sonia tried hard to put her discomfort behind her and give him the warmest smile she could. She was tempted to tell him about Papi's, her new favorite Mexican restaurant, but chose not to get into it.

With that, Sonia slid past Johnny, grabbing her coat off the rack in one swift motion and heading as quickly as she could to Brad's side. He turned to her. "Everything alright, Babe?"

"Yes, absolutely." Her words came quickly, intense. "Can we go now? We're going to need some rest before tomorrow's trip."

Brad tipped his head dramatically. "Honey, it's eight o'clock.

I'm sure I can get you home to your place in plenty of time to get your ten hours of beauty sleep before tomorrow's," he paused, "*trip*."

"Okay, fine." Sonia's words faded away as she brushed past Brad, out the door, and down the steps into the misty and now colder night.

In the parking lot, Brad helped Sonia into his Corvette. "Can we get something to eat together? I haven't seen you all day and I'm starving."

Sonia waited for him to walk around the car and slide in. She gave him a tight smile, it was the best she could muster. "That would be fine."

Brad paused a moment. "Are you sure?"

"Uh huh."

Brad started the car. "Where?"

"What?"

"Where did you want to go to eat?" He spoke slowly, deliberately.

Sonia started to focus on the topic of the conversation. The idea of Papi's had crossed her mind a few minutes earlier and now it seemed like exactly the right place to go—more for the comfort of the place and the people who ran it than for the food, although that was always great. "Papi's. I want to go to Papi's and get one of their chimichangas."

Brad pulled the car out of the Magee's parking lot, turning right and then right again onto Ashland Avenue. "You going to tell me?"

"Tell you what?" Sonia was looking out the passenger side window as if she was suddenly enthralled by the beautiful homes on that street—homes she'd seen a million times.

"Tell me what's got you so upset."

"Nothing. I'm fine. Let's just go get something to eat. I'm starving too, and I'm whipped." Sonia was relieved when Brad let things slide, though she didn't, for a moment, think he believed her. She'd already had one run-in with him that evening and the thought of telling him about Johnny's request sent a sudden quiver of nausea into her stomach. By the time they had parked and walked up the steps into the inviting warmth of Papi's, the only thing on Sonia's mind was one of their famous raspberry margaritas.

JOHNNY ADAMS PULLED his car under the portico in front of the Holiday Inn Express and walked through the front door. As he stood before the simple two-computer front desk, there was only one thing on his mind—book a clean, quiet room as cheaply and quickly as possible.

Once inside the room, he threw the simple leather bag he'd picked up earlier in the day on his bed and walked directly into the bathroom. The fluorescent light gave his face a strange, greenish tint as he looked in the mirror, but it wasn't his face he was most concerned about.

Loosening his belt and lifting up his shirt and undershirt, Johnny was frustrated. The bandages with which he had dressed his own wound were soaked with blood. He was simply not healing as quickly as he had hoped and he was more and more concerned that he might have to seek real medical attention. With that would come questions—questions he hoped he would never have to answer.

DAY FOUR

32

Sonia woke around eight o'clock on Monday morning, restless. Still lying in bed, she interlocked her fingers and stretched deeply. Day Four, only forty-eight hours to wrap this thing up. A moment later, a tiny, tentative smile touched the corners of her mouth. But I'm pretty sure we've got you, Missy Charles. I'm not sure how we're going to prove it, but I'm pretty sure we've got you.

Sonia stepped out into the kitchen/living room/dining area only to find the coffee pot already fired up and half the normal amount in the carafe gone. She stepped over to the back of the couch and looked down. Blankets, sheets, pillow, but no Tee. Hmm. She's up and out early.

As Sonia sat down at her tiny kitchen table, she was certain that what she and Brad had to do first was go out to Eastern Kentucky. After all, the story of the two brothers was significant enough for Holiday to have held it back, and it was also the very information that he brought forward after someone took a potshot at them. Twenty-year-old bourbon, Victor sloshing around in a bourbon barrel—there had to be a connection—*and* a way somebody got his body into that barrel.

Still, Sonia was haunted by the fact that her gut told her she needed to get back into Carl Rasmussen's computer and find some proof that Missy Charles was trying to take over the Rasmussen company. That would indicate a clear motive for her taking Victor Rasmussen out of the picture and bring Sonia and her team a giant step closer to wrapping up this case.

After showering, Sonia slipped into jeans, a light-brown sleeveless top, and sneakers. She let her wavy, layered, hair dry on its own as she gobbled down a quick bowl of raisin bran and a half-glass of OJ. Eight minutes later, she was down the steps and walking up Ashland Avenue toward the BCI offices. Though it was bright and sunny out, she got a little chill as she recalled last evening's events. By the time she reached the bottom of those wooden steps, she was more grateful than usual to be able to duck into Magee's to pick up not one almond croissant but two, and two coffees as well.

As she stepped out of the bakery and headed for the wooden stairs, Sonia saw Brad pull his Corvette into the parking lot. She went directly to the car and slipped in.

Normally, Brad would have given Sonia a brief but meaningful kiss. She loved how his lips would linger on hers just long enough to convey the fact that he loved her, that he was really *kissing* her, without being so long as to imply the beginning of a romantic interlude. This morning, the kiss was a bit perfunctory. She didn't mind. It fit with the stress that was churning in her own stomach.

It wasn't long before Brad had the car on I-64, headed for the Mountain Parkway and Eastern Kentucky. Try as she may, Sonia was unable to sustain any light-hearted banter as they traveled. Brad seemed equally focused on the day's challenge. When they reached Hazard, Kentucky, Brad turned the car east on Route 80. Sonia watched the town go by. "So, this is the place that the *Dukes of Hazzard* are from."

"One Z," was Brad's only response.

"What?"

He gave her a quick look. "Hazard, Kentucky, H A Z A R D. The *Dukes of Hazzard*, H A Z Z A R D. There's only one Z in the town's name, two in name of the show.

"Oh."

"And since we're already through the town of Hazard," he turned to her and smiled, "Hindman, Kentucky, here we come. GPS says it's another 28 miles."

About thirty-five minutes later, they took a left onto Route 160 and came into town on East Main Street. They made a left at the fork and pulled into the parking lot at the Redi Mart. "Well, here we are, sweetheart. Hindman, Kentucky. Population, according to the 2010 census, seven hundred and sixty-seven. I'm guessing that most folks around here know exactly who Ephraim and Ezekiel Bartley are." Brad tapped Sonia's leg. "Stay here, I'll go inside and ask around."

It wasn't long before Brad was back in the car. "Here we go." He smiled at her. "We just stay on 160 'til we get to Tadpole Hollow, take a left on Frogtown Road and follow it to River Street. Their house is at the end of that road."

Sonia gave him a look. "Seriously, did you find out where they live?"

"Honey," Brad backed the car up, palming the steering wheel, then drove out of the parking lot, "that's *exactly* where they live."

Approximately nine minutes later, Brad pulled the 'Vette up to the home of Ephraim and Ezekiel Bartley. It's rustic stone and wood construction was obvious, but this was no simple log cabin hidden in the woods. Its size and design indicated it had been, at one time, quite grand. Closer inspection, however, revealed a screen door that barely closed, windows in desperate need of paint, and a light bulb above the front door that was actually broken. Standing on the wide front porch that ran the length of the building, Brad gave Sonia a silent nod and then knocked. She stepped back three or four steps.

Several long moments went by before a man who appeared to be in his late fifties or early sixties made it to the door. He was slender, almost skinny, with a thin mouth that seemed filled with teeth that belonged to a much larger person. The hair on his head was cropped extremely short on the sides, yet hung from the top, flopping across his face. Dressed in work boots, sloppy jeans, and a tattered University of Kentucky T-shirt, he didn't give the impression they had interrupted any important work he might have been doing. In fact, even from outside the house, Sonia could hear the sound of a television and some sort of game show. The man opened the screen door wide, though it squeaked in the process, peering out of the darkness that filled the house's interior. "Can I hep you?"

"Mr. Bartley?" Brad tried to sound as respectful as he could.

"Who's askin'?"

"Mr. Bartley, my name is Brad Dunham." He turned to Sonia. "This is Sonia Vitale. We'd like to talk to you if you don't mind."

"You from the *po*lice?"

"No, we're not, sir. Actually, we're from a private investigation firm in Lexington, Bluegrass Confidential Investigations. Any chance we could have a few minutes of your time?"

The man behind the screen door looked them over. He took in Brad's stature first then spent too much time drinking in Sonia's attractiveness. His head bobbed gently as he waited a long moment before answering. "What's this about?"

Brad took a half-step forward. "Actually, Mr. Bartley, we're not sure."

"Then why the hell are you botherin' me?" The words came out fast. So did the smell of alcohol, perhaps bourbon, perhaps not.

Brad took a moment, scratched his ear. "Damn good question, sir. Damn good." He smiled. "You see, we're trying to figure out what happened to a man in Lexington, and somehow, the names of you and your brother came up."

"And?"

"And honestly, we don't know how important it is, but some folks are paying us pretty damn well to find out what happened to that man. We didn't want to leave any stone unturned. Know what I mean?"

The man raised his head in the direction of Sonia. "What's she doin' here?"

Sonia could see Brad struggling a bit with the answer. She was pretty certain he wasn't clear as to how well things would go over if he told the man that she was in charge. Neither one of them were sure how far into the mountains of Eastern Kentucky women's liberation had made it.

Brad gave it his best shot. "We work together."

The man pulled a dirty, yellowed handkerchief out of his pocket and wiped his nose. As he did, Sonia noticed the redness in his eyes. *This man has done some serious drinking already today, and we're just a little past noon.* "We'd appreciate your help," she called out.

The man gave Brad a crooked smile. "She your boss?"

Brad's smile was authentic this time. "Actually, sir, she damn well is."

The man pushed the screen door open and spit some brownish substance right past Brad's shoulder. "Knew it. She's the brains. Just brought you along for the muscle."

Brad's head dropped as he chuckled. "I'm afraid you got that right sir." He paused. "Now, about this man."

"What's his name?" The question came quickly.

Brad took a quick breath. "Victor Rasmussen. Know him?"

The man's chin dropped as he shook his head. "Shee-it," he said quietly. "Come on in."

Sonia was surprised by the invitation. She looked quickly at Brad, who had turned to get her response, and used her eyes to tell him to accept. She pushed a wisp of hair out of her face. *We're not going to accomplish anything playing coy with this guy.*

The man pushed the screen door open a few more inches and waited for Brad to take hold of it, then turned his back and disappeared into the darkness. Brad went in first, clearly choosing Sonia's safety over chivalry. Sonia followed. As she did, her eyes scanned the main room—large plank oak floors, fieldstone fireplace with a stack of firewood next to it, wooden rocking chair, open passage to the kitchen divided by a wooden counter with a varnished, wood countertop. It was an all-natural, log cabin motif, everything wood except the sixty-inch flat screen TV. He picked up the remote and turned the TV off, the room getting noticeably darker, even at mid-day.

The man swept his arm in the direction of a tired-looking couch. "Have a seat." When Brad and Sonia sat on it, springs popped and groaned. The whole thing sagged under their weight. "So, you want to know about Victor Rasmussen." He picked up a Coke can and spit into it. He said nothing more. Clearly, like many folks from the hills and hollers of Eastern Kentucky, he wasn't the kind of man who was eager to share private information with strangers.

Sonia put her hand subtly on Brad's arm. She thought that since they had made it this far, she might have more luck getting answers out of the man than Brad. "First, are you Ephraim or Ezekiel?"

"Ephraim, ma'am. I'm the oldest. Zeke is my little brother by twelve minutes."

Sonia gave him a gentle smile. "Oh, I see." She struggled for a minute, wondering if she should make some family oriented comment like, "So, you're the responsible one." She decided against it. Looking around, she asked, "And is Zeke here today as well?"

"Nope."

Sonia waited, hoping for something else to come. Silence filled the darkened room.

Though Bartley was not being combative, the tension in the

room was thick. Sonia took a quick breath and dove in again. "Well, Ephraim, the reason your names came up is that Victor Rasmussen has recently made some claims about bringing a twenty-year-old bourbon to market."

"What of it?" There was a real, new edge to his question. He moved forward a few inches in his chair.

Brad must have felt the need to back Ephraim down, because he picked up the thread. "Well, here's the thing Mr. Bartley. Victor Rasmussen hasn't been in the bourbon distilling business long enough to make a bourbon old fashioned, no less bring a twenty-year-old bourbon to market." Bartley's only response was to wipe his nose, sans handkerchief.

Finally, Sonia tried again. "Some of the folks we spoke to back in Lexington said it was possible you'd have some idea as to where he might be able to get some of that vintage bourbon. Do you?"

Ephraim Bartley picked up his Coke can and spit into it again. He sat quietly for a long moment. Sonia could tell he was mulling over his options, deciding whether or not to tell these folks from Lexington anything about anything. Finally, he took a deep breath and spoke. "Yes, ma'am. I do. But before I tell you about it, I've got to explain something else to you, something most folks just don't seem to understand."

33

Ephraim Bartley leaned forward in his chair, a wooden, slat-backed affair with a faded floral cushion. His elbows leaned on his legs and he rubbed his hands together as he spoke. "Now y'all need to listen, and listen careful." His words were not angry but not friendly either. "I'll tell you about that bourbon, but first you got to understand where you sittin'."

Sonia and Brad glanced quickly at each other then back to Bartley. Neither responded.

"This is coal country. You know," he said, narrowing his eyes, "ever since they found coal in Kentucky in 1750, it's been important, real important. First, they mined it out west, in Muhlenberg County. That was in the 1820s. But come 1900 or so, they started commercial mining in Eastern Kentucky, right there in Floyd County. Some people say that over the years we've taken over eight million tons of coal out of this state. And all that meant work to some, good work, and money to others, real money. Me and my brother Zeke, we got our share. Done real well twenty, twenty-five years ago." He paused a moment. "That's when we started."

Sonia raised her eyebrows. "Started?"

"Started with the bourbon ma'am." Ephraim sat back in his chair, a little smile on his face. "Actually, it was my brother Zeke's idea. We was doin' real good with coal back then, but it was hard work—hard, hard work. And Zeke, he thought about those boys down there in the bluegrass, sittin' around all day sippin' bourbon and talkin' 'bout its complexity and its finish, stuff like that. He come to me and said, 'Eph, we got to get us some of that kind of livin'. We got to finish the day with clean hands and clean clothes.' "

His words drove Sonia's eyes immediately to his hands. They were the hands of a man who had worked hard all his life—worked with dirt and coal and heavy machinery—hard work—honest work.

Ephraim noticed Sonia checking him out and looked directly at her. She averted her eyes, instantly embarrassed. "Anyway," he continued, "I said, 'How we gonna do that, little brother?' And he tells me all about his plan to start makin' bourbon." He stuck his chin out and squinted his eyes again. "But not a lot of bourbon, just the very best bourbon, like Pappy, you know?"

He reached down for his Coke can and spit some more tobacco juice into it, a tiny drop trickling down his chin. He wiped it away with the back of his wrist and continued. "So, I heard him out, how we should have our own still and rackhouse and all, and wait twenty years before we ever sold a drop. He said, 'By then we'll be wore out on this coal mining thing, and good and wealthy to boot. Then we can just sit back and start sellin' the best bourbon anyone ever tasted and live the good life on some nice piece of land out of these mountains. Maybe run us a few horses. Be able to get into town easy and eat fine steaks at one of those fancy restaurants they have there.' "

"The best bourbon?" Brad asked. "How were you going to do that without a lot of experience making it?"

"Without your own yeast recipe?" Sonia's question elicited a quick look from both Brad and Ephraim.

"There's ways, ma'am. There's ways."

Sonia leaned in, pressing the point. "You mean like hiring one of the Benningtons to be your master distiller?"

The question set Ephraim back in his chair. At first, he didn't say a word. Then a big smile crept across his face. "Now, ma'am. Sounds like you been talkin' to some of the gentlemen of the bourbon brotherhood. That right?"

Sonia sent a quick look over to Brad, then turned back to Ephraim. "Well, yes. That's true."

"And they told you all about how they help each other out because they're all one big happy family?"

Sonia didn't respond. She looked back at Brad, who shrugged his shoulders.

"Now let me ask you a question, ma'am. You ever know a family that didn't have a little bit of trouble in it? A little competition? Maybe a little back-stabbin'?"

"Wouldn't be surprising," Brad said, clearly hoping to direct Ephraim's attention away from Sonia.

Ephraim rubbed his nose with the back of his big, rough hand. "Then I guess it wouldn't surprise you that all the jumpin' around those boys did from one distiller to the other might just have to do with some backroom deals. Maybe *stealin'* a boy from one place to another."

Sonia jumped in. "And a yeast recipe?"

Her question caught him off guard. He just grinned. "No comment, ma'am."

Sonia could tell that she could waste a whole afternoon listening to Ephraim's take on the bourbon brotherhood and trying to wangle the truth out of him about how he and his brother got started with their bourbon. She needed to get him on track again. "So, Ephraim, we get it. You and your brother built that distillery and the rackhouse and started making bourbon that you wouldn't sell for twenty years, right?"

"Oh, not just twenty-years-old, ma'am, but the best. See our inventory was so small that we could rotate the barrels every year. That meant that every barrel would spend some time at the best level, the third or fourth level, right in the middle. We only had the six levels."

He glanced at Brad, then turned back to Sonia. "Anyway, that meant that every barrel would be like a honey barrel."

She gave him a quizzical look. "A honey barrel?"

"Yes, ma'am. A barrel that spent its time in the best part of the rackhouse. Not too hot, not too cold. And then, when the master distiller opens that barrel, he doesn't mix it with any others. It's not just small batch, it's single barrel. And that master distiller, he works that whiskey until it has the very best taste he thinks he could ever get out of it." He looked up at the ceiling. "Now that's good bourbon." His whole upper body bobbed up and down as his eyes met Sonia's. "Good bourbon."

There was silence in the room for a few moments. Finally, Brad took a breath loud enough for both of the others to hear. "Okay, you went ahead and made the bourbon, drinking, we've heard, one small portion a year yourselves. So, what happened to your plan?"

Ephraim was slow to respond. When he did, his voice was filled with frustration. "What didn't happen? The economy went up and down, the mines around here started to play out, Eastern Kentucky coal became the most expensive coal in the world." He glanced at Brad. "That didn't help. Then the government put stiffer and stiffer rules on us. Hell," his voice was rising, "did you know that since 2000, coal production in Eastern Kentucky has gone down from around twenty-seven million tons a year to about four million?" He looked directly at Sonia. "You think people get that? They hear about the loss of coal jobs, but they don't get it. They don't know what it's like in the coalfields now." He turned to Brad. "Listen, in 2016 we mined less coal in Eastern Kentucky than we did in 1915." His voice reached a peak. "What the hell do you think that did to the economy out here? What the hell do you think that did to Zeke and me, to this whole region?" He turned slowly to Sonia, his voice softening, "We haven't made a decent wage in years."

There was silence in the room. For the first time, Sonia noticed that there was some sort of small radio playing softly in a back room of the house. She wanted to say something comforting to this tired, broken man. Instead, she had to push forward. "So, Ephraim, how did that affect the plan for your bourbon?"

His face bent downward, then he raised his eyes to her. "Pretty much skunked us, ma'am." He fell silent.

After a few moments, Brad made an attempt to get things moving again. "You and your brother are pretty much broke. You're sitting on some very, very fine twenty-year-old bourbon, but you don't have the resources to get it to market. Is that it?"

Ephraim raised his head and nodded. "That's it exactly. Costs money to get the master distiller to finish off one barrel at a time. It takes money to bottle the stuff. It takes money to promote it, to advertise, even a little. Hell, just to make the damn labels." He looked back to Sonia. "And we just didn't have it. Not a bit of it."

Sonia thought for a moment then asked. "Couldn't you just sell it? Just sell the barrels of aged whiskey and let some other company do all the rest. Wouldn't that work?"

Ephraim used his Coke can again. "Not 'wouldn't,' ma'am. Can't." He looked up at Brad, then back to Sonia. "See, Zeke, he just couldn't let it go. It was his dream, and he'd made it happen—almost. I tried to talk him into sellin' those barrels, but he just couldn't get himself to do it. Said everything we ever hoped for was in those barrels and someday, somehow, we were the ones who were goin' to get rich on 'em." He fell silent.

Brad prodded again. “Sooo?”

Ephraim sat up tall and put his palms on his legs. It was obvious to Sonia he was about to say something important, maybe the one thing they needed to learn from a trip that was using up most of the second to last day they had to solve this case. He started. “So, one day Zeke says to me, ‘Come on. Get your ass off that worn out chair and let’s drive down to Lexington. We can still afford a decent steak somewhere. Let’s do it before we can’t afford to do it at all.’

“I wasn’t real excited about the idea, but I figured, what the hell, maybe he’s right. So, we pile in his truck and drive down to Lexington. We go into a decent place, not that fancy Malone’s, but somethin’ decent. We have to wait a bit for a table, so we take a seat at the bar. We’re watchin’ UK basketball on the TV, they was playin’ Tennessee, and sittin’ next to us is this guy, dressed up kinda nice, but he’s alone, drinkin’ and watchin’ too. All of a sudden, he leans over to Zeke and says somethin’ like, ‘I’ll bet UK sinks its next shot. Come on. Twenty bucks. What do you say?’ ”

Sonia shot a look at Brad, clearly remembering what Patricia Huntington-Jones, Victor’s first wife, had told him.

“Well,” Ephraim coughed as he spoke, “Zeke probably knew he shouldn’t bet the guy, but I guess when you’re feelin’ really down on your luck you figure it’s got to change some time, so he says, ‘Sure,’ and dang if he doesn’t win the bet.” Ephraim used the can again. “So, the guy says, ‘Come on, let’s go again. Double or nothing. Next UK shot goes in.’ Again, Zeke shouldn’t have done it, but he does, and he wins.

“This goes on for a while and the guy says, ‘Hey, you play poker?’ Zeke, he turns to me and smiles, ‘cause Zeke is one hell of a poker player. Wins all the time. He turns to the guy and says, ‘Well, I know some of the rules.’ ”

Ephraim let out a sad, tiny chuckle. “Next thing you know, we’re leavin’ the place.” He turned to Sonia, “We didn’t even get to order that steak.” He turned back to both of them. “Anyway, a little while later we're at this guy's place, in his fancy basement, with a green, felt card table, and Zeke and him are playing poker, head to head, just the two of them." He took a deep breath. "Long story short, at the end of the night the guy has pretty much cleaned Zeke out. So, he says somethin' like, 'You got anything else you can put up?'

"I should-a seen it comin'. Zeke looks at me and smiles like he's been playin' this guy a sucker all night. Then he tells the guy about our bourbon, and that they can play one more hand, five card stud. If Zeke wins this guy has to front our whole production and promotion process and all he gets is ten percent of the profits. If the guy wins, he gets all the bourbon, lock stock and barrel."

Sonia couldn't believe her ears. "And Zeke gambled twenty-years of bourbon development on one hand of cards?"

Ephraim took another deep breath. "Again, ma'am. When you're down on your luck . . . ." He wiped his nose one more time with the back of his hand. "And yes, ma'am, he did. They played one hand, the longest five minutes of my life. In the end, Zeke, he lays down a pair of aces, queen high, pretty good for five-card stud. But the guy, this Victor Rasmussen, he lays down three kings. There it was. Zeke lost. All of his dreams gone, and mine too. No coal money, no bourbon money, no bourbon. No nothin'."

Brad waited a few moments before he asked another question. Finally, he rubbed his hands together and spoke. "So, Ephraim, how did Zeke take it in the end?"

"Terrible." Zeke scratched his head. "Terrible. He's a broken man. Like he's got nothin' to live for."

Sonia sensed Ephraim's concern for his brother. "And you said he's not here right now?"

"No, ma'am. He's not."

She pressed. "Do you know where he is?"

Ephraim scratched his chin, considering his answer for a long time. Finally, he spoke. "Can't rightly say, ma'am. He left over a week ago. But wherever he is, it's the same place his pistol has gone."

Sonia's eyes widened. "Do you think he might have gone after Victor Rasmussen?"

"Ma'am, if I didn't, I never would have told you any of this."

34

After a restless night, Johnny Adams had slept later than he'd hoped. When he rolled over and swung his legs out of bed, his side hurt like hell. The whole process put him in a foul mood.

Still in his underwear, he sat on the edge of the bed and picked up his phone. The screen indicated it was ten minutes after eight. "Damn." He dialed a number that wasn't in his new phone but that he knew by memory.

"Officer Oliver. How can I help you?"

"Ricky, it's me, Johnny Adams."

"Hey, man. How are you? Where are you?"

"I'm fine, pretty much. I'm back in town for a little bit."

"Wow. I was pretty sure I'd never see you again after what happened a couple of months ago. Where you been living?"

"Out West. I'm living out West. You, uh, still at it—you know, running stuff?"

"Me? No. Things got way too hot after you all iced that Hensley guy. Man, if you hadn't wasted those three at the Coroner's Office, I'm afraid we all would have been rolled up."

"Yeah, well. I did Dimitrov and the farm manager, but it was that Marine guy, Dunham, who actually shot the Medical Examiner."

"Still. If Dimitrov or Hollings had flipped on us, you and I would be doing time for pushing drugs and worse. Man, that took some balls, blowing them away right there in front of that DEA guy."

"Yeah, well, you do what you've got to do."

"And what about that chick? You told everybody you were leaving town because she picked the marine guy over you. Was that true?"

"No, no. I was just trying to stay close to her while she investigated the Hensley thing. You know, just to keep up with what she was learning. So, listen, with Dimitrov gone, I thought I'd be cool with Toro, but I'm pretty sure he sent some bitch after me. Damn near killed me a couple of nights ago."

"Really? You okay?"

"Pretty much, but I've got two problems. First, I need to see a doc real soon. She caught me in the side with a nine-millimeter slug and I can't get it to stop bleeding. It sucks. Second, I've got to talk to Toro, get him off my back. You still know how to get in touch with him?"

"Toro? Hell, he's still in Mexico."

"Yeah, I figured. But can you get in touch with him?"

"Yeah, I guess. Might take a day or two."

"No, no. It can't take a day or two. I've got to talk to him right away. I saw two guys pull into a motel I was staying at in Little Rock. Pretty sure they were looking for me. I've got to get him to call off his goons before it's too late."

"Okay . . . I guess . . . . Look, let me make a phone call or two. Where you staying?"

"Don't worry about that. Just call me back at this number when you've worked out some way for me to talk to him. Can you do that for me?"

"I'll do the best I can, Johnny. Just stay cool. I'll get back to you."

Johnny Adams ended the call, not sure if maybe he'd done more harm than good.

Having gotten up early, Tee had thrown on jeans and an old sweater, grabbed a quick cup of coffee, and left the apartment. She'd jumped in her little, blue Chevy and driven the two blocks to Magee's. She was right on time, seven o'clock. The plan was for Johnny Adams to meet her there and work out a strategy for getting to as many Rasmussen Company customers and vendors as possible in one day. The BCI team had to know if any of those people had a reason to send Victor Rasmussen to the great bourbon barrel in the sky.

By seven-thirty, Tee was pretty certain that Johnny was probably not coming. She had no idea why, though she had noticed that he'd looked kind of sickly the night before. She wondered if he had overslept. Unfortunately, she had no phone number for him and didn't know where he had spent the night.

At seven-forty-five, eager to prove she could do things on her own, Tee packed up her notes, refilled her paper cup with Southern Pecan coffee, marched out the door, and headed for her car. Struggling to open its door with coffee in one hand and a large notebook in the other, she was glad she hadn't locked it. Then again, she never locked it—who would bother to steal this old piece of junk. As the car noisily came to life so did Tee's level of frustration. Sick or not, that jerk should have called me by now. Screw it. I'll do this without him. A few moments later, Tee had turned left on Main Street and was on her way to meet with the first of the companies on her list of Rasmussen Company vendors.

Jet walked into Magee's and checked her watch—twelve forty-five. It was time for lunch and she was good and ready. As she stood, looking up at the electronic menu, she was nudged from

35

The Corvette's engine purred as it made its way along the country roads, back toward the Mountain Parkway and Interstate I-64. The sun faded slowly behind the mountains as Brad and Sonia sat in silence. It was clear to her that each of them was trying to get a grip on Ephraim's story. "Well, at least we know now why Victor Rasmussen was so certain he would soon be putting his hands on some fine, twenty-year-old bourbon."

Brad checked his rearview mirror before he answered. "We most certainly do. I guess the guy was on a roll. First, he makes a bundle in his dad's business. Then he lucks out and winds up with a winning racehorse." He glanced over at Sonia, "Then, with just one winning hand at poker, he winds up with twenty years-worth of prime bourbon, crafted by one of the Benningtons, at that."

Sonia gave Brad a crooked look. "If you can call winding up dead in a barrel of Oscar Blevins' finest," she snorted, "on a roll."

Brad inhaled. "Well . . . let's just say mostly on a roll." He turned to her and grinned. She answered with a chuckle and a smile of her own.

Sonia thought for a moment, then she spoke. "Okay, though.

Where do we go from here? Do you think Zeke Bartley has already done Victor in? Is he the one who killed him?"

Brad had his right hand on the wheel while he tugged on his ear with his left. "I don't know. Sure sounds like he could be our guy." He watched a pick-up going well over eighty fly by him in the passing lane. "It certainly sounded to me like Ephraim was trying to tell us that's what he was planning on when he left over a week ago."

Sonia let her eyes drift to the mountains as they seemed to disappear into the fading light. "Does that fit our timeline?"

"Actually, it does." Brad stretched his back, already stiff from a long day of driving and sitting. "It's just killing me that we can't take advantage of any of my NCIS connections to get fingerprints or even an approximate time of death."

Sonia turned to him. "Are you sure? I mean, couldn't there be DNA on the barrel?"

"Too hot to handle, babe. I can't ask any NCIS technicians to put themselves on the line by going to a murder scene and tampering with evidence when the police haven't even been notified about the murder."

"Well," Sonia sighed, "I hate to say this, but we may have to do exactly that come Thursday."

Brad checked his rearview mirror again. "Right. Time's up tomorrow night."

Sonia pursed her lips. "And I hate it." Her voice began to rise. "We wanted so much to help out—to learn something before the bourbon brotherhood had to go public with a story that could create havoc in the industry, in the whole state. Especially when it would all be nonsense anyway. One barrel. One body. Not even a whole batch would be affected, no less a whole distillery or a whole industry." She sat silent for several minutes.

"Okay." Brad broke the silence. "Let's understand that Zeke either killed Victor or he didn't, right?"

"Figured that out yourself, did you?" Sonia's voice was on full snarky.

Brad gave her a look. "So, let's think this through. If he did kill Victor, then we have twenty-four hours to find the guy and prove that it was him."

"And if he didn't?" Sonia's voice was taking on new life, if only slightly.

"And if he didn't, then where the hell is he? Is he in Lexington? Is he still waiting to kill Victor because he doesn't even know Victor is already dead?"

Sonia sat up in the soft leather seat. "Or . . . what if he killed Victor and now he's waiting to do something more?"

"Like what?"

"Like kill somebody else." Sonia was fully engaged, energized by the terrible possibilities.

"Like whom?"

"Like the old man, the son, the ex-wives, Missy Charles, anybody." She was becoming animated.

"Okay." Brad nodded. "You could be right, but let's think this through." There was a tiny pause before he spoke again. "So, you think it's possible that Zeke's our killer *and* might be thinking of hurting someone else?"

Sonia's voice was a bit calmer. "Well, could be."

Brad watched another pickup pass him going eighty or more. "Damn, these boys fly in these mountains." He gathered his thoughts. "But listen. I think, one way or the other, you're right about this, at least about the fact that we have to take the threat seriously. We need to find Zeke Bartley as fast as we can. Either he's our guy now or he might be later."

Again, Sonia let a few moments go by while she thought. Then she asked, "So, how do we do that?"

Brad reached for his phone as he answered. "Actually, for the first time in this case, we really *can* use some of my old contacts. I'll put in a sort of emergency call to some guys in the electronic communications department and see if we can find out where ol' Zeke Bartley has been keeping himself for the past two weeks."

Sonia watched as Brad made the phone call, asking for any information his old colleagues could pull together based on cell-phone and credit card information. They were already back on I-64, headed for Lexington, when he got a response. He put the call on speaker.

"Brad Dunham."

"Hey, Brad. Billy Stapleton here. I've got that info you asked for."

"Great. Let me have it."

"So, this Zeke Bartley you're looking for. Seems like he left his usual hangouts in Eastern Kentucky about ten days ago. Been in Lexington almost the whole time since then. We've got credit card usage and phone logs that make all that pretty clear."

"Do we know where he's staying?"

"Looks like he's been paying weekly rates on some place called The Embers Motel. Based on what he's paying, it's certainly no Hilton."

"Excellent." He gave Sonia a quick smile. "Anything else you can give me?"

"As far as I can tell, there must be a lounge there at the motel, something called The Embers Lounge."

"How do you know that?"

"Because he's been running up a bar bill there every night for the past nine days."

"Got it."

"And Brad?"

"Yeah."

"If I were you, I'd be hoping this guy's not an angry drunk."

"Yeah? Why?"

"Based on his bar tab, this boy's been doing some serious drinking, real serious drinking."

"Got it. Thanks, Billy boy. I owe you." Brad smiled at Sonia. "Thanks, again. Talk to you soon."

"Wow." Sonia was still impressed with how much a federal

organization could learn about a person in a matter of hours, or even minutes.

"Well, there you go, babe. One Zeke Bartley, staying at the Embers Motel and drinking himself into a stupor every night." He tugged on his ear again. "Looks like the boy's looking for trouble."

Sonia turned in her seat, her concern reflected in her voice. "I know, Brad. We've got to do something before he gets away, or worse, hurts someone else."

Brad changed lanes to pass a slower car. "You're right. The first thing we've got to do is get eyes on him and we're still a good two hours away. Who do we have that we can send to the Embers tonight?"

Sonia was quick to answer. "Johnny. We can send Johnny." She was careful not to glance at Brad, certain that the look on his face was less than enthusiastic. "Let me call him." She reached into her purse and pulled out her phone. After a long moment, she ended the call. "No answer. Dang."

Brad kept his eyes on the road. Sonia sensed it was a clear attempt to hide his pleasure at Johnny's failure to fulfill his responsibility—one of which he wasn't even aware. He chuckled quietly before he spoke. "Okay. Not Johnny. Who else do we have?"

"Brad?" The look on Sonia's face was incredulous. "Do you think I'm going to send Jet down to the Embers to babysit Zeke Bartley? Do you really?"

"Oh." He kept his eyes forward.

"Oh, is right, mister." She shook her head. "Or maybe I should send my baby sister down there."

"I'm sorry." He sounded honestly contrite. "It's just . . . . It's just that I spent years having a team of professionals who were always totally prepared to do whatever I needed them to do. I forgot." He turned to her. "I'm sorry. I really am."

There was silence in the car as the night fell down around

them. Finally, Brad spoke again. "Listen, babe. We really do have to get eyes on this guy, and right now we're lucky enough to have a pretty good idea where he is. We really can't let him slip away into the dark. I'll take you home once we get back to town and then I'll stop by The Embers Lounge for a little nightcap. Know what I mean?"

"Yeah, right. I sit at home while you go looking for Zeke Bartley? I don't think so."

Brad gave her a quick look. "What's that mean?"

"Nothing."

"No, really. What do you mean?"

Sonia turned back to him. "Well, no offense, but I know that part of town."

"And?"

"And I'm afraid you'll stick out like a sore thumb there."

Brad's voice started to rise, clearly a sign that he was feeling insulted. "And why, Ms. Professional Investigator, is that?"

"Well, with your short hair and hairless face, I'm afraid you don't exactly look like you just crawled off your Harley and stumbled into The Embers Lounge reeking of dope and ready to take on half a bottle of tequila."

"So," Brad was clearly getting pissed, "you don't think I can pull this off?"

Sonia reached out and put her hand on Brad's leg. "Now, I didn't say that, sweetheart, but I'm pretty sure I've got a better idea."

36

She walked into the Embers Lounge just past eleven o'clock at night, a beautiful woman, approximately thirty-five years old. Thin, shapely body, black hair, dark Hispanic eyes. Her choice in clothing left little doubt that she hoped, expected, to be noticed. Black jeans that hugged, really hugged, her body, a red satin top that plunged all the way to Mexico, red five-inch heels, black and red earrings that dangled almost to her shoulders; she gave off the unmistakable aura of a flamenco dancer.

Every eye, male and female, followed her from the entrance, through the smoke-filled room, to one of the several empty seats at the bar. Journey's *Don't Stop Believin'* played on the PA while no one danced on the small wooden floor that sat tucked up against the back wall. It was only moments before the sandy-haired, female bartender—late fifties, in black slacks, white shirt, and a red vest—moved to take her order; she had, after all, only two other customers at the bar, both of whom were adequately supplied at the moment.

"What can I get you, sweetheart?" The woman's voice was as pleasant as her smile, though clearly rasped by years of smoking.

"Jose Cuervo, please." Her eyes settled on the mirror behind the bartender.

"Chilled?" A smile accompanied the question.

"No, *gracias*."

The bartender tipped her head, inquisitive. "Salt? Lime?"

"Neat." No explanation followed.

The bartender must have sensed the quiet power the woman possessed because she poured the single shot extra heavy, then stepped back as if she planned to stand and watch her down the shot.

The woman engaged the bartender's eyes. She lifted the glass and smelled deeply without averting her gaze. Tipping her head back just slightly, she tossed the shot down almost motionlessly then placed the glass back on the bar very gently. "Again." Her voice was almost a whisper, but not without intensity.

The bartender repeated her routine. This time, however, the woman lifted the glass and smelled it but returned it to the bar's wooden surface without taking a sip. The bartender tipped her head as if to ask, "*something wrong*?" The woman, her forearms now resting on the bar, waved one wrist and finger without moving her arm at all. Her gaze remained focused on the mirror behind the bar. The bartender seemed perplexed as she backed away. "Let me know if you need anything else."

Minutes ticked by. Journey gave way to Bon Jovi, then Queen. Of the two men residing at the bar, one seemed lost in thought. In his mid-forties, paunchy, wearing a black T-shirt, black jeans, a black leather vest, and a wallet chained to his belt loop, his phone sat on the bar in front of him. It appeared to hold no interest for the man. The other resident, much younger, perhaps early thirties, also dressed in jeans and a T-shirt, though more hippy than gothic, dared a surreptitious glance at the woman. It was rebuffed by a sharp pulling together of her dark eyebrows. He turned his attention immediately back to the near-empty glass in front of him.

The woman continued to search the mirror, her eyes darting between the reflections of the call liquors that sat on the shelf in front of it—Jack Daniels, Johnny Walker Red and Black, James Bennington, others. From her vantage point, she could see each of the two tables that were currently occupied by other patrons. The one on her left held a couple, mid-forties, early fifties. She sported red hair, teased to within an inch of its life, a blue and white top with stripes that failed in their mission to de-emphasize her girth, and a full week's worth of Mary Kay's best. She'd applied it in a manner that would have made Sherwin Williams proud. Her partner gave nearly the opposite impression. Thin to the point of looking sickly, the only hair on his head was the overly long fringe low around his ears. His skin looked sallow and yellowish, even in the smoke and darkness of the lounge.

The woman's eyes spent little time on the couple. It was the solitary figure sitting at the table on her right that held her interest. She watched as he sat motionless at times, that stasis interrupted only occasionally by his lifting a rocks glass filled with amber liquid, taking an almost imperceptible sip.

The woman called the bartender over with the subtle move of a single finger. Leaning forward, she spoke softly as she nodded to her right. "He come here often?"

The bartender looked down at the cooler just below the bar, wiping it aimlessly with a bar towel as she spoke. "Every night the past week or so." It was obvious to the woman that the bartender wanted to ask something. She was glad she didn't.

Spinning on her stool, the woman left the bar and turned toward the tables. As she did, the boys in AC/DC reminded her that they were *Back in Black*. She walked over to the single soul, slowly, feeling every eye in the room follow her, even the four attached to the couple that sat intertwined with each other. When she reached his table, she stood silently before it, waiting.

He was slow to lift his gaze. Eventually, however, he looked up at her, a slight squint in his eyes. His skin had a darkish hue as if he had worked in coal mines all his life and the fine black dust could no longer be completely removed from its pores. His face showed clearly his sixty-plus years, though his hair was still mostly black and the impression was more rugged and worn than old. His body was lean. "Can I help you, ma'am?" The voice was soft, flat, deep.

"You have room at the table for one more?"

"You got a name?"

She gave him a tiny smile, but only out of one side of her mouth. "Gabriela." She paused for a moment. "You have a name?"

He stirred in his seat. "Zeke. Folks call me Zeke." He nodded to his right. "Have a seat."

Gabriela sat, turning the simple action into a long, slow, sexy process. She took a small sip of her tequila. "You are alone tonight?"

"Alone every night." They danced a slow, dramatic tango with their words.

AC/DC gave way to Van Halen. "Do you mind me sitting here?"

Zeke ran his index finger along his upper lip and reached for a cigarette from the pack of Marlboros that sat on the table in front of him. "Up to you."

Gabriella slowly moved her gaze around the walls and windows behind Zeke's seat, the flickering red lights of a beer sign reflecting in the room. As she did, she could feel his eyes drinking her in. She knew he was being drawn to her. Eventually, she reached out and took another sip of her golden liquid. Waiting.

Finally, he lit the cigarette then spoke. "You know I can't afford what you're selling."

A tiny smile in the corner of her mouth, her eyebrows raised. "Now, is that any way to start a new friendship?"

He paused, clearly thrown a bit off stride. "Then what do you want from me?"

Gabriela let her eyes travel from his, downward, along his chest, toward his waist. "A woman can want lots of things."

He waited in silence for more. It didn't come. Finally, "Like?"

She reached out and lifted her glass to her lips again. She spoke before drinking. "It would depend."

He didn't wait to respond. "On what?"

"On whether what was available was worth the effort."

He took a sip of his drink. "I reckon it would be worth the effort."

She smiled and tipped her head, innocent. "What would?"

"Whatever you've got in mind, ma'am."

Gabriela took a deep breath and leaned back in her chair. She looked around the room, as far as her position at the table allowed, taking her time. Van Halen faded away, Survivor took over. Slowly, she finished her drink. "Not here."

Zeke sat up taller. He nodded. "Not here." He waved to the sandy-haired bartender. Somehow, she knew to bring the tab for both of them rather than another round. As soon as she turned and left, Zeke stood, threw a wad of cash on the table, and started walking. "Come on."

Gabriela followed Zeke through the smokey room and outside into the warm night. As they walked, he made a feeble effort to put an arm around her waist. He wasn't surprised when his move was rebuffed, though he never realized that what she was protecting was the sweet little Diamondback 9mm pocket gun tucked inside the tiny purse that hung over her shoulder.

Even at the late hour, the Embers' location on a main drag assured there would be plenty of traffic noise, lights, energy. The fact that a liquor store sat in the parking lot directly next to the motel accounted for the young men standing outside, next to their cars, holding brown paper bags that concealed the shapes of tall bottles. Gabriela was just barely aware of it all.

They walked across the lot to the motel proper, down the side of the long building, until they reached his room. Using the large key, attached to a reddish-brown piece of plastic in the shape used for motel room keys for the last fifty years, he opened the door to the room's darkness. Stepping in behind him, watching him turn on the dim light, Gabriela could smell the muskiness of an old air conditioner and bedding used way beyond its functional limit.

He walked directly over to a worn, six-drawer dresser with a full mirror in which the silver reflective material had been eroded by moisture and time. Looking at her in the mirror as he poured bourbon into a partially clean water glass, he asked, "Want some?"

She moved toward the broken-down chair sitting in the corner of the room, next to the long heating/air conditioning unit. Its moan quietly filled the room with ambient sound. "Sure." She took a seat, crossing her long legs as she sank into the worn-out cushion.

He poured a second glass, then walked over to her, his arm extended. With no other options, he sat on the edge of the bed, two feet or so away from her. "So, what's your story?"

Gabriela took a sip of the bourbon. "Do you really need to know?" She waited, then gave him the biggest smile of the night, her eyes lighting up. "I don't think so. Just think of me as some sort of gift the gods have sent you in your time of troubles."

His head and shoulder rocked back. "My troubles. What do you know about my troubles?"

She put her drink down on the tiny, scratched and stained wooden table that sat next to her chair and stood. She moved across those two feet until she was standing right in front of him, between his legs. His eyes had nowhere else to look but at the red satin blouse and its downward trajectory. She waited as he sat silently, his breath deepening, though he was probably unaware.

Finally, she reached down and lifted his chin, forcing his eyes to hers. “Not enough.”

His forehead furrowed. “Not enough what?”

She smiled, a gentle smile, knowing the man was totally under her spell. “Your troubles. I don’t know enough about your troubles.” She reached out and put her hands on either side of his head. She ran her fingers through his oily hair. “And I can’t help you if I don’t know what your troubles are.”

He pulled back, almost angry. “You here to help me? Is that it?”

She responded immediately, pulling away from him, turning toward the door. “Not if you don’t want me to.”

She took a step, but he reached out and grabbed her arm. She spun on him, fire in her eyes. “You don’t touch me until I say you can.” She didn’t need to hit him.

“Sorry, sorry.” His voice fell away as his hands withdrew. He shook his head. “Sure, sure. I guess I can tell you. Hell, I ain’t told nobody else, ‘cept my brother.”

She stepped back between his legs, fully aware that her fragrance was filling his nostrils. She put his hands on the sides of her blouse but in a way that made it very clear that they should go no further until invited to do so. She lifted his chin again. “Now, you tell Gabriela what has given you so much trouble that you sit here every night, alone, angry.”

It took Zeke a solid five minutes to tell her the story of losing his coal business to progress and a collapsing economy and his bourbon business to a man who cheated him in a card game. The whole time he spoke, Gabriela stood patiently, feeling his breath on the bare skin between her breasts, tolerating the invasion of her personal space for the sake of the mission. Finally, she asked. “And why do you sit here night after night. What are you waiting for?”

Zeke looked at her and took a deep breath. “Vengeance, woman, vengeance.”

DAY FIVE

37

Sonia woke early, five thirty in the morning. She rolled over and was awake again at six ten. By six thirty she knew why she couldn't sleep. It was Day Five.

She dragged herself out of bed by six forty and decided she needed one of her three-mile runs to get the day going. She did some of her best thinking while she ran. This time, however, she'd have to work hard to push aside the sound of the clock ticking in her mind.

Sonia had checked in with Jet and Tee when she and Brad had gotten back to town. She had been disappointed when Jet told her that she hadn't found anything definitive about who might or might not have had access to the Horatio Blevins property at night. There were surveillance cameras on the site, but Jet's trained eye found several paths by which a person with knowledge of the property could avoid being caught on them.

Sonia had been even more disturbed when she heard that Johnny had been a no-show for his assignment with Tee. She worried about him, but when she'd followed up with a phone call, he hadn't responded. At least Tee and Jet had picked up the slack and continued working on the list of Rasmussen clients.

As Sonia turned into her third mile, she continued to struggle with the day's time-crunch and the fact that she was caught between two theories. On the one hand, what she and Brad had learned in Hindman made it quite clear that Ezekiel Bartley had a solid motive for murdering Victor Rasmussen and a lengthy absence from home which created opportunity. Since she couldn't examine the body, she wasn't certain if his pistol met the benchmark for means, but it wasn't hard to imagine it fit the bill one way or the other. Motive, opportunity, and *almost* means. An *almost* perfect case against Ezekiel Bartley as a murder suspect.

On the other hand, Missy Charles met a few of those benchmarks herself. With Carl Rasmussen on the verge of dying and her believing she could run the company better than Victor or his son, Davey, Missy had plenty of motive for eliminating Victor. If Victor was out of the picture before Carl died, she would have every opportunity to convince the old man that she was the one who should take over the company, not the young man who was currently out living the high life in Dubai, searching for a new racehorse for his daddy. As for opportunity, no one knew more about Victor's patterns and whereabouts than Missy Charles. Maybe this whole story of him "gallivanting around Europe" and communicating by email was pure bull, made up to cover her tracks for a long time. And, unfortunately, Missy had never opened the bogus email that Sonia had sent her—not unusual for a busy executive, but it meant that the virus Sonia had embedded had not yet had a chance to do its work.

Now, as for means, Sonia wasn't quite sure, but there might well be something on Carl's computer that not only locked down her motive but gave a hint or two as to how she had planned to accomplish the dirty deed. Maybe there would even be information that would shed some light on how the murderer had gotten access to the Horatio Blevins facility. She just had to get to that computer and find out what it was that Missy and her co-conspirator had erased.

When Sonia got back from her run, she jumped immediately into the shower then dressed as quickly as possible. Finishing her makeup, she looked at her watch. Almost nine o'clock. Not too early to visit Frieda Schiessl. She hated to admit it, but she hoped Carl was still in the hospital. If he was, she might be able to get another shot at that computer, a shot that might expose the very thing she needed to close this case.

She finished her coffee and stepped into her living room. "Tee, Tee. Wake up, sleepy head. It's Day Five and I've got something I need you to do with Jet."

Tee looked at her sleepy-eyed. "Yeah, what?"

"Listen, I'm going out to Carl's house to see if I can get into that computer again. But we're running out of time and maybe, just maybe, Missy Charles will do something today that proves she's the one. I need you and Jet to team up and follow her around today. See where she goes, what she's up to."

Tee sat up on the couch. "Why both of us? Can't I do it alone?"

"Right. Well, here's the thing. It's hard enough to follow someone for a little while without getting noticed, but to do it all day, that's really tough. I'd like you and Jet to switch off. One follows for a while, then the other. That way, she's much less likely to figure out she's being tailed. Okay?"

Tee rubbed the sleep out of her eyes. "Yes, ma'am, boss lady." She stood and stretched. "I'll give Jet a call then grab a quick breakfast. We'll be on her like white on rice."

Sonia chuckled. "Whatever. Thanks. I'm out of here. Check in with me during the day, okay?"

Tee nodded, still stretching, then gave her sister a silent wave goodbye.

Sonia moved quickly down the steps of her apartment and headed for her car. Sliding into her old Subaru, she could only hope that somehow the clock would move exceedingly slow on this last day of the investigation. No such luck. She could feel each minute of it slipping through her hands.

Sonia drove down New Circle Road to Tates Creek Road, then another mile to Carl Rasmussen's community. Using her smile, her big brown eyes, and her knowledge of Rasmussen's housekeeper's name, she was able to get through the security gate and drive directly to his home. She walked up to the front door and rang the bell, practicing her speech about needing one more chance to look at Carl's computer because the last two-some that had come had failed to extract the proper file. As she waited for Frieda to answer the door, she put a frustrated pout on her face. It got easier when she had to try and then try again to get Frieda to respond.

It finally hit her. Frieda was not there. Sonia hoped, for his sake, that her absence didn't mean that Carl had passed away. Taking a deep breath, she realized that whether it did or not, she still needed to get inside that house and find out what was on his computer.

As she looked around, hoping that no one was paying any attention to her as she stood at the front door, Sonia knew that there were now two things she always kept with her when she was working. The first was the .38 she had strapped to her ankle, something that had seemed cumbersome at first, but to which she had become quite accustomed. And since the episode the other night, something she would never be without. "Sending a message," or not, when someone shoots in your direction, you want to have something more to respond with than your stapler.

The other thing, actually two things, she always had with her were the binoculars and lock picks that Brad had given her when they had first agreed to work together in a loose partnership. Professional level tools, all of them, she kept the binoculars in her car. They were too cumbersome to carry and were rarely needed. The lock picks, on the other hand, were in a neat little leather case, not much more to deal with than a cellphone.

Sonia waited until she had walked around the side of the house before she slid the little leather case out of her pocket. She found a back door that was partially hidden from the view of others by a flower-covered trellis. She was relieved that, it being a back door, there wasn't one of those new computer-based doorbells that let people see you on their phones if you approach the entrance. In fact, as she thought about it, she hadn't seen one on the front door either. She let out a tiny chuckle. I guess it all feels too new-fangled for an old man like Carl Rasmussen.

Before Sonia went to work on the door with one of the lock picks, it struck her that she wished she was wearing rubber gloves to avoid leaving fingerprints. Oh well, something else I should be keeping in my car at all times. It took her about ninety seconds to get the lock to spring. She was proud of herself for getting the door open, though a little frustrated that it had taken her so long to accomplish the task.

She was also disappointed, though not surprised, when the home's alarm system went off. It wasn't as if she hadn't thought about the alarm or tried to figure out how to disarm it. This was a high-end community with expensive homes and a security guard. They all had sophisticated alarm systems that weren't easily defeated.

Sonia stepped into the house, rattled by the sound of the alarm, but determined to get the task accomplished. She was grateful that she knew exactly where the computer was and that she wasn't going to be stymied by any sort of internal security. Carl never even used a password.

Sitting at the computer, Sonia found it hard to concentrate with the alarm blaring in her ears. Finally, it stopped. She knew, however, what that meant. It indicated that the signal had been sent to the security system's dispatcher and that the phone would ring any moment, asking if there was some reason why they shouldn't send the police.

She worked as quickly as she could. The list of recently opened files came up. At its top was the WOCR file, Carl Rasmussen's will. She let a tiny smile cross her lips. The fact that the WOCR file was at the top of the list indicated that no one had been on the computer since Sonia had opened it the other day.

The phone rang. She jumped in her chair. Though she had expected the call, it still jarred her. She was aware of the fact that when the phone stopped ringing, she could be certain the dispatcher's fingers would go immediately to the phone number of the local police. It would now be a matter of minutes before the police were there.

Sonia was looking for deleted files. Not files that were sitting neatly in the "Deleted Files" folder, but files that had been completely "erased" from the computer.

Trying to keep her focus as she felt the minutes ticking by, Sonia bore down. She was using knowledge that the average person didn't have, even folks with "good computer skills." She was doing things she had learned as a computer science major at a significant university, finding files that other people were certain no longer existed.

Working in DOS, a computer language unknown to most mortals, Sonia was able to find three files that, though encrypted, seemed promising. She pulled a forty-gig memory stick out of her pocket, slipped it into the computer, and began the process of transferring the information from the computer to the stick. Unfortunately, as she waited for that to happen, it struck her that her car was sitting on the street, right in front of the house. If she was going to have any chance of getting away with this intrusion, an illegal intrusion, she was going to have to be in her car and gone before the police even turned the corner of Bellevie Road.

After what seemed an interminable amount of time, the computer finally indicated that the transfer was complete. Sonia shut the computer down, jumped out of her chair, and was just about to wipe her fingerprints off the computer when she realized that Frieda Schiessl would certainly recall her being there the other day. Better to have her fingerprints still there. Having literally run through the house, however, she had no hesitation about wiping her fingerprints off the doorknob as she left the house. She was certain that she had been careful to touch nothing else while she was in there.

Sonia desperately wanted to run to her car. She realized, however, that the alarm was no longer sounding. She forced herself to walk at a normal pace, though it felt like she was slogging through waist-deep water in the ocean. The whole time, she knew that there was no chance she was going to make it to her car and drive away before the police showed up. And yet, she did.

Not only was she gone before the police arrived, but the big smile she received from the security guard at the gate made it clear to her that he wasn't in the loop. No one had alerted him. Of course, she realized as her stomach flipped yet again, he would remember letting her on the property in order to visit Carl Rasmussen. She shuddered. That's a problem I'm just going to have to deal with at another time.

38

Tuesday morning, Brad Dunham was sitting at his desk in the white house across the street from Magee's. It was the building in which his own firm, Semper Fi Investigations, was located. Although he had agreed to drop everything and help Sonia and Jet with their BCI investigation, there were still lots of things going on in his world. He was fully aware that it was Day Five, but that didn't mean it wasn't important for him to be in touch with several of his own clients. He had been at his desk since six-thirty that morning.

Around ten-thirty, Brad received a text from Gabriela Castillo. SITTING IN MY CAR AT THE EMBERS MOTEL. NEED TO LEAVE SOON. CAN YOU MEET ME?

Brad replied. ON MY WAY. Brad really didn't know much about Gabriela, but what he did know was that she could take care of herself. She had proven that when she was part of an investigation that centered around three young women. He felt confident that she was okay but was still eager to get to her, just to make sure. Before he took off for The Embers, Brad tried to call Sonia. He was surprised and a bit frustrated when he couldn't get through. Instead, he sent her a text. ON MY WAY TO THE

EMBERS TO RELIEVE GABRIELA. WILL LET YOU KNOW WHAT I FIND OUT.

As Brad drove down Richmond Road, out to New Circle Road, and around to the north end of town, he thought about the hundreds of investigations he had done as a Marine assigned to NCIS. So many of them had been intense, really intense, but he could think of only a handful that had been brought to completion under a five-day time constraint. He hoped for Sonia and Jet that somehow they would have this case wrapped up by the end of the day. As complicated as it was, he had his doubts.

Brad pulled into the parking lot at The Embers and waited. It was just a few moments before he saw the exotic woman in clothing much more suited for an evening rendezvous than a mid-morning meeting approach his car. Without knocking on the window, or even saying a word, she opened the door and slid into the supple leather seat.

"Nice." Her hand reached out and touched the dashboard, the console, the sun visor. She turned and looked at him, running her fingers through her hair just above her ear. "Very nice."

Brad simply nodded. "Thanks." He took a long look at her. "So, where are we? You look beat."

Gabriela yawned before she spoke. "You would too if you had spent most of the night sitting in your car, making certain the person you were watching didn't just get in his vehicle and drive away."

"That's it?" Brad seemed perplexed. "You just watched his room from the car?

Gabriela rolled her head on her stiff shoulders. "No. I found our guy sitting alone in the lounge last night. We had a drink and then he invited me to his room."

Brad looked at her. "Just like that, he invited you to his room?"

Gabriela's next words reflected an inner confidence. "I don't think he had any choice." The smile on her face made it clear that she was not going to say any more.

"Okay." Brad let out a subtle chuckle. "Then what?"

As Gabriela answered, her head turned to the right, her eyes roaming the empty parking lot as if the conversation were boring her. "Let's just say we had a heart to heart conversation."

Brad had worked with plenty of different agents and informants over the years. Perhaps one of his greatest strengths as an investigator was the ability to have discussions with all kinds of people—straight ahead people, coy people, honest people, liars. That didn't mean that this conversation was any less interesting. A tiny smile worked its way across his lips. "And are you going to share with me any of the highlights of that heart to heart?"

Gabriela was still playing coy. "Well, he did tell me an interesting story about losing his coal company and then losing his bourbon. He said the man he was looking for had cheated him at cards. But I'm not sure I believed him."

"Why is that?"

Gabriella played with the ends of her long, black hair. "A man who feels cheated, really cheated by a thief, his anger is hot, white hot." She pouted her lips. "But a man who feels cheated by life, that's different. That kind of man is angry, but it's a dark, hopeless anger."

"And?" Brad's eyebrows rose. "Which one was he?"

Gabriela let out a short breath. "The second. The man is hopeless, hopeless and angry."

Brad's fingers tapped on the steering wheel. "And?"

Gabriela turned her face to his, suddenly serious. "And, he said these words to me. 'I came to Lexington to kill them both, the Rasmussen's, both of them. One is already a dead man. I'm just waiting for the chance to finish the other.' "

Brad's fingers stopped tapping. He had hoped that the trip Sonia and he had taken the day before, and the surveillance Gabriela had done that night, might lead them to a real suspect. He'd never expected an out and out confession. He paused a moment, then looked at Gabriela. "And how, exactly, did you get Zeke to tell you that?"

She turned slowly and looked directly at him—dark brown eyes, almost black. "There are two things, Brad, that will make a man bare his soul in the middle of the night." Her voice became increasingly breathy. "One is bourbon," she paused and looked away, "the other is sex."

Brad had dealt with too many different people in his life to be shocked by almost anything. Still. "And?"

Gabriela turned back to him. "And last night he had too much of one, and less than he had hoped for of the other." Gabriela pulled on the fancy door handle and pushed the door open. "After a while, I left him alone in his room and just watched from my car to make sure he didn't leave." She swung her legs and slipped out of the car. Turning back to Brad, she smiled. "I've got to go to work."

Brad watched her walk back to her own car, her hips moving back and forth in a way few women's could. "Wow." It was all he said. As he did, he dialed Sonia's number.

39

Johnny Adams had gotten a phone call from Ricky Oliver, telling him to meet Ricky in an abandoned warehouse on Manchester Street, just past some rock'n'roll club called The Burl. The warehouse was more than abandoned, it was almost hidden, lying behind a decaying old factory building and accessible only by a dirt driveway and down a steep hill.

As Johnny pulled up to the building, he noticed Ricky's car. Although Lexington police officers are able to use their official vehicles when they're off duty, Ricky had chosen to drive his personal car, a sharp-looking, red Dodge Charger. Slipping out of his own Accord, Johnny walked toward the large, garage-door opening in the front of the building. Out of habit, as he passed the Charger, he put his hand on the hood of the car. Still warm. He's only been here a few minutes.

As Johnny stepped into the building, Ricky called out to him. "Johnny, back here!"

Johnny stopped for a moment, taking in his surroundings. The building was all but empty, though there were ten or twelve used oil drums stacked to his left and a pile of broken and discarded wooden crates farther into the building and on his right. "Coming!" He wanted to ask Ricky to come out to him but was trying not to arouse any suspicions. He had enough of his own.

Johnny found Ricky sitting in a broken-down swivel chair next to an ancient metal desk by the back wall. Sitting on it was an old, black telephone that was plugged into the wall. "Hey, man. Sorry I couldn't set this up for you sooner. Not easy to get hold of Toro, know what I mean?"

Johnny couldn't help but hold his left side with his right hand as he spoke. "Yeah, that's okay. But why here?"

Ricky gave him a big country-boy grin. It fit with his large frame, straw-colored hair, and broad, clean-shaven face. "Security, man. Security. You were a cop. You know how it goes. Nowadays we're all about plucking conversations out of the ether, listening in on fools who think their conversations are private. But you can't listen in on a landline conversation without a warrant. This is the only way Toro will talk to you, and damn, there ain't too many landline phones around anymore—not that you can talk on freely."

"Yeah, sure." It made sense to Johnny. Still, he certainly had his antennae up for anything suspicious.

He got another big grin from Ricky. "You ready to do this?"

"Let's do it." Johnny watched as Ricky dialed the phone number then handed the phone to Johnny.

"Hola. Este es Toro."

"Toro. Johnny Adams here.

"Sí. Yes, Johnny. How are you?"

"Been better. Seems like one of your female acquaintances was pretty intent on helping me leave the country—on a permanent basis if you know what I mean."

"Well, my friend. Apparently, she is not as, how did she put it, proficient, as she said she was. Are you okay?"

"Like I said, I've been better. I've got a hole in my left side that won't stop bleeding and I really need to see a doctor soon, one who won't ask any questions."

"Ah, sí."

"More importantly, I'm thinking that might be a waste of time unless I can convince you to call off your people and let me be."

"Hmm. Now, Johnny, why would I do that?"

"Listen, didn't I take care of things for you in Lexington when that Vitale chic and her Marine friend managed to snag Dimitrov and Xin Li? Seems that if it weren't for me, the *Federales* would have heard from the US DEA and your whole operation might have been rolled up. As it was, all they got were a few drivers who didn't know much more than where the drop-off points were. The way I see it, I saved your ass. And now, you're trying to burn mine. Doesn't seem fair, now, does it?"

"Johnny, Johnny. You're right. I know you're right. You're a good soldier. I should be very grateful for what you've done, and I am."

"Right. So, we're good then?"

"Almost. You see, Johnny, I know it. I know you're a good soldier, one who protected me. Or was it you that you were protecting yourself?" Johnny's pulse started racing as he felt the conversation shift. *"Right, Johnny? Weren't you just protecting yourself?"*

"Well—"

Toro's words quickened. *"No, Johnny. Too late to explain. I know that you were trying to protect yourself and I congratulate you for that. But, you Johnny, you are a soldier, right?"*

"I guess."

Toro was racing now. *"And if a soldier will shoot the captain who was in charge of all of Kentucky just to protect himself, what will he do to the general if he gets himself caught?"*

Johnny scrambled. "I see, but—"

"Oh, mi amigo. If you shoot the captain to save yourself, you will surely turn on the general if you get caught. True? Now what—"

Johnny didn't hear any of the words that followed. What he did hear was the sound of Ricky's sidearm sliding out of the leather holster at his hip.

Ricky hadn't realized that Johnny had been careful to nonchalantly keep his back to his former colleague. And though, from behind, it looked as though Johnny had the old black handset in his left hand and was holding his hurting left side with his right, that right hand had slipped into his lightweight jacket and was now firmly grasping his Glock 17. He spoke with a lift in his voice. "Okay. Thank you so much. I really appreciate it. I'll tell Ricky. I'm sure he can get me to that doc without anyone being the wiser." He waited. "Yes, thank you. Just let me say . . ."

With that, Johnny spun around. BLAM! The gun roared in his hand as he fired at Ricky before his former colleague could grasp what was happening.

"Shit!" Ricky dodged to his right. BLAM! BLAM! The explosions filled the room as Ricky fired wildly, running for cover behind a sturdy metal support post. "What the hell, man?"

Johnny was in no mood to have the kind of conversation that viewers see in a police drama on TV—the kind in which people explain their motives while trying to kill each other. He had only one decision to make—the wooden crates that were closest or the oil barrels that were furthest away. No brainer. BLAM! BLAM! BLAM! Shooting wildly himself, he ran for the oil barrels.

Stumbling over a barrel that was lying on its side, his ears ringing from the echoing sound of handguns discharged in the empty building, Johnny slid behind another barrel, peeking out, wondering where Ricky had gone.

Moments of silence ticked by as Johnny wondered if he could make it out of the building and to his car without being gunned down by his former friend. Hell, he didn't want to kill Ricky. Maybe he could—

SNAP. Ricky appeared suddenly behind Johnny and to his left, at the other end of the barrels. BLAM! BLAM! BLAM!

Falling backward to the floor, Johnny could hear bullets whizzing past his head and his police training echoing in his mind. "One well-aimed shot always beats a crazy barrage from a gun that keeps rising in the hand of a man firing wildly." He froze, aimed, squeezed. BLAM! Ricky fell to the floor.

40

It took Sonia's heart quite a while to settle down after leaving Carl Rasmussen's home. The toughest part of the trip had been smiling at the security guard as she left the property, knowing full well that in a few minutes the police would be coming to ask him questions about anyone who might have been involved in setting off the alarm at Rasmussen's home.

Sonia turned into the parking lot at Magee's, slipped out of her car, and headed for her office. As she reached the bottom of the wooden stairs, however, she had another thought. It would take a strong cup of coffee to settle her nerves after this morning. She stepped into Magee's and walked toward Hildy's smiling face. For once, the notion of eating an almond croissant really didn't appeal.

Coffee in hand, Sonia marched up the steps to her office and sat at her desk. Plugging in her thumb drive, she pulled three files onto the computer's desktop and then into some decryption software she had downloaded long ago. She picked up her phone and pressed the CALL icon next to the pretty face with the ever-present ponytail.

"Lordy. Is that you checking up on us, Ms. Sonia?" Jet's accent was in full bloom.

"Not checking up. Checking in. Where are you two?"

Jet's accent disappeared. *"Well, I sat in the Rasmussen Company parking lot until Missy arrived. When she took off about an hour later, I had Tee follow her. Apparently, she checks in on some of the bigger work sites, so we've had to switch off twice already. What about you?"*

"I've managed to get my hands on three files that may give us a clearer picture of Missy Charles' motives and plans."

"And where did you get those files?"

Sonia finally took a sip of her coffee, then answered. "From Carl's computer."

"And how did you get files from Carl's computer? Did you go and lie to that nice German lady again, tell her you were with the company?"

Sonia sat up taller and raised her chin. "Actually, I did not." She paused. "Okay. I was going to do that, but it turned out that Frieda wasn't there. Anyway, I broke into the house with the lock picks that Brad taught me to use. I got to the computer and found those files. They're encrypted, so I'm running them through some software on my computer now. I'm hoping we'll learn everything we need to know about Missy's plans from one or more of those files."

"How long will that take?"

"It's going to take a while. And while I'm sitting around waiting for it, all I'll be able to hear in my mind is the clock ticking and a little cuckoo bird popping out of his box, chirping, "Day Five, Day Five, Day Five." She sighed. "Meanwhile, I'm afraid we're really not going to be able to lock this thing down until we understand one more thing."

"What's that?"

Sonia ran her fingers through her hair. "Look. We've got the encrypted files from Missy Charles. I'm all but certain it could be her, or someone she hired, who stuck Victor in that barrel of bourbon. She went to Carl's house. She deleted files from Carl's computer. We know she thinks she can run the business better than Victor or the son. She had the motive, and as soon as we see those decrypted files, I'm telling you, we're going to see that it's her. But the first thing we're going to be asked when we report that to Mason Holiday is how she did it. How did she kill him? How did she get him into that barrel? And right now, I think the only one who can give us any help with that is John O'Neal out at Horatio Blevins."

"The guy who runs the place."

"Right."

"So, are you going to go see him?"

"Absolutely, but I'd like to take Tee with me. I'd like as many eyes as possible out there looking for . . . well, for whatever."

"Sure. I can stay on Missy myself unless something else breaks."

"Thanks so much, lady. Tell Tee to get over to the office as soon as possible. We're running out of time."

Sonia could hear Jet snort. *"Not as quickly as Missy Charles is, not with you on her tail."*

BRAD SAT IN HIS CAR, wondering how long it would be before Zeke Bartley made an appearance. There was no question in his mind that Zeke was the one who had killed Victor. He rubbed his chin. Hell, he admitted it to Gabriela last night. Unfortunately, Brad no longer had the official capacity he'd enjoyed as an NCIS agent, he couldn't just barge into Zeke's room and arrest him. In fact, given the complications that had arisen from the non-disclosure agreement Sonia and Jet had signed, there were some significant problems with him even calling the police. Brad tapped out his frustration on the 'Vette's steering wheel. What would I say? I've got a guy here who has admitted to killing the guy you didn't even know was murdered? Nope, I've got to have more than that.

Brad took out his phone and dialed Gabriela's phone number. "Gabriela. It's Brad."

"Sí. Having fun sitting in the parking lot?" There was a certain snarkiness in her voice.

"Yeah, yeah. Just like you did last night. I'm just guessing, though, that you used some tequila or something to help the time slide by. I'm stuck with coffee."

"Well, then, mi amigo, maybe you should have been the one who sat with Zeke in the bar and got invited back to his room."

"No, thank you, ma'am." He laughed. "Not my cup of tea. In fact, probably not his either." Brad heard a tiny chuckle at the other end of the line. "So, listen. I'm sitting here thinking we need more to go on than just Zeke's confession. Let's face it, all he has to do is deny saying anything to you."

"Sí."

"And come to think of it, when you tell the police you picked the guy up in the bar and took him back to his room . . . well, I'm not sure they're going give anything you say any credence. In fact, they may be wondering how you make your living."

"Hmm."

"So, this is what I need you to do. I need you to call Zeke at the motel. They'll connect you. Tell him you want to meet him for coffee, sometime real soon."

"But I'm getting ready to go to work."

"Doesn't matter. Just pick a place that he'll be able to find, but something that's not too close. All I need is to get him out of the room. You don't actually have to meet him. Just get him out of there. I'll take care of the rest. But listen, find some phone other than your own to use. I don't want him to be able to track you down sometime in the future."

There was silence on the other end of the line for a few moments. Then Gabriela answered. *"It will be my pleasure."* The line went dead.

A few minutes later, Brad's phone pulsed. He had a text.

Looking at his phone, he saw it was from Sonia. QUITE CERTAIN MISSY IS OUR KILLER. FOUND 3 ENCRYPTED FILES ON CARL'S COMPUTER. DECODING IN PROCESS. ON MY WAY TO HORATIO BLEVINS FACILITY.

Brad gave his phone a funny look. "Oh, really?" he said out loud. "I don't think so, sweetheart." He let out a big breath. "Oh, well. I'm not telling her she's wrong in a text."

"*Yeah. Hello.*"

"Zeke?" Gabriela was sitting on her bed, looking at herself in the mirror.

"*Yeah?*"

"This is Gabriela."

A moment went by. "*Yeah?*"

She gently pushed the mascara brush into its tube, then drew it out and worked on her left eyelashes while she held the phone between her shoulder and her ear. "I was thinking of you."

"*Oh yeah? Then why were you gone when I woke up in the middle of the night?*"

She switched to the other eye. "Zeeeke? Do you think I call you so you could give me problems?"

"*I guess not. But where the hell were you?*"

"Goodbye, Zeke."

"*No, wait. Wait a minute.*"

She put the brush back in the mascara tube and twisted it closed. She reached for a tissue. "Will you be nice, Zeke?

"*Yeah. Okay. So, what do you want?*"

"Zeke. I'd like to see you, you know, in the daylight." She wiped some excess mascara from below her left eye. "Do you think that you would like to come and join me for a cup of coffee somewhere?"

"*Why don't you just come to my room?*"

"Zeke, if I wanted to come to your room, you would be hearing me knock on your door right now. Can you hear me knocking, Zeke?"

"No."

"Okay. Then meet me at the coffee place on North Lime near East sixth street. It's called North Limestone Donuts or something like that. I'll be there in ten minutes, gone in thirty. Goodbye, Zeke."

BRAD WAS NOT SURPRISED WHEN, a few minutes later, he saw Zeke Bartley emerge from his motel room. Not having seen him before, Brad was taken by the ruggedness of the man in the denim shirt, jeans, and work boots. Yeah, that's a man that could take a soft business guy down, for sure. From what Brad could tell, Zeke hadn't taken time for a shower and shave before leaving to meet Gabriela.

Brad watched Zeke walk to his pick-up, climb in, and drive away. He was wasting no time, and certainly, Brad felt, wasn't at all interested in the dark blue Corvette sitting at the other end of the parking lot.

As soon as Zeke left, Brad slipped out of his car and walked nonchalantly to Zeke's motel room door. After years as an NCIS agent, and given the flimsiness of the door's lock, it took Brad less than fifteen seconds to get into the room. The dampness and musty smell of the room struck him as he entered. Even Gabriela's perfume, lingering from the night before, had lost its appeal when mixed with the room's ambient odors.

Brad wasted no time admiring the furnishings. Taking gloves out of his back pocket, he went first to the drawers in the dresser, then to the closet. He knew those were the least likely places to find some hidden piece of evidence, but he had learned over the years that some criminals were simply dumber than a box of rocks, putting things in places where even a novice investigator could find them.

Having found nothing of interest in the dresser or closet, Brad was not the least bit surprised when he looked into Zeke's duffel bag and saw a Colt Python 357 Magnum revolver. He pulled the gun out of the bag. With its four-inch barrel, it was a hefty piece of hardware and one that could do serious damage. Brad spun the cylinder. Wow, no wonder Ephraim mentioned Zeke's pistol. A gun like this would have special meaning for a man, make him feel invincible.

It struck Brad that Zeke must have shot Victor in the chest or back, or maybe even in the stomach. Not being willing to tamper with evidence, he hadn't seen Victor's body. Nonetheless, he was certain that if Victor had been shot in the head with that weapon, the men who had looked down and seen Victor's face floating in bourbon would have certainly mentioned that there wasn't much left of that face.

Brad lifted the gun to his nose. It was a habit he had developed over the years. As he thought about it, however, he realized that Victor had probably been shot at least a week ago. That was too long for the smell of cordite to be significantly obvious on the weapon. He would just have to wait for the police to be brought into the investigation. They would pull the body, and now, at least, they would have a gun to compare ballistics on.

Brad poked around the room for a few minutes then took the gun with him as he left. Fully aware that taking it might be considered tampering with evidence, he was more concerned with trying to keep Zeke from completing his mission. Not sure the bastard can't get his hands on another one, but I sure as hell don't want him coming at me with this baby.

41

Around one forty-five, Sonia drove down the picturesque road that led to the Horatio Blevins Distillery. Parking right in front of the lovely visitors' building, Sonia and Tee stepped inside, Sonia asking one of the guides to direct her to John O'Neal's office. Frustrated, she was told that he was in a meeting and wouldn't be available until at least two-thirty.

As she waited for O'Neal's meeting to end, Sonia kept fighting off the feeling that time was slipping away from her. Confident that she would find something incriminating in the files she had gotten from Carl's computer, she was still uncertain she would have enough on Missy Charles to be able to bring the case to Mason Holiday. He needed more than conjecture and incriminating files. If he was going to go to the police and shut the case down so fast that it wouldn't damage Kentucky's bourbon industry, he needed proof.

Finally, right at two thirty-five, things got rolling. Sonia and Tee were escorted into O'Neal's office. "Have a seat, ladies." O'Neal's long arm stretched out in the direction of the two leather chairs that sat a few feet in front of his massive, oak desk. Sonia noted that this was yet another wood-centric bourbon official's office. She felt the oak arm of her chair under her fingertips. Bourbon. Corn and water and wood. Corn and water and wood. She sat taller in her chair and ran her fingers through her hair. "Well, Mr. O'Neal—"

He smiled. "John."

Sonia started. "Okay, John. I know you must have thought about this long and hard, but I just have to ask. Is there anyone on your staff who has, or I should say had, any kind of connection with Victor Rasmussen?"

O'Neal's answer came quickly. "You're right. I've thought and thought about that, but the answer is no. Not that I can think of. And trust me. I've gently asked around, you know, among my staff. Nothing."

Sonia was not surprised by the answer. "So, then, let me ask you this. Somehow, someone got into your facility and plopped Victor Rasmussen into one of your barrels. Do you have any idea how that person or persons got access to your facility?"

O'Neal's face lowered just slightly. When he spoke, however, he looked directly into Sonia's eyes. "Listen. I'd love to tell you that it was some sort of magic, that no one can get in here without our knowing about it. But it's just not true. Sure, we have security, but we also have a long-standing staff that we trust. Over the years, so many different people have needed to know codes for one reason or another—people who work here now—people who used to work here. And there's nothing to say that someone couldn't worm those codes out of one of our unsuspecting workers. Lord knows how many people could sneak in here at night." He took in a deep breath and let it out slowly. "Oh, I know. We've got to deal with that issue and we will. Unfortunately, right now, as concerns Rasmussen, I just can't help you with any information about how somebody got in here and when."

Sadly, Sonia knew she simply had to accept O'Neal's answer. She moved on. "John, we've spoken to everyone on Mason Holiday's list that he marked as crucial. I should tell you that at this point, we have a pretty good idea of who is responsible for Victor Rasmussen's death. But I'm not sure I want to share my thoughts with you until I have solid proof. Still, I was wondering if you had anything at all you wanted to add."

O'Neal looked at her, quiet, calm. "Actually, I've spoken with Mason as well. I'm pretty much aware of everything you've learned from the gentlemen of the bourbon brotherhood, and I can't say that I have anything important to add. What I'd like to know from you is if you learned anything from Ephraim and Ezekiel Bartley."

Sonia instinctively glanced briefly at Tee, then turned back to O'Neal. "Actually, we have learned a few things about the Bartley's, but I'm afraid that's something else I've got to keep confidential for just a little longer."

O'Neal sat forward, leaning his forearms on his desk. "Ms. Vitale. I do understand that there are certain protocols in your profession," his voice was soft but strong, "protocols you feel obliged to adhere to. But let me remind you. We're paying your firm a lot of money to conduct this investigation and we want to know what kind of progress you're making." He leaned even further forward, a dark firmness setting on his face. "Need I remind you that our contract ends at nine o'clock this evening?"

Sonia sat taller, unconsciously trying to match John's intensity. "Yes, sir. I do know that. However, I really can't say anything that might imply that someone is guilty until I know, for a fact, that they are."

O'Neal's face tightened, his eyebrows lowering. "And there's nothing you can tell us?"

Sonia tried to sound as upbeat as she could. "Actually, I have in my possession some files I believe will make quite clear who the perpetrator is," she brushed that wisp of hair out of her face, "or, at least, who is behind Victor Rasmussen's demise."

Long moments passed as John O'Neal sat silently, sliding his long, interlocked fingers in and out of each other. He looked first at Sonia, then at Tee, then back again to Sonia. Finally, he scratched the back of his neck. "Have it your way, Ms. Vitale. Just know that I'll be meeting with Mason Holiday at ten tomorrow morning. Mason will have invited a detective from the Kentucky State police to join us."

Sonia interrupted. "The state police? Why not the local police department?"

"I see your point." O'Neal nodded as he spoke. "On the one hand, the Woodford County Police Department, as small as it is, would have jurisdiction over the case. And, in fact, would really be scrambling to help protect a major producer located within their jurisdiction. On the other hand," he gave them a sly smile, "the Kentucky State Police, now, they have a lot more clout than a small local constabulary. We're thinking we bring them in first and try to get the governor to help give us cover. Then we bring the Woodford County folks in, apologizing for going over their heads."

Sonia took in a long breath and nodded. "Makes sense."

"Anyway," O'Neal pushed his rolling chair back from his desk, "that meeting takes place at ten tomorrow. If we can't button up this case by then, all hell's going to break loose." He looked at Tee. "Excuse my French, ma'am." He turned back to Sonia. "In fact," he shook his head, "even if we can close the case for them, things are still going to be pretty rugged when this gets out."

Sonia stood, extended her hand. "Mr. O'Neal, you have our word that we will do everything humanly possible to bring this to a conclusion by nine o'clock this evening," she glanced briefly at Tee, then back to O'Neal, "certainly by ten tomorrow morning."

42

Sonia led the way, as Tee followed her out of O'Neal's office. The weight of the situation's time press felt even heavier on Sonia's shoulders than before. As she walked, Sonia sensed that Tee had fallen behind. Turning, she realized her sister seemed fixated on one of the photos in a collection of portraits entitled, "The Horatio Blevins Family." It hung on a wall they had just passed. "What is it? What are you looking at, Tee?"

Tee turned to her, eyebrows and mouth turned downward, anger in her eyes. "Nothing." She stormed past Sonia and headed directly for the exit.

Sonia scurried behind her, "Tee? Tee?" She reached out and grabbed Tee's arm. She spun her around. "What is it? What's going on?"

Tee looked around furtively. "Not here." She turned again and pushed through the doorway, out into the late afternoon sun that filled the parking lot. A few steps out into the gravel she stopped, tears running down her face.

Sonia moved quickly around her, then turned and stood only inches away from her. "Tee. Tell me. What is it? What's wrong?"

Tee was silent.

Sonia reached out, one hand on each of Tee's arms. "Tell me. I can't help you if you don't tell me. What is it? What did you see?"

Tee took a deep breath. "Inside. On the wall. The pictures." She stopped.

"What about the pictures?" Sonia was bordering on frantic.

"He's in there. On the wall. It's him." She was choking for air.

Sonia was struggling to get control of the situation, of herself. "Calm down. Take a breath. Who is on the wall?"

Tee wiped a tear away from each cheek with the backs of her hands, first the right, then the left. She looked into the surrounding trees as she spoke, her eyes still brimming with tears. "That night. When I went to the Burl." She took another deep breath. "There was this guy." She stopped again.

Sonia was struggling to stay calm, patient. "And?"

Tee rubbed her running nose with her forearm. "And he was inside." She stopped again, but this time she turned her head and looked directly at Sonia. "It felt like he was checking me out, almost like he was stalking me."

Sonia blinked, "Stalking you?"

Tee struggled to swallow. "So, just when I was going to leave, I looked around to see if I could find him. I wanted to know where he was . . . so I could avoid him. But he wasn't there. He was gone."

Sonia looked deeply into Tee's eyes. She was confused. "Wasn't that a good thing?"

Tee's emotion exploded. "No. It wasn't a good thing. He was waiting for me in the parking lot."

"What?!"

"In the parking lot. I got into my car, and when I turned around to back up, there he was. He was coming at me. He had something in his hand. Something long. It scared me."

Sonia took a deep breath. Trying again to calm herself. She squeezed Tee's arms harder and spoke softly. "Then what happened?"

"I just gunned it. I hit the gas and drove right at him." Her eyes widened even more. "I just barely missed him." She stopped.

Sonia waited. Finally, she reached out and pushed some tear-soaked hair out of Tee's face. "And you were okay?"

Tee nodded silently, wiping her nose again with her forearm.

Sonia reached into her purse and pulled out a half-used tissue. She gave it to Tee who blotted the mascara that had run down her face, then wiped her nose again. Sonia waited patiently before she asked. "Then what did you do?"

Tee was getting herself under control. Sonia could sense her shift from totally rattled to pissed. "Then I came home, to your place. I had a couple of beers and went to sleep."

"And you didn't tell anybody? Did you call the police?"

Tee was becoming even angrier. "No, I didn't. I just took care of it. I knew you'd be pissed if I got in trouble at that bar, like it was my fault, like I'd done something wrong."

"Tee?"

"Come on. You know it. You would have been giving me the lecture about not going out to a club by myself, especially in a town where I didn't know anyone."

It hurt Sonia's heart to think that Tee believed that. "Tee, I'm on your side. I'm always on your side. That was not your fault. You should never think that."

Tee was silent, clearly processing what Sonia had just said.

Sonia let a moment go by. Finally, she took a quick breath. "And you saw a picture of him inside?"

Tee was silent, her head nodding.

"And you're sure it was him?"

Tee's face tightened. "Yes. And now we go find out who the hell that is and I kick his ass."

Sonia spoke through clenched teeth, seething. "Hang on. I'm with you on finding out who it is, but let's be careful. This guy could be dangerous."

"Careful? I'll give you careful. If I find this guy—"

"We. When *we* find this guy, we're going to handle this the right way."

"I don't give a f—"

"Tee." Sonia's voice was firm. "Listen. You have to think this through. We've got to be careful."

Tee stood there in silence, stewing.

Sonia stood in silence as well, thinking. Finally, she spoke again, softly, "And besides, we have some resources that most people don't have."

Tee asked the question with her eyes.

"He drives a dark blue Corvette." Sonia smiled, reached out and drew Tee to her. She gave her a hug that was half-way between sister and mother, then pulled back just a bit and gave Tee a nasty smile. "Now, let's go find out who that piece of garbage is."

43

When they walked back into the Horatio Blevins Visitor's Center, Tee headed directly to the ladies' room to clean herself up. As she did, Sonia strolled nonchalantly over to the gallery of photos on the wall, wondering if she could pick out the perp just by his looks. She had a few ideas, but nothing jumped out at her.

Tee returned from the ladies' room and walked up behind Sonia. She moved directly toward one of the photos and pointed surreptitiously to a picture of a man named Steven Belcher. "That's him. That's Creepy Guy." She took a deep breath, staring at the photo as if to burn into her mind every tiny aspect of his face. When she turned back to Sonia, she noticed that Sonia was staring as well. "What?"

Sonia rubbed the back of her neck as she spoke, her eyes glued to the photo. "I've seen this guy before. I know it. I just can't remember where."

Tee had herself under control. "Well, he works here. Maybe you just saw him earlier or something. Maybe you noticed him and I didn't."

"No." Sonia shook her head, her eyes still searching the

image. "No, I've seen this guy before and it wasn't here. It was . . . wait a minute. I do remember. It was at Magee's."

Tee's eyes opened wide. "Oh my God, do you think he was following me?"

"Well," Sonia twisted her lips, "he had a cup of coffee in his hand. But . . . . Damn, the son-of-a-bitch *was* tailing you."

The look on Tee's face was one of complete disgust. Her Italian blood boiled. "*Figlio di puttana.*"

Sonia's eyebrows lowered. "Okay, Steven Belcher, your life's about to get a whole lot harder." She slipped her phone out of her jeans and took a photo of Belcher's picture. "Come on, Tee, let's go."

Sonia started walking. Tee reached out and grabbed her arm. "Don't we want to find out where this guy is?"

Sonia stopped, turned around, and smiled. "Honey, we don't ask these folks where Steven Belcher is and leave people wondering why we wanted to know. We go to the man with the dark blue car and the bright blue eyes. He goes to his friends in NCIS and, within the next few hours, we know exactly who Steven Belcher is and where he's likely to be."

As soon as she got back to her car, Sonia put in a call to Brad. She put him on speaker.

"Hey, babe." There was real warmth in his voice. *"Where are you?"*

"Tee and I are at Horatio Blevins. Something has happened."

Brad was quick to speak. *"With O'Neal? Did you get something from him?"*

"No," Sonia started the Subaru, looked over her shoulder, and drove out of the parking lot. "This is something else, something that happened to Tee."

"What? What happened to Tee?" Sonia could hear Brad shifting into protective mode.

As she drove, Sonia looked over to Tee momentarily, a tender look on her face. "Something happened the night she went to the Burl."

"The what?"

"The Burl, it's that rock club she went to alone on Saturday night." As she said it, Sonia could sense how long ago that all seemed, all that had happened in the past three days. She also felt the sting of knowing that something terrible had happened to her sister days ago and she hadn't done anything about it, hadn't even known about it. She was determined to do something about it now. "Anyway, while we were out here, Tee saw a picture of a guy who hassled her while she was at the club. Someone we need to find."

Brad's voice was filled with more energy. *"What'd he do to her? Was she hurt? Is she okay?"*

"No, no." Sonia tried to calm the situation with the tone of her voice. "She's okay, but we've got to deal with this guy and see if he's somehow connected to the case. Where are you now?"

"I'm downtown. I got Gabriela to lure Zeke Bartley out of his motel room and send him on a wild goose chase for a cup of coffee. As soon as he left, I got into his room. And remember what Ephraim said about Zeke's pistol?"

Sonia looked at Tee, then back to the road. "Yeah?"

"Well, I found it. It's one hell of a piece. Colt Python 357 Magnum. I'm telling you, honey, if Zeke shot ol' Victor with that, he put quite a hole in him."

Sonia gave Tee a raised-eyebrow look. "Wow."

"Anyway, Gabriela told me where that coffee shop was. I'm down here now. Pretty sure he'll be coming out soon, and pissed for sure. Maybe he'll do something stupid."

Sonia felt the need to get Brad back on her wavelength. "So, listen. We've got to find this guy. His name is Steven, S-T-E-V-E-N Belcher. He works at Horatio Blevins. And here's the thing, Brad. Not only did he threaten Tee down at that club. He followed her to our offices."

"Wait a minute. How do you know that?"

Coming off the Bluegrass Parkway, Sonia made the turn onto Route 60. "Because I saw him there, hanging around Magee's."

There was silence for a moment. Then Brad asked, *"And you're sure that he was trying to get to Tee?"*

"Sure?" Sonia sent Tee a quick look. "Yes, I'm sure. Why else would he have been there?"

"I don't know, babe, but somebody took a pot shot at us when we were in your offices. Any chance the guy was interested in more than Tee, maybe in all of us?"

Sonia pondered the thought for a moment. "I'm thinking that's exactly right."

"Then we need to find out for sure. Where is this guy?"

Sonia smiled. "Hey, cowboy, that's your department. We didn't want to make anyone suspicious by asking around about Belcher, so we figured we'd let you and your tech-savvy friends find him for us."

"Oh, you did, did you?" There was a pleasant, collegial tone to Brad's voice. *"Do my best, babe. I'll do my best. S-T-E-V-E-N Belcher. Works at Horatio Blevins. General scum of the earth, right?"*

Sonia's smile was returned by Tee. "Right."

"Okay. I'm on it. As soon as I find out where he is, I'll get back to you. Till then, I'm keeping my eye on Zeke. I'm pretty sure he's our boy. What about you? Where are you going now?"

Sonia made the dog-leg turn in Versailles and headed for Lexington. "Wait a minute. Why do you say that Zeke's our man? Just because you found his gun?"

"Well, yeah. That, and the fact that he told Gabriela he'd come to Lexington to kill both Rasmussens and that one of them was already a dead man."

"What?" Sonia looked quickly at Tee then back to the road. "Zeke confessed to killing Victor and you didn't tell me?"

"Babe, I tried. I just found out a little while ago and I tried to call you as soon as I was done with Gabriela. You didn't answer."

Sonia's frustration showed on her face. "I guess I was with O'Neal. I had to silence my phone. But, really, are you sure?"

"Babe. Don't you get it? He said he's already killed one of them. Has to be that he means Victor. He must be waiting for Carl to get out of the hospital so he can get to him and finish him off as well."

Sonia was torn. Here was Brad telling her that Zeke was the killer, yet she felt in her gut that it was Missy Charles.

"Sonia?"

"Yeah, well," Sonia was trying to get strength back into her voice. "Listen. I still need to find out what's on those files I've got decoding. You know, just to clean up loose ends. I'm on my way to my office now. Let's see what the computer has for me."

"Just let me know, babe. I'll be out here watching Zeke and waiting for info on Belcher. Love you truly, babe."

"Love you, too."

"Wow." Tee looked at Sonia smiling. "Guess you two have some different ideas about things, don't you?"

"I guess we do."

44

When they reached the parking lot at Magee's, Sonia and Tee climbed out of the Subaru. Sonia was charged up but torn. She couldn't wait to get upstairs and find out if she was right about Missy Charles. On the other hand, Brad had just told her that he was certain that Zeke had killed Victor Rasmussen. And then there was Steven Belcher.

Sonia scurried up the stairs, Tee right behind her. There were no fewer wooden steps to climb than there had ever been, but Sonia's legs were driven by the energy and frustration in her mind. At the top of the stairs, she pushed open the heavy door and went directly to her desk. She was pleased to see that her computer had finished decoding all three files she had taken from Carl Rasmussen's computer.

Sonia sat down, taking a yellow pad from a neat stack on the left side of her desk. Tee pulled up the wooden chair that normally sat in the corner of Sonia's office and took a seat next to her.

Sonia opened the first file, ready to take notes. She was only half-way through reading the file when her phone sang to her,

The Star-Spangled Banner. She checked the screen. It was Brad. "Hey. What've you got?" She put the phone on speaker.

"Listen. My buddies came through. Seems like Mr. Belcher and his colleagues get off at different times, depending on what's going on at the distillery that day. Today's a late day. They're off at six."

"Okay."

"And it turns out that Belcher lives on the south side of Lexington. Little street called Longview Drive. Simple houses, shingle, built in the fifties."

"Are you going to pay him a visit?" She was still scrolling through the Rasmussen file.

"I'm planning on it."

"What about Zeke? Anything happening there?"

Sonia thought she heard Brad chuckle. *"Ol' Zeke seemed plenty pissed when he walked out. Not sure he even bothered to finish his caramel macchiato, skinny, no whip, no cherry."*

Sonia stopped reading. "His what?"

"Never mind. Just a joke. I'm just saying he was pissed. But, unfortunately, not pissed enough to do something stupid. I've followed him back to his motel room. I'm going to hang here until it's time to go wait for Belcher to come home. I'd like to give him a nice homecoming for the evening."

Sonia flashed Tee a snarky look. "I hope he enjoys it."

"I'll do my best. But listen. I need someone to get out here and cover Zeke when I leave. Give Jet a call. Find out if she can do that for me, okay?"

"Okay. I'll call her and get right back to you."

"Thanks, babe. Take care. Love you."

"Love you, too." Sonia was still touched every time she heard those words, even when the pressures of her challenging and sometimes dangerous job bore down on her. From one perspective, the familiarity of the way they ended their phone calls made those words seem less special. On the other hand, it was exactly that familiarity, the fact that she could count on his simple and daily expression of his love, that made them even more important. It had been a long time since she'd felt the joy that came with that security.

Sonia took an unconscious moment to look around for a cup from which she might take a sip—preferably hot coffee—or maybe even something a little stronger. She found none and was certain there was no time to get something. She plowed on, finishing her review of the first file. It had to do with The Rasmussen Company but was mostly projections for several large commercial projects. She turned to Tee. "Nothing of great import here, but those were some hefty profit projections, weren't they?"

Not having read the file as carefully as Sonia, Tee responded as best she could. "Yeah, wow."

Sonia moved on to the second file. It didn't take long before her eyes widened and she spoke out loud. "And there it is. A letter from Missy Charles to Carl Rasmussen." She directed Tee's attention to the screen. "Look, she's explaining why, in her opinion, Victor is no longer the right person to run the company. 'Lack of responsibility.' 'Loss of interest.' 'Defamation of the company's reputation.' Those are some powerful indictments." She pointed to some comments near the end of the letter. "There's even something here about getting useless emails from him while he's in Europe."

Sonia sat back, drumming her fingers on her desk. "Just as I thought. She was going for the company and trying to get Carl on board."

Tee smiled at Sonia, almost smirking. "Gotcha, bitch. We gotcha."

Sonia's phone sang to her again. Without looking, she answered. "Bluegrass Confidential Investigations. Sonia Vitale."

"Well, my, my, my. Aren't we just the professional one?" The southern accent was unmistakable.

"Jet. Where are you?" She put her phone on speaker for Tee's sake.

"Just doing what I've been told to do. Following the scurrilous Missy Charles all about town."

Sonia was excited. "And?"

"And you'll never guess where she just wound up."

"I'd rather not." Sonia's voice was just a touch impatient. She wasn't really in the mood for playing. "Can you just tell me?"

Jet didn't seem to catch her drift. *"Well, in the last hour she has gone right from First Bluegrass Bank to the offices of James Peterson."*

Sonia was really getting itchy for a sip of something—warm or strong. "Who's that?"

"That, little lady, happens to be a lawyer who does a lot of corporate work. Handles business transfers, small corporate take-overs and such."

"Okay. And?"

"Aaand. I couldn't help but wonder if she might be talking to him about some sort of change in leadership at the Rasmussen Company?"

Sonia smiled. "Well, it turns out, dear friend, that you're absolutely correct. I just found a letter from her hidden on Carl Rasmussen's computer. The letter made it clear that she was making a move on the company and she wanted his help. In fact, she even mentioned the emails from Europe. I guess she's simply been making them up, trying to keep people thinking he's alive until she gets some sort of deal worked out with Carl."

"And in case she didn't?"

"And if she didn't, then it would turn out that Victor's unfortunate encounter with that barrel of bourbon would throw the whole thing up for grabs anyway. Given her experience with the business, she's still got a chance of winding up with the company and getting it away from Davey."

Jet paused for a moment, clearly thinking things through before she spoke. *"So, she tries to get Carl to turn the company over to her but does poor Victor in just in case?"*

Sonia glance at Tee again. "Looks like it."

"Wow, that's some cold lady."

"Wow is right. And get this. She must have known that Carl wasn't much for computers, so she very specifically told him to delete the letter and then empty the trash so the file couldn't be found."

"Of course, not knowing that our very own computer genius would be poking around on said computer and finding that exact file." Jet let out a long, *"Awww, isn't that just cunnin'?"*

Sonia couldn't help but appreciate the compliment. "Whatever. Anyway, my dear partner, thanks to your work and mine, it looks like we've got her. We know exactly what she was up to."

Jet spoke, sans accent. "Yeah, but how do we prove it . . . by nine o'clock tonight?"

45

Sonia had finished her conversation with Jet by telling her about what Steven Belcher had done to Tee, that Brad was leaving soon to go talk to Belcher, and that Brad needed Jet to relieve him at Zeke's motel room. When Jet pulled into the Embers' parking lot, it wasn't hard for her to locate Brad's car. She pulled into a space right next to his and rolled down her window as he rolled down his. "What up, Semper Fi?"

"Just livin' the dream. What about you?"

Jet stretched her arms out over the steering wheel, trying to relieve her fatigue. "Me and the Camry have had a long day, pal. Been following Missy Charles all over creation." She nodded gently and gave him a warm smile. "But looks like it paid off."

"How so?"

"It seems," she was too tired to fall into an accent, "that Sonia found a pretty damn incriminating file on Carl's computer while I was tracking Missy to a bank and a lawyer's office." She gave Brad a giant smile and winked a pretty blue eye. "No question about it. Looks like Missy had big plans for the future, and they didn't include Victor Rasmussen. Sonia's still got a bee in her bonnet about Missy being the one who did Victor in."

Brad's bright blue eyes were on high beam. "Is that so? Even after I let her know that Zeke told Gabriela he'd come to Lexington to kill both Rasmussens and that one of them was already dead?"

"Really?" Jet furrowed her brows. "Gabriela got him to admit that he'd already killed Victor and was planning on killing Carl?"

"Either Carl or the son, Davey. We're not sure."

She tipped her head. "How'd she do that?'"

"Jet," Brad chuckled, "do I need to tell you that Gabriela has certain, uh, charms?"

"That's one way to put it, now ain't it?" Jet paused and thought for a moment. "And you already told Sonia that?"

"That I did." Brad got more serious, "Anyway, I've got to get out of here. It's getting late and I've got to go check on this Steven Belcher guy. I don't think Zeke's going anywhere tonight, except maybe to drink himself into a stupor in the motel lounge over there. But I need you to keep an eye on him for me, nonetheless." Brad pointed in the direction of the motel building. "He's in room 114."

Jet looked at the poorly kept motel and room 114's faded red door. "I've got you covered, Captain. Now, off you go, and I hope this Belcher guy can finally understand what happens to a man when he messes with someone on our team, especially the youngster."

Brad fired up the Corvette. "Count on it." His eyes roamed the property. "Something happens, you call me." The 'Vette's window slid silently upward. The sound of gravel was louder than the purr of the powerful engine as the car moved out of the parking lot.

As Jet relaxed back into her seat, a chill ran down her spine. A realization struck her. She loved being a PI. She loved helping someone find a missing child or spouse. She *more* than loved tracking down cheating lovers, especially husbands. But now, she found herself sitting in a parking lot keeping an eye on a man who had already confessed to one murder and admitted that he was simply waiting for the opportunity to commit another. Scary. She let out a deep breath. She also reached into her purse and let her fingers find her recently purchased handgun.

Jet's other realization was that she was starving. Following the subject of an investigation all day doesn't always allow for a union-required sixty-minute lunch break. They may be sitting somewhere eating a heart-healthy lunch and drinking bottled water, but you're stuck, hoping you might just get lucky enough to slip through a fast-food drive-thru lane without losing them. Today hadn't been a "lucky day" for Jet.

About thirty minutes after Brad had left, Jet started thinking about the liquor store that sat in the adjacent parking lot. She knew liquor stores sold all kinds of liquor. She could almost feel the sensation of a glass of Horatio Blevins Black in her hand. But it was the other thing that she knew about liquor stores in Kentucky that had higher priority for her. They sell Slim Jims, the *"Meat Stick for Real Carnivores,"* and Mingua Beef Jerky. Not exactly roast rack of lamb, either one of them, but the thought of one of those, when the red needle in her stomach was on "E," became harder and harder for her to resist. She also had to pee.

Jet slipped out of the Camry and headed for the liquor store. She figured she could be in and out in less than three minutes, and she'd already spent ten times more than that staring at a red door that hadn't budged.

The jingle bells over the door jangled when she entered the small, narrow building she assumed had a bathroom. Of course, she was quite certain it wouldn't be for patrons. Few liquor stores offer that courtesy, given the types of things that might well go on behind those closed doors. However, she was pretty certain that the batting of her blue eyes and the tossing of her silky blonde ponytail could convince any young man behind the counter to let her use the employee's facility. She stepped to the counter, smiled at the young Hispanic man, went through her act—eyes then hair

—and found herself in the bathroom within minutes and just in time. She finished, washed her hands without soap, and was not the least bit surprised to find that there were no paper towels to be found anywhere in the nasty little room. Oh well.

Jet stepped out quickly, drying her hands on her jeans, and moved directly to the counter. She grabbed a package of beef jerky and an Ale-8 One, a unique, Kentucky soda with a huge, cult-like following. She reached for her tiny wallet. As she did, her eyes noticed movement beyond the flashing Coors sign in the window. It was Zeke. He was throwing a duffle bag into his car.

Jet threw her "lunch" on the counter and hustled out the door. She thought about calling Brad, but she knew Zeke would be long gone before Brad ever got back. She decided she'd just have to follow him, wherever he was going. When Zeke stepped back into his room, Jet headed for her car, walking slowly, casually. Then it hit her. If this guy takes off for Eastern Kentucky, there's no way we would have him in custody by nine o'clock. The contract might be blown. She stopped. Standing still, she made one of the toughest decisions of her life.

46

Jet started walking again. Just as she reached her Camry, she saw Zeke come out of his room, throw a blanket or heavy coat into his car and then head back inside. She assumed it was for the last time. Opening her passenger side door, she reached in, opened her purse, and pulled out her handgun. Holding the 9mm tucked slightly behind her leg, she walked directly toward Zeke Bartley's room. Her heart was pounding, her breathing difficult.

Jet was only a few feet away when Zeke appeared in the doorway. He stopped, a surprised look on his face. Glancing quickly left then right, she lifted the gun. "Don't move, you bastard." Her voice was soft but strong. "Don't you lift one little finger."

Taking advantage of Zeke's surprise, and realizing he could shut the door at any moment, Jet moved quickly, right at him, driving him back into the room with the fierce look on her face and the gun in her hand. Fortunately, Zeke, not being the most considerate of motel guests, had left the lights on, so Jet's eyes didn't have to adjust to any darkness. She kept moving right at him, driving him further back, until he was standing in the middle of the room, confused and apparently stunned into inaction.

Looking around, Jet realized she didn't really have him where she wanted him. In the corner, right next to the heater/air conditioner unit, was a beat-up old chair. That's where she wanted him, sitting in that chair. Unfortunately, she was standing between him and the chair, and in order to get him there, she would have to let him walk past her. Damn.

Jet took a deep breath and pulled herself back into the corner, behind where the door would open. She motioned him toward the chair. "Not a single quick move or I'll blow your f'ing head right off." As he slipped past her, the thought crossed her mind that it was probably a good thing she'd made it to the ladies' room.

Fortunately, Zeke complied readily. In Jet's mind, he seemed broken. He took a seat in the ratty old chair and spoke in almost defeated tones. "So, what's this all about?"

"Oh, I think you know." Jet was trying her damnedest to be strong. "It's about you and the Rasmussens."

Zeke narrowed his eyes and leaned a bit toward her. "How do you know 'bout that?"

Jet's insides were shaking, but she was determined to do her best playing the toughest role of her life, badass. "Let's just say that Gabriela and I are friends, really good friends."

Zeke hung his head. "Damn. Shoulda known." He looked up at Jet, truly inquisitive. "What'd she tell you?"

Jet could feel sweat in the palms of her hands, particularly the one that was holding the pistol. She wanted to switch hands, so she could wipe her palm on jeans. She didn't dare exhibit that weakness. "Let's just say that I'm not sure why you're leaving town now," a snarky smile crossed her lips, "your work unfinished and all."

Zeke looked up at her again and let out a muffled laugh. "Yeah, me either."

Jet furrowed her brow. "What?"

Zeke leaned forward, his forearms on his knees. He had the look of a person who was about to explain something, something that would take some time explaining. "Look, little lady. I'm on my way home because things just don't seem to want to go my way." He shook his head and actually smiled, "You know the old saying, 'If it weren't for bad luck, I'd have no luck at all?' Well, I ain't had no luck worth talkin' 'bout for the last ten years."

Jet leaned against the wall to steady herself, her gun pointed at a man who, it appeared for the moment at least, presented no real threat to her. In fact, the closer she looked at him, the more she could see the humanity in his eyes. It was as if he had morphed from a monster into a real man, a real man with real problems.

"See, me and my brother, we done good in the coal business, but then that all went to hell." His eyes searched her face as if he were looking for a reaction. "Then we come up with this plan to get rich makin' great bourbon, but I go and lose it all to a cheatin' son-of-a-bitch in a card game." His head dropped again. "So, I get all pissed and come here to Lexington to kill the guy and his ol' man, only to find out the guy's in Europe and the old man's dyin' anyway." Zeke sat up taller. "Then last night," his voice grew rougher, "and again this mornin', I got played for a fool by some hot Mexican gal." Sitting back and putting his hands on his legs, Zeke almost laughed when he spoke. "And then wouldn't you know it, while I was out chasing that damn piece of ass, some local bastard must've snuck into my room and stole my gun." He smiled at Jet, a sad smile. "If it weren't for bad luck . . . ."

"Wait a minute." Jet had to remember to keep the pistol pointed at Zeke. "You mean you think that Victor Rasmussen is still in Europe?"

Confusion crossed Zeke's face. "Well, ain't he?"

Jet took a deep breath. "Actually, before I say anything else, explain something to me. Last night you told Gabriela that you were here to kill both the Rasmussens, and that one of them was already dead. Isn't that so?"

Zeke thought for a moment. Then he shook his head. "No, I told her that one of them is already a *dead man*." He huffed "The old man. Don't you know he's dying of cancer or some such? He's a dead man. He ain't never comin' out of that hospital."

It was Jet's turn to stop and think things through. "So, the reason you were still hanging around Lexington—"

"Was to kill that cheatin' son-of-a-bitch Victor. Soon as he gets back from Europe. But I'm tired of waitin', and now I don't even have a gun. Not here. I was goin' to go back home and get another." He stopped and took a breath. "Though I'm startin' to wonder if it's such a good idea." He scratched his head. "Or maybe I'm just losin' my stomach for the whole thing."

Jet took a breath, a deep, long breath, then moved to the bed across from the chair. Sitting as far away from Zeke as she could, and still being careful to keep the gun pointed at him, Jet said, "Maybe you're a luckier man than you thought, Zeke."

He shook his head, indicating he didn't think so. "How's that?"

"Okay, so listen. The reason Gabriela came looking for you last night, the reason I'm watching you right now, is because our firm has been hired to investigate something."

"Yeah, what's that?"

"The murder of Victor Rasmussen."

Zeke's head popped backward. "How can that be? I ain't done it yet. The son-of-a-bitch is still in Europe."

Jet shook her head gently. "No, Zeke. For the last week or so, Victor Rasmussen has been marinating in a barrel of Horatio Blevins' finest."

"Bourbon?"

"Yeah, bourbon. Somebody killed him and shoved his body into a barrel full of bourbon. Left it right there in one of the rack-houses on the Blevins property."

Zeke was having trouble comprehending. "So, he's dead already?"

Jet's whole body was nodding. "Absolutely. And you are one lucky son-of-a-bitch yourself. Instead of running from the law the rest of your life, you get to . . ." Jet didn't know how to finish the sentence.

Zeke seemed to come to life. He sat up taller. "I get to leave this damn room and go home." He tipped his head. "Really? He's dead?"

Jet smiled. "Yup." Then it struck her. It was nothing she should have been smiling about. She shrugged gently, sadly, "And I guess you're getting your wish about the old man as well."

Zeke took a deep breath, capitulating to the truth. "Oh, I never really meant the old man harm. I was just so pissed. I just . . . . . Actually, I feel bad for the old guy."

A long minute passed while Jet and Zeke sat in room 114, at the ramshackle Embers hotel, digesting what they had each learned. Finally, Zeke stood up. "Well, I guess I'm out of here."

Jet jerked backward, standing, holding the gun higher. "Now, I didn't say—"

Zeke waved her off. "Put the gun down, little lady. I knew all along you never had the gumption to shoot me. And you're certainly not going to shoot me now, seein' as how I ain't done nothin' wrong," he chuckled at himself, " 'cept be a fool." He turned around, looking at the chair as if to check that he hadn't left anything there. "Now, if you'll excuse me, my stuff's in my truck and I've had about all of Lexington a man like me can handle." He walked right past her and out the door. "Evenin' ma'am."

Jet still had the gun in her hand, had even kept it pointed at him as he'd walked by her. But she knew that there was no way she was going to stop him from leaving. In fact, she really couldn't come up with a reason why she should.

47

Brad Dunham was a pro. A combat-hardened Marine and a veteran of years as an NCIS agent, he seldom took unnecessary chances. He could have gone to the Horatio Blevins property and waited in the parking lot for Steven Belcher to leave work at six. However, that would have meant a long, one-car surveillance on a two-lane country road, followed by a trip on an open four-lane highway, and travel through town. Too many chances for him to be noticed.

On the other hand, as much as he was convinced that Belcher would take the Bluegrass Parkway to US 60 and head for Lexington, he couldn't take the chance that Belcher had other plans. There was only one solution in Brad's mind, using the same type of GPS tracking device he'd recently used to follow some criminals all the way down to Memphis and back. Accordingly, by six o'clock, Brad had been to the Horatio Blevins facility, placed the device on Belcher's car, and then driven back to Versailles. He waited in the parking lot of a KFC, confident that he would pick up Belcher's signal on his laptop, wait for him to pass, and then follow him back toward his home.

He was right. Around fourteen minutes after six, Belcher's car came to Versailles, took the left at the dog-leg turn and headed for Lexington. Brad moved in right behind him. A few moments later, he dropped back over a mile, certain that he was following the right car. It wasn't long before Brad's laptop indicated to him that Belcher had turned onto his own street, Longview Drive.

A few minutes later, Brad pulled up to Belcher's home. Though many of the homes in the neighborhood had recently undergone fortuitous facelifts, the small, white, shingle house that Belcher owned had not been so fortunate. Able to see clearly that Belcher's car was now in the open-fronted garage at the back of the property, he had already decided not to fool around. This situation would demand a full-frontal attack plan. He knocked on Belcher's front door.

Steven Belcher opened up and looked out through the glass storm door. Tall and thin, his scraggly goatee and dirty comb-over sat sadly over his brown, Horatio Blevins T-shirt.

Brad stepped back two feet and spoke softly, so softly that Belcher opened the storm door a few inches in order to hear better. It was exactly what Brad had counted on. He lunged for the door, grabbing it with two hands before Belcher could get the door completely closed. Yanking it open, Brad forced his way into Belcher's home.

Brad pushed him backward, driving Belcher against the wall. The only words spoken were Belcher's. "Hey, hey. What the—" His head slammed against the wall. He was stunned into silence.

"Okay, creep." Brad was not playing nice. "You and I are going to have a little talk. Right?"

Belcher's eyes were opened wide, fear emanated from every pore on his body. He said nothing.

"Yeah, I thought you'd agree. Now, sit down." Brad pushed on Belcher's shoulders, driving him to the floor. Standing over him like a giant pin oak dwarfs a rose bush, Brad slowly drew his Colt 1911 out of his shoulder holster. The move was mostly for effect, but Brad could tell it had been more than successful. "Now that we've come to an understanding, friend, let's you and I have a chat. Where would you like to start, the Burl, the BCI offices?"

Belcher sat silently while Brad wondered if the poor guy might actually be about to pass out. Perhaps he might have come on stronger than he'd needed to. He took a deep breath, looking around the shabby living room—maroon plush couch, worn gray chair, fifty-inch flat-screen TV sitting on a scratched imitation wood table. "Okay, Steven. Let's start over. My name is Dunham. I am not your friend."

By the look on Belcher's face, Brad could tell the calm words were making the man even more frightened. He continued. "But Steven, although I am not your friend, I am not yet fully committed to hurting you. In fact, Steven, if you tell me everything I want to know, you may well be able to survive our little discussion. Would you like that, Steven?"

Belcher's eyes were wide as he spoke. "Are you a cop?"

Bad grinned. "I'm afraid you're not nearly that lucky, Steven. Now, let's begin with the Burl. What was that all about?"

Belcher started to speak, but no words came out.

"Calm down now, Steven. We really need to get to the bottom of things. Take a deep breath, swallow, and start slowly." He smiled again, "We'll get through everything, I hope."

Belcher did take a deep breath. He did swallow. "I didn't mean to hurt the girl."

Brad lifted his chin. "Tee?"

"Yeah, the Italian one. I didn't mean to hurt her. I just wanted to scare her."

"And," Brad used Jet's over-the-glasses look, "why would you want to scare her?"

"I had to. Just like I had to scare all of you by shooting into your office."

Brad looked at him silently, motionless.

"You've got to believe me. I knew I wouldn't hit anybody. I shot real high, to make sure that no one got hurt."

"Steven?" Brad said his name slowly. "I'm glad you're telling me this, but I really do need to know why you had to scare Tee, why you needed to scare all of us at BCI."

Belcher looked at Brad as if Brad should already know. "Because of the investigation. She said the investigation could get us both in trouble. Don't you see? All we wanted was for you all to stop poking around."

Brad took a moment to inspect his weapon. Then he asked, "And who, exactly, is *she*?"

"Carla. Carla Lombardi. She's my girlfriend."

Brad thought for a second. Lombardi. It sounded familiar but . . . . He squinted and looked closely at Belcher.

"Carla Lombardi, Victor's half-sister?" Belcher was on a roll. "She's the one who made me do it."

Brad gave Belcher an encouraging look and used his gun to signal that Belcher should continue.

"She's the one who made me try to scare the young girl, and the rest of you."

Brad rolled his head and shoulders as if all of this was making him tense. "Now, Steven. Or should I call you Steve or Stevie?" Belcher didn't respond. "I get the feeling you did something else, is that true?"

Sweating, Belcher was almost breathless as he spit out the rest of the story. "Listen. I didn't kill him. That wasn't me. All I did was help her get him into that barrel." He shook his head. "I'm telling you, she did that, she killed him. All I did was help her with the body."

"Him, who, Steven?" Brad knew the answer, but he wanted to hear it directly from Belcher.

"Victor Rasmussen. Her half-brother. She killed him. Asked him to come meet her at the Irish bar where she works then tricked him into going out back with her. Stuck a knife right in his gut and twisted. Guy bled out like a pig in just a couple of minutes. Blood was everywhere. She called me and told me to come help her. I was freaked out, but I had to do it. We wrapped him in a bedspread and dumped him in the back of her pickup. We took him out to the distillery." He blinked at Brad. "We could get in late at night because I know the codes. I work there."

Brad smiled. "Yes, you do."

"Don't know why she felt she had to stick him in a barrel of bourbon. I guess it was because she couldn't stand hearing him bragging about the fancy, new bourbon he was going to start selling."

Brad looked at him sideways. "How'd you get him into that barrel?"

Belcher scratched behind his ear. "You know, you can't just kind of open a full barrel of bourbon." His voice became less scratchy. He began to calm down. "I had to start by putting in a tap then emptying some of the bourbon into a big pan, just enough to kind of fill the barrel back up after we had him tucked away. The rest of the bourbon just went down the drain. After that, I had to knock off the hoops, take the lid off, lift that heavy sucker up and drop him in. Then I had to put the whole thing back together, bourbon and all."

Brad paused before continuing. He knew Belcher was ready to tell him everything he needed to know and he didn't want to overplay his hand. "All right, then, Steve. How 'bout you tell me why Carla Lombardi killed her brother."

Belcher was starting to regain his composure. He spoke almost calmly. "It was the old man. She hated the old man."

Brad tipped his head to the right. "Carl Rasmussen?"

"Yeah, the old man, her father. He kicked her and her mother out of the house when Carla was just a little kid. He never had a single thing to do with either of them all these years, nothing."

"So?"

"So," Belcher had become a willing confidant, "she hated his guts. Then, he goes and becomes real wealthy putting roofs on buildings, lots of buildings." He coughed several times, his mouth clearly very dry.

Brad was earnestly trying to understand. "And, how did that hate turn itself against Victor? Carla told Tee she'd never met him. Wished him luck."

Belcher looked beseechingly at Brad. "Could I have some water, man? I'm dying here."

Brad stood up slowly, extending his hand to Belcher. "Come on, Steve. Stand up. Let's go get you a drink of water. Which way to the kitchen?"

Belcher led the way into the drab, off-white kitchen, the highlight of which was 1970's vintage, avocado green appliances. Walking directly to the kitchen sink, where he used a dirty glass, he drank down two big glasses of water. He turned back to Brad. "Thanks."

Brad motioned toward the little two-person kitchen table with his gun. "Okay, Steve. Let's have a seat at the table, both of us." Belcher complied. The table wobbled as Brad leaned his left elbow on it, his right hand holding the gun under the table in order to make Belcher feel a little less threatened. "Now, Steve, tell me why Carla hated her brother."

"No," Belcher shook his head. "She didn't hate him. She just hated the father. It's just that the father brought Victor into the business, eventually made him head honcho. Carla followed all of that stuff in the business section of the newspaper. Anytime something big would happen with the Rasmussens, Carla would read about it, then she'd have a hissy fit." He took on the woman's voice. " 'That piece of crap. He didn't have a minute for me and my mother. Not a minute's time. Not a f'ing dime.' "

Brad nodded and shrugged. "I get that, I guess."

Belcher didn't need to be asked any more questions. "So, then Victor gets lucky with that racehorse of his and Carla gets even crazier." Belcher dropped his jaw and rolled his eyes. "And then this bourbon thing, that really pushed her over the edge."

"How so?"

Belcher's eyes widened. "Are you kidding me? She's a damn bartender down at McCullen's, and now Carl's prized son is going to become one of those bourbon-making guys, and twenty-year-old bourbon at that. That was it, she snapped."

Brad would have waited for Belcher to continue, but he sensed that Belcher was running out of gas, and he didn't have the key information he needed yet. "Okay, Steve. I get all that. But what I don't get is why Carla wanted Victor dead. Can you help me out there, Steve?"

"Yeah." Belcher took a deep breath. "Here's the thing. My sister, she works down at St. John's Hospital. You know, where they took Carl when he first got sick." Belcher stopped and looked at Brad, a question in his eyes. "You do know that Carl's sick, real sick, right?"

"Yeah, Steve. We know."

"So, my sister, she knows Carla and I are together, so she tells me that he's sick, probably going to die. She tells me. I tell Carla."

"And?"

"Well, first, she's walking around the house kind of singing to herself. You know, 'Ding, Dong, the bitch is dead,' and all. But then, she says to me, 'Hey. I'll bet there's no one home at Carl's place. Don't you think we should go slip in there and take some of the stuff he should have given to me over the years?' "

Brad gave Belcher a "*Did you buy that?*" look.

"Yeah, yeah. I know. I should have talked her out of it, but you don't know Carla. She's got a mean streak, a hell of a mean streak. I guess I just went along with it." He paused and rubbed his head like he was trying to erase the memory. "But here's the thing. First, she says we should dress up. We'll be less noticeable in his fancy neighborhood if we have good clothes on. Then, when we get to his house, just to be sure no one's home, Carla walks up to the door and rings the bell, bold as can be." Belcher's mouth dropped as if the next part of the story were a surprise to him.

"Son-of-a-bitch, some German lady answers the door. And instead of asking us what we want, she just asks us if we're from the company."

"And, of course," Brad interjected, "you said, 'Yes.' "

Belcher shrugged. "Well, not me. But Carla did. So, the lady invites us in and asks if we want to go into his office." Belcher raised his eyebrows. "Who says 'No,' to that? So, in we go. Now, I'm no computer genius, but it wasn't hard for me to figure out how to get into his computer. We poked around."

Brad was pleased that the whole story was finally coming out, but he was getting impatient with the pace. The night was wearing on. Nine o'clock was on its way. "So, did you find anything?"

Belcher nodded and smiled. "You bet your ass we did. We found a copy of the old man's will." He gave Brad a snarky look. "And what do you think it said?"

Brad simply shrugged.

"He was leaving everything to Victor. Everything. It pissed Carla off so bad she could have taken a dump right there. She starts walking around and around in the office. At first, I thought she was looking for something to take. Then I figured she was just looking for something to break. But damn, I was wrong."

"How so?"

"All of a sudden Carla stops. She turns around to me and smiles. Then she asks me a question." He stopped to take a breath, or maybe just more for effect.

Brad couldn't wait. "Come on, Steve, my man. Let's get to it. What did she ask you?"

"She asked me, 'If the old man dies and Victor's not around, who gets all his money, all his stuff?' She got really excited, smiling. 'All his everything?' " Belcher's smile got even bigger. "So, I told her that if the old man died, and Victor wasn't around, it would go to his wife or to one of his other kids. And since he was divorced from Carla's mom, and his second wife was already dead. Everything would go to Carla." He laughed. "She was grinning like a kid on Christmas morning. She'd already figured that out."

Brad took another deep breath. "So, that's the deal? Carla knew Carl was dying and figured if Victor was dead, she would inherit everything?"

'Yeah," Belcher raised his finger, "but she's no fool. She also figured that if Victor died before the old man did, then the old guy might change his will."

Brad perked up. "So, she had to keep Victor alive, right?"

Belcher rolled his head on his shoulders. "Well, kill him, but make it *look* like he was still alive."

Brad shook his head. "Yeah, Steve, that's what I meant. And she stole Victor's laptop and started sending messages to Missy Charles, saying he was in Europe. Am I correct?"

"Damn," Belcher's eyes widened again, "you *are* good. That's exactly what she did. And every day that lady, Missy Charles, would send him an email asking him questions about the business, and Carla would have to come up with some bullshit answer that made it sound like it was Victor answering them."

"Quite a plan." Brad nodded. "So, Carla kills Victor and is still waiting for Carl to kick the bucket, right?"

"Uh huh."

"And as soon as he does, Carla's going to step in and claim the inheritance, right?"

"Well, kind of."

Brad's head popped up. "What do you mean, kind of?"

Belcher thought for a while, then he sat up taller and asked, "Do you know much about legal words?"

"I guess I do. Why?"

"Well," Belcher seemed to be enjoying himself, "do you know the legal term par stirps?"

"You mean, per stirpes? Like purr stir peas?"

Belcher shook his head, embarrassed. "Well, I guess, something like that. Anyway, before we left the old man's place, Carla asked me to print out a copy of the old man's will. After she killed Victor," Belcher wagged his finger at Brad again, "and remember now, I had nothing to do with that, she started reading that will every day. It just made her happy to read it, to know that that was the legal piece of paper that was going to make her rich."

"Let me guess," Brad wagged his finger back at Belcher, enjoying the turn-about, "she kept stumbling over the term, per stirpes. Am I right, Steven?"

The energy seemed to slip out of Belcher. "Yeah, she finally went to the internet and looked the damn thing up."

Brad smiled. "And it said that per stirpes means, 'by the root,' or 'by the branch.' That there are two ways to pass things down in a will. Per capita, by the head, and per stirpes, by the root. In other words, if the old man died and the estate went to Victor, per capita, and Victor wasn't around, it would go to Carl's other child, Carla. But if it's left per stirpes, then it wouldn't go to Carla. It would go to Victor, and per stirpes, by the root, it would go to Victor's heirs. In other words, when Carl passes, everything goes, through Victor, to Carl's namesake, Carl David, you know, Davey." Brad sighed and smiled again. "And did Carla lose it when she figured that out, when she realized she'd killed Victor for nothing?"

Belcher looked at Brad with dead earnestness. "Oh, no. She just figured that now, before the old man died, she had to kill Davey, too."

48

When Sonia got off the phone with Jet, after sending her to relieve Brad at The Embers motel, she felt uneasy. No matter what Brad had said, there was still something that told her that Missy was guilty. She had the incriminating files, but she had no hard proof. She stood up at her desk, convinced she should go follow Missy Charles, at least until nine o'clock, "game over" time. Missy seemed to have a lot of plans in motion. Maybe, just maybe, she would do something that Sonia could bring to the bourbon brotherhood. Something solid.

Missy's home, where Jet had seen her last, was on Lakeshore Drive, not far from Sonia's office. It would take her only a few minutes to get there. Before she reached her destination, however, her phone sang to her. Driving, she picked up the phone without looking at it. "This is Sonia Vitale."

"Sonia." It was Brad, his voice terse. *"Big trouble. I'll explain later, but it turns out that Carla Lombardi is the one who killed Victor, and now she's after Davey. It's past seven. That means his plane has already landed. Do you know where he lives?"*

Sonia was instantly alert. "No, I don't. I don't."

"Babe, we've got to get someone out there fast. Someone who can keep Davey safe. Where are you?"

"I just left the office, headed to watch Missy. Her place is on Lakeshore. I'm almost there now."

"Where's Jet?"

"She's out at The Embers, where you told me to send her." Sonia pulled her car to the curb and switched her phone screen to Google Maps.

"Damn, that's right. That's around the top of New Circle Road. Where's Tee?"

Sonia's voice reflected the tension in Brad's. "She said she was going to get something to eat. I think she's up at Saul Good."

"Listen. I'm going to put in an emergency call to my buddies—"

"Don't bother. I just found it. He lives in an apartment on Village Green Ave, that's out in Hamburg—maybe ten minutes from here."

"Isn't there a Saul Good up there, too? Do you think that's where Tee is?"

Sonia was already doing a three-point turn, palming the wheel hard. "Yes, I'm pretty sure that's where she went." Sonia sensed the strength in Brad's voice and was aware of it in her own. They were two partners, two equals, working together to save a life. "I'm going to call Tee and send her to Davey's right now. Then I'm heading up there myself."

"Copy that. Village Green Ave, near Hamburg, right?

"Yes."

"Be there soon."

TEE WAS SITTING on a bench just inside a cool, local place called Saul Good. The atmosphere was relaxed but somewhat up-scale. Still, Tee knew that for nine bucks she could get a small, take-out pizza and a drink. She liked the fact that their pizzas were all unusual, Thai, and stuff like that—right up her alley. Her phone rang just after she got her order in.

"Tee." The voice on the other end was abrupt. *"It's Sonia. This is critical. I need you to drop everything and go to where Davey Rasmussen lives."* The words came out rapid fire. *"Carla Lombardi is the one who killed Victor. Now she's after Davey. I need you to get there as soon as possible to warn him."*

Tee was momentarily caught off guard. "Okay, but I just—"

"Tee! Drop everything. Go. If Carla gets there first, you may be too late. Go. Go now. I'll text you the address."

Tee stood up, a little dazed. She looked around for the hostess, but the young woman was not at her station. Not knowing what else to do, Tee reached into her jeans pocket, pulled out a crumpled ten-dollar bill and threw it on the hostess stand. She hustled out of the restaurant and headed for her car. Jumping in, she checked her phone. Sonia had already texted her the address.

As Brad talked to Sonia on the phone, Belcher sat still, watching, enthralled, as if he were part of some sort of TV show or action movie. When Brad stood and motioned for him to follow, Belcher did exactly as he was told, no questions asked.

"Okay, Steven. Here, put your hand on the refrigerator door handle."

"Okay."

"Good." Brad took one of the plastic ties he had with him out of his pocket. He slipped it through the refrigerator handle and around Belcher's wrist.

"Hey? What the hell are you doing?"

Brad smiled at Belcher while he worked quickly. "Come on, Steven. Did you really think that since you told me the whole story about you and Carla things were all good now?"

"I guess not. But . . . ."

"Listen. This way if you get thirsty or something, all you have to do is open the door. I'm sure you've got something worth drinking in there."

"Yeah, but what if I have to—"

"Steven. That's your problem." Brad was wrapping up as quickly as he could. "As you can tell. I've got to get somewhere fast. Listen, I'll call the police—" Brad stopped, interrupting his own speech. He knew he couldn't call the police, not yet. He looked around the kitchen, finally finding a large pot, the kind you might cook spaghetti in. He walked quickly over to the stove, picked up the pot, then laid it on the floor next to Belcher. "You might be here for a while." Brad turned and headed for the front door. "Hope you've got more than beer in that refrigerator, Steve. Probably be some time tomorrow before we get back to you." He walked quickly out the door, almost running, climbed into his car, and was on his way to Davey's apartment.

~

THOUGH IT FELT like an eternity to her, it took Tee only a few minutes to find Village Green Avenue. Watching the apartment unit numbers go by, Tee instinctively stopped a half-block before she reached Davey Rasmussen's apartment, which was on her left. She looked at her watch, seven fifty-seven. Remembering that Davey was supposed to arrive back in Lexington from the UAE right around seven o'clock that evening, she assumed he would be driving up to his apartment in the next few minutes.

Unclear as to what she was looking for, but determined to carry out her part of this rescue plan, Tee climbed out of her old Chevy Caprice, crossed the street, and began walking nonchalantly down the block. As she passed Davey's apartment, she realized there was a car parked across the street, on the right. Though the inside of the car was dark, Tee was pretty certain there was a woman in it. A chill, a deep chill, ran through her body.

Calming herself, Tee made the instant decision to keep on walking. As she did, she casually slipped her phone out of the back pocket of her snug jeans. She hit FAVORITES, then tapped on a picture of Sonia's face.

"Yes, Tee. I'm almost there. Everything okay?"

"Sonia. There's a woman in a car waiting across the street from Davey's place. I can't see her clearly. But I can tell, it's not some young girl. It's an older woman. I'm pretty sure it's Carla."

"Don't do anything, Tee. Promise me you won't do anything. And for God's sake, don't let her see you. She might recognize you. Just wait for me to get there. Find a place where you can see the woman without her seeing you, then just keep watching."

"But, what if she—"

"Tee! Don't do *anything. Carla has come there to kill Davey. She's got to have a weapon of some kind, probably a gun. I don't want you getting hurt. Just stay on the line. Keep watching her. Keep talking to me. I'm on Liberty Road. I'll be there as soon as I can."*

WHILE SHE WAS TALKING to Tee on the phone, Sonia, who had taken a back route to the very busy Hamburg area, was speeding along curvy, winding, Liberty Road. With no concern for the speed limit, she approached a traffic signal that was glowing red. She blew right through it, turning left across traffic. Fifteen seconds later, frustrated, she waited for two cars to pass before she could take one last left. The next turn to the right was Davey's street.

Sonia saw Tee's car and pulled up behind it. "Okay, Tee. I'm parked behind your car. I'm getting out. Where are you?"

"I'm at the end of the block, on the left side of the street, tucked behind some bushes. I doubt that you can see me."

"No, I can't. Just stay still. I can see a car in front of me. Some sort of dark sedan. Is that the car?"

"Yes. I haven't seen any movement. I'm pretty sure she's still in there."

Now that Sonia felt Tee was safe, she wanted to take advantage of the fact that her quarry was unaware of Sonia's presence. She bent down close to her steering wheel and pulled her .38 out of the holster around her ankle. She sat up and took a deep breath. "Okay, Tee. Here we go. I'm going to try to catch her off guard. Let's hope she doesn't have her weapon in her hand or anything and I can take her into custody without a hassle.

"Sonia, can't we just wait for Brad?"

Sonia thought for a moment. That would be a lot simpler and safer for her. "No. I can't take the chance that Davey shows up and Carla gets out of the car. Once she does that, we might get caught in a real shoot-out. God knows how that might turn out. No, I've got to take advantage of the fact that we have the element of surprise. I'm going in. If anything goes wrong, hang up and call 911 right way. Don't you dare come running at us. Got it?"

"Please, Sonia, be careful."

SONIA'S CAR might have made good time on its way to Tee and Davey's place. It was nothing compared to the way Brad maneuvered the 'Vette. Seventy, eighty, ninety miles per hour, blowing through red lights, screeching around corners. He was determined to get there before Sonia or anyone else got hurt.

SONIA GOT out of her Subaru, walked in front of it to the passenger side, and stepped up onto the curb and then the sidewalk. Walking as calmly as she could, she approached the dark sedan, pretty certain it was some kind of old Ford, or maybe nondescript Chevy. She couldn't help but stop when she saw the silhouette of a woman's head in the car. She thought it was strange that Tee was right, that even without direct light she could somehow tell that it wasn't the head and shoulders of a young woman she was looking at.

She started walking again, her pistol at her side, remembering all the instruction she had received about keeping her finger off the trigger until the moment she was sure she was going to fire. The thirty or so steps it took for her to reach the car seemed like the longest walk she'd ever taken. Eventually, she was standing on the sidewalk, at the right rear of the darkened car. She closed her eyes. Okay, Sonia. It's now or never. She stepped forward, turned, bent over, and pointed the gun at the woman in the car.

Having taken the same route Sonia had, Brad was finally on Liberty Road. Same curvy, winding road, same dangerous places to pass other vehicles. Bigger engine, lighter car. The 'Vette flew down the street, eating it up in mere minutes. He made the same screeching, illegal turn at the light that Sonia had. Just a minute or two until he'd get there.

"Carla Lombardi!" Sonia was surprised at the volume of her own energized voice. "Don't move! Stay still! Raise your hands!"

"AHHH!" The woman in the car screamed in fright. Even in the darkness of the vehicle, Sonia thought she could make out the fear on the woman's face. "All right! All right! Just don't shoot! Please don't shoot me!"

Sonia leaned forward and opened the passenger side door. "You just stay still, Carla. You just stay still. I'm not here to hurt you, but I will if I have to." She was pointing the gun right at the woman, something she had never done before, something she had hoped she would never have to do. Unfortunately, Sonia was now chagrined to find that she had approached the car from the wrong side. Sure, it was easier to sneak up on the woman from that side, but now she didn't quite know how to get the woman out of the car without putting herself in danger. Fighting to keep the gun from shaking in her hand, she took a deep breath and plowed on. "Okay. Carla. I want you to gently open your door and step out of the car. Just remember. I've got my gun pointed right at you and I'm pretty damn sure you're armed. If you make the slightest move I'm going to have to shoot. Please don't make me shoot you, Carla."

The woman did as she was told. When she had, she stood, hands raised, looking over the top of the car at Sonia. "Please. Please don't hurt me. But I'm not Carla. I don't even know who Carla is. I'm Sherry. Sherry Rasmussen. I'm just waiting for my son Davey to come home. He's coming home from the airport. I'm just here to welcome him home. Please don't hurt him. If you have to, please shoot me, but please don't hurt him."

Sonia was stunned. She'd never met Sherry. For that matter, she'd never met Carla. Was this really Sherry, Victor's ex-wife, or was this a bluff?

Tee watched from down the street. She held her breath as she saw Sonia bend over and point her gun at the woman in the car. Sonia's voice was so loud Tee could actually hear everything Sonia shouted at the woman. She was drawn to what was happening. She began walking slowly down the street, closer and closer to Sonia and the car. She watched the woman get out of the car, her hands raised, talking to Sonia over the top of the car, though she couldn't quite hear what she was saying.

Suddenly, a car turned the corner. Headlights on, it spilled light across the whole scene—a woman standing by her car, hands raised, while another woman held a gun on her.

The car pulled to a screeching stop. A man—young, tall, blond-haired, well-dressed—jumped out. "Mom! Mom! Are you okay?" He ran toward his mother—a strange but instinctual attempt at protecting her.

Sonia was shocked. Her eyes wide. Her whole system in overdrive. She turned the gun toward the man in self-defense. "Stop! Stop right there! Stop so nobody gets hurt!"

Tee was mesmerized by the scene playing out in front of her—Sonia holding a gun on the woman, a strong, young man jumping out of the car, running at them. It was wild, crazy. She kept walking slowly toward the center of the storm.

Just as she heard Sonia yell, "Stop so nobody gets hurt," Tee saw a reflection out of the corner of her eye, a glint, some movement. She turned to look. To her horror, it was the real Carla Lombardi, the woman she had interviewed days ago at McCullen's, the woman she now knew had murdered Victor Rasmussen. What she held in her hand, what had glinted in the street light, was a gun, a silver-plated gun, and she was pointing it right at somebody. She looked ready to shoot.

Tee didn't know what to do. Her mind flashed with images of guns and blood and death. She froze for a second. Pure adrenaline kicked in. She screamed. "Sonia!! Look out!!"

The sound shocked everyone, including Carla, who hesitated then turned. She looked right at Tee. She raised the weapon. She fired. BLAM.

Fortunately, it was a long and not-well-prepared shot. Still, Tee heard the bullet whip past her. She gasped. Diving into a space between two buildings, she tried to find real shelter, she tried to stay low, she tried not to die.

Sonia heard the scream. It stopped her. She turned toward the sound. Then she heard the shot. It had the opposite effect. Realizing that someone was shooting at Tee, at her little sister, the little girl that Sonia had taught to braid her own hair and how to flirt with boys, she flew into action. Running right at Carla Lombardi, Sonia traveled twenty yards in a split second. Getting close enough, while at the same time watching Carla turn the handgun on her, Sonia stopped. Drawing on every bit of self-discipline she could, she took in a breath, whispered to herself, "squeeze don't jerk," and pulled the trigger. BLAM. The gun jumped in her hand. She focused. "Squeeze don't jerk." BLAM. And again. BLAM. And again. BLAM. Carla grabbed her chest with the first shot. She stumbled to her knees with the second. Within seconds, Sonia watched her crumple to the ground as if someone or something had simply turned off every function of her brain.

49

The sound of the gun rang in her ears. The smell of cordite filled her nostrils. Her hand felt the tingle that came from firing her weapon. Sonia was frozen, her gun still pointed in Carla's direction.

A car screeched around the corner. Another pair of headlights. More light on the now-eerie scene. Sonia turned. A low-slung car, dark. A big man flying out of it, running toward her. Something dark in his hand. New sounds in her ears. "Sonia, Sonia, babe. Are you ok?"

It took a second before Sonia recognized the voice, Brad's voice. "I'm okay." She'd spoken so softly she was the only one who had heard it.

Brad got to her, his eyes searching the scene, trying to understand. A dark car sitting by the curb. Another, newer car, door open, lights on, still running. A young man holding an older woman close, the woman's face buried in his chest. Tee walking gingerly toward something or someone crumpled on the ground. And Sonia. Sonia, standing seemingly shell shocked, her pistol in her hand, tears running down her face. Holstering his own weapon, he gently reached out and took her gun, slipping it into his pocket. He pulled her close to him.

"I," Sonia's voice was shaky. "I shot her." She looked into Brad's bright blue eyes. "I shot her, Brad. I think I killed her." There was disbelief in her voice. "I think I killed someone."

Brad put his hand on the back of her head and pulled it close to his chest. "Yes, babe, you shot someone. You also saved Davey. You saved his life."

Sonia pulled her head away from his chest while he held her tight. She tried to look around her. "And Tee, Brad. Is Tee okay? She shot at Tee and I couldn't help it, I couldn't stop. I, I had to do something. I ran at her. I shot. I shot and shot and shot. Brad?"

"Tee's okay." Brad pulled her head back to his chest, muffling any words she might say. As he did, he noticed Tee walking toward him slowly, carrying something. He also saw the young man helping the older woman sit down on the curb. The man was speaking softly to her, comforting her.

Tee finally stepped close. She looked at Brad and motioned with her head. "That's Davey. I think the woman may be his mom."

Sonia's head popped up. "Tee." She ripped herself out of Brad's arms and threw her own around Tee, frantic. "Are you alright? Are you hurt? Tee, are you okay?"

Tee was calm, overly calm. "I'm okay Sonia. Really. I'm okay. You?"

Sonia pulled back as if she were going to say something to Tee. She didn't. She just pulled Tee close again and hugged her as hard as she could.

Brad looked at Tee. He gave a nod of recognition toward the woman. "You're right. That's Sherry Rasmussen, Davey's mom." He motioned at the crumpled body lying on the grass across the street. "Carla?"

Tee twisted her lips. "Yeah, Carla. She was here for Davey, but Sonia ruined the plan." She raised her hand, holding Carla's handgun gingerly between her fingertips. “Then she shot at me and Sonia shot her. Shot her three or four times.” She shook her head, “I called 911, but I’m pretty sure she’s gone.”

Brad took the gun from Tee without saying a word. He tucked it into his belt, behind his back.

Sonia was finally regaining her composure, though the shock of having taken a human life was difficult for her to absorb, as it would be for a very long time. She pulled away from Brad, trying to speak calmly. “Tee. Tee’s the one who saved everyone’s life, not me. She’s the hero. She’s the one who saw Carla with the gun, who called out—who stopped it all.”

Wiping tears from her cheeks with her fingertips, Sonia saw Davey Rasmussen approaching her. She brushed damp hair out of her face and moved to meet him. “Davey? Davey, I’m Sonia Vitale with Bluegrass Confidential Investigations. Are you and your mom okay?”

Davey moved slowly and carefully as he approached Sonia. He spoke softly, more shaken than angry. “What’s this all about? Who was that woman?” Then something struck him. “And why were you holding a gun on my mother?” He was clearly starting to get his bearings. He was starting to recognize his own anger.

Brad stepped forward. “Now, just stand down, son. Let Ms. Vitale explain.” Davey stopped, turning his attention first to Brad, then back to Sonia. “Okay, explain.” It was a command.

Sonia’s body was still full of adrenaline. She took a breath, trying, again, to calm it. She started. “That woman is your aunt, Carla Rasmussen Lombardi. She came here to kill you tonight.”

“What?” Davey’s chin dropped. “Why would she want to kill me?” He hesitated for a moment. “And that can’t be true. I don’t even have an aunt.”

Sonia’s voice became more compassionate. “I’m afraid you do, Davey. She was your father’s half-sister, the daughter of your grandfather’s first wife. And, I’m sorry to say, I have some more bad news for you.”

Davey turned his head partially away from her as if to ward off the pain that might come with that bad news.

Sonia explained the whole sordid mess, Carl disowning his first wife and child, Carl's illness, and worst of all, Victor's murder. Even Sonia and Tee were stunned when Brad stepped in to explain why Carla had murdered Victor and why she had come there to kill Davey. Sonia could see from Davey's face that it was really more than he could absorb all at once. By the time Brad had finished reciting the facts, Sherry Rasmussen was standing next to Davey, her arms around him, comforting her son.

Sonia and Brad had shared the entire story quickly. While they did, they could hear sirens approaching, sirens responding to calls from neighbors about gunshots in the neighborhood. As the first red and blue lights came flashing onto Village Green Avenue, Brad looked at his watch. He gave Sonia a tiny smile. "Eight thirty-seven. Looks like you made it with plenty of time to spare, babe." He bent down and put Carla's weapon, Sonia's .38, and his own gun on the ground, then he spoke in a voice loud enough for all of them to hear. "Everyone, raise your hands and smile at the nice police officers. Let's not make anyone nervous."

50

It was ten forty-five the next morning before Tee and Sonia shuffled into Magee's. Jet was already there, sitting at one of the larger tables, reserving seats with her purse, her keys and the pink sweater she'd brought. They all looked exhausted.

Sonia pointed Tee toward the coffee bar, then walked up to the counter where she was greeted by a smiling Hildy. "Small coffee and an almond croissant?"

"Large coffees," Sonia shook her head wearily, her voice a bit raspy, "and just keep track of what folks in our group order. You'll know who they are. We're putting it all on the business credit card this morning." She managed a tiny smile. "And I *will* take that croissant."

Hildy put the croissant on a paper plate and handed it to Sonia with an especially warm smile. "It'll be okay, honey. Whatever it is."

Sonia simply smiled in response then turned and headed for the table. Tee showed up at the same time with two coffees. Jet already had hers.

A few minutes later, Brad arrived. He'd been across the street in the offices of Semper Fi Investigations since seven o'clock. He was still trying to catch up on his own casework. He walked directly over to Sonia, stood behind her, and kissed the top of her head. "Morning, babe." She turned her head awkwardly toward him and made a gentle, kissing sound in the air. Eventually, all four of them were seated, quietly eating pastries and drinking hot coffee.

It had been quite a night. When the police had arrived, hands on their weapons, Brad had stepped forward and informed the police that there had been a shooting, that everyone involved wished to be taken into custody, though not arrested, and that no one would explain anything until they'd had a chance to confer with a lawyer.

It had been almost an hour before Revelle Boudreaux, a lawyer Sonia had recently conferred with, had arrived at the precinct to represent everyone from BCI. Davey Rasmussen and his mom had called their own lawyer. Sonia had given Boudreaux a thumb-nail sketch of the situation and told her that she believed no one should say anything until Mason Holiday showed up. Boudreaux had agreed.

It was well past eleven o'clock that evening when Holiday appeared, his own lawyer in tow. Sonia never quite knew how he did it, but using the clout of the bourbon brotherhood, Holiday had managed to significantly shift the legal jeopardy that arose from the non-disclosure agreement to the brotherhood. There was still, however, the possibility that BCI and all its agents might be charged with obstruction of justice.

Sonia had sat in a holding cell until well after one o'clock in the morning. Still in shock from the events of the evening, she worried that the local DA might not fully grasp the panic she'd felt when Carla had shot at Tee and then turned her gun on Sonia. She'd been relieved when Boudreaux had come to the cell, announcing that she'd been able to secure Sonia's release on her own recognizance. Boudreaux had already made plans with the DA to meet again in the morning.

Jet was just finishing catching everyone up on the specifics of her final conversation with Zeke Bartley when Boudreaux walked into Magee's. She was a stunning woman with bright brown eyes, straight black hair, a wide, engaging smile, and mocha skin. Her Cajun bloodline came through in her voice and speech patterns. Slender and shapely at five-foot-seven or eight, her obviously expensive black suit and teal silk blouse completed the impressive package. Sonia spoke softly to the group. "That's Revelle Boudreaux."

Sonia stood as Boudreaux approached the table at which they were all seated. "Good morning." She motioned toward the others. "This is Brad Dunham and Teresa Vitale. We call her Tee. And this is Joyce Ellen Thomas. She goes by Jet."

Boudreaux smiled. "Lots of short names. Easy to remember." The words were almost syrupy as they flowed out of her mouth in smooth rhythms covered in Cajun spice. "Do y'all mind if I sit?"

Sonia gestured toward a wooden chair. "Please, have a seat. Can we get you something?"

"Yes, thank you. Coffee." Boudreaux scanned the table again, smiling gently—clearly absorbing impressions while Tee popped up to get her a drink. Boudreaux turned to Sonia. "Now, I've got nothing but good news, so I assume you don't mind me sharing it with y'all as a group. Yes?"

Sonia took the lead, relieved. "Please. Go ahead. But first, thank you, again, for getting us all released last night. I don't know if I could have made it through the whole night in that cell."

"Not a problem." Boudreaux's smile warmed the whole table, "Working with Mason Holliday, who I must say has some serious connections, we've been able to take your obstruction of justice charges completely off the table. Now," she shrugged, "John O'Neal, he's in some pretty hot water for asking Bobby Ray to move that body."

She turned to Sonia with increased warmth in her eyes. "And

you, sweetheart. I've just come from my meeting with the DA. Given the fact that you are licensed to carry, and that Carla Lombardi fired first and was aiming at you, you will not be charged with any culpability in her death." She leaned back and smiled at the whole group. "It appears this entire incident is completely behind all of you." Sonia's relief was reflected in the faces of the whole group.

"Oh, and one other thing." Boudreaux looked at Brad. "The DA mentioned you left that Steven Belcher fellow tied to his own refrigerator. Apparently, the police found him with his arm still locked to the door handle, sitting on the ground next to a pot of . . . . Never mind. What matters is that he corroborated the story y'all told the police about Carla Rasmussen."

Sonia was a bit confused but figured she would have plenty of time to ask Brad about Boudreaux's comments later. She took a deep breath before she spoke. "It's been one hell of a five-day case, ladies and gentleman. And let us lift our coffees in a toast to a successful completion."

Everyone at the table complied, including Boudreaux. The sound of the quiet, celebratory comments was followed by a long moment of satisfied silence. Jet broke the spell. "Well, I have two questions. First, are the Bartley brothers still out that bourbon?

It didn't take long for everyone's eyes to drift to the only lawyer at the table. Revelle thought for a moment before she spoke. "It seems to me that if they haven't already signed the property over to anyone else, it would be difficult to enforce a verbal agreement based on the fruits of illegal gambling."

Heads at the table bobbed in silent agreement before Jet spoke again. "Okay, second question. What the hell happened to Johnny Adams? Did he just disappear off the face of the earth?"

Tee was quick to follow. "Yeah, right? What *did* happen to him?"

Sonia sat up taller, almost defensive. "I'm sure something

must have come up with his own work. He's very busy and successful out there in, uh, Denver, you know."

Jet gave Tee a look, while Brad's eyes drifted to the large mural on the back wall of the bakery. Tee couldn't help but speak. "The least the jerk could have done was let us know what was happening."

"Johnny Adams?" Boudreaux's curiosity was clearly piqued.

Jet gave Sonia a quick look. When she got no response, she began explaining Johnny's relationship to BCI, all the way back to the Hensley case. While she was speaking, Sonia sat quietly, a thought plaguing her. Though she had made a work-based excuse for Johnny's sudden disappearance, she feared a different motive was at play. She unconsciously ran her fingers through her hair. It's me. He still has feelings for me and I rejected him. I know it. That's why he left. She certainly didn't feel comfortable sharing the thought with the group, especially Brad.

As Jet continued filling Boudreaux in, explaining in detail the very sudden and bloody end to the Hensley case, a second thought crept through Sonia's mind as well. She brushed a wisp of hair out of her face. And how could I have been so wrong about Missy? I felt it. I could have sworn it was her. I even found the letter. Yet, there's no question that Carla Lombardi killed Victor. She swallowed her frustration and joined the conversation. "Yeah, that was quite a night."

Brad put his coffee cup on the table. "Quite a night."

Boudreaux stood, drawing everyone's attention. "Well, y'all. It's been a pleasure, but I've got a client on his way to court, and I've got to get over there before," she winked, "he says something less than beneficial to his case." She waved a gracious hand. "Y'all have a good day now. And Ms. Sonia. I'll check in with you tomorrow to make sure everything is still copasetic."

Everyone at the table responded, and Boudreaux left the bakery. After a moment, Sonia leaned forward. "Okay, now, let's get back to the present." She smiled, "I think it's time we talk a little business." The others all turned their attention to her. "Ms. Jet. I believe it's time we offer our temporary employee zero-zero-three a permanent position. What do you think?"

Jet played coy. "I don't know. She did help save your life and all, but does that actually deserve the offer of a full-time position?"

Tee gave them her best pirate voice and wink. "Damn well better."

"And I agree." Sonia's smile filled her face.

Jet banged her fist on the table. "Done."

There was laughter all around. Tee wagged her finger at the group. "Now, wait a minute. You're not going to make me an employee without giving me my own desk, are you? I'm tired of sitting in a folding chair or stealing a few moments at one of your desks."

Sonia was having great fun. "Actually, I'm glad you brought that up. Given the size of the check we're about to receive from an informal group known as the bourbon brotherhood, I believe it's time we make some changes to our facilities. I propose that you not only get your own desk but that you get your own glass-enclosed office." She turned to Jet. "How does that sound, partner?"

"Sounds good to me." Jet closed one eye and raised the other eyebrow. "Maybe that will keep her from making such a mess on my desk."

"Wait a—"

"Hold on, ladies." Brad raised his arms to quiet the whole table. "I have an offer to make myself." Silence fell on the table. He took a big, almost majestic breath. "If you can find the funds to build a glass-enclosed conference room as well, I just happen to have a large, beautiful wooden table that will fill that space." He smiled. "It's a family piece, been in storage since my folks passed." His grin turned mischievous. "Of course, we'll all miss the shaky, white, plastic table.

Sonia looked at Jet, got the response she hoped for, and turned back to Brad. "Well, kind sir, what a lovely gift, and one we will be glad to accept." She shifted her expression. "However, try as you may to ingratiate yourself to us, please do not hold out any hope of ever becoming employee number zero-zero-four."

Brad looked at her, surprised confusion on his face. "And why is that?"

"Because BCI is now, and shall ever be, an all-female investigation firm." She paused for a moment, then spoke directly to her partner. "In fact, Jet, I believe we'll be installing *two* offices and a conference area."

Jet seemed truly puzzled. "Two? Why?"

"I'm quite certain," said Sonia coyly, "that by the end of the day we will be hiring our first Latina investigator, one that's quite a red-hot pistol."

51

After the celebratory coffee had broken up, Tee and Jet went off to start the process of looking for some furniture for Tee to put in her new office. Not counting the TV in the waiting area, not a single piece of brand-new furniture had ever made its way into the BCI offices, and Sonia made it clear to Tee that the tradition was not about to change. Nonetheless, Tee was excited about searching for some things that would be functional and yet fit her personal style. Jet was pleased to be a part of the process of searching.

Tee had, of course, invited Sonia to join her on her search, but Sonia had declined. She was just too exhausted. Instead, she went upstairs to her own space with the intention of clearing off her own desk. When she walked into the room, however, she realized there was very little clutter to deal with. Sonia kept her space neat, always.

She sat at her desk and decided there was one bit of business she still needed to attend to. She opened her computer and began the process of transferring the files she had taken from Carl's computer to a back-up hard drive she used for all important BCI files. She was about to transfer the third file when she realized that she'd never even opened it. The case was closed now, but sheer curiosity drove her to open it anyway. She started reading. It was a letter from Carl to Missy.

Missy,

I know that you found my recent suggestion a little hard to believe, Victor being my only son. Still, I ask you to consider what it is like to invest your entire life in building not only a successful business but a personal reputation—a reputation for being an honest man who built quality roofs for people, who gave them the quality they paid for. And then, what it is like to turn that business over to your son, your own flesh and blood, and watch him squander, not the business, but the reputation—to have your name become synonymous with low-quality, over-priced roofs.

But you, Missy, you always understood. Right from the time you joined the company, you had the same vision I did, high-quality roofs worth what people paid for them. As I said to you the other day, you are the only one I can trust to restore my good name, because you were there when things were right, and you know how to make them right again.

Now, I know that won't be easy. If I try to move control of the business from Victor to you, he will fight tooth and nail, declaring me incompetent, and probably win. Davey, on the other hand, is another matter. Honestly, I don't know how else this can be accomplished. You know my plan. You know how I want things to turn out. If you have the courage for it, you can call the number I asked you to put in your phone the other day. The man who answers the phone will not be surprised to hear from you. Simply say the words, "Do it," and hang up. He will know exactly what to do. He has already been paid. But it must be done before I pass. If he does not hear from you, do not fear. I have asked a lot of you and done all that I can to make things right. One way or the other I will die in peace.

Respectfully,

Carl

AUTHOR'S NOTE

As I'm sure you can imagine, Victor Rasmussen wasn't really murdered, nor did he wind up in a barrel of bourbon. THE STORY YOU HAVE JUST READ IS NOT TRUE. NONE OF THE EVENTS OR CHARACTERS PORTRAYED HAVE ANY RELATION TO ACTUAL EVENTS, ORGANIZATIONS, OR ANY PERSONS LIVING OR DECEASED. That having been said, I hope you've enjoyed our bourbon-soaked adventure.

Now, a word of advice. Do not go to your local purveyor of fine bourbons and try to purchase a bottle of Horatio Blevins, Settler's Pride, Woodland Acres, James Bennington, or any of the other fine bourbons mentioned in the book. Remember, ***I just make this stuff up!*** On the other hand, if you know your bourbon brands and facts, I hope you feel that I have captured an authentic sense of what bourbon is, how it is made, and why so many folks, in Kentucky and around the world, consider it so special. Let's be clear, however, that ***no actual distiller, brand, or company, real or inspirational, was involved in anything untoward that was described in this book***—other than providing beautiful, delicious bourbon in which some of us may or may not have over-indulged.

Also, for those of you whose interest in bourbon, its history, and its production has been piqued by the reading of this book, I would recommend, *Bourbon: A History of the American Spirit*, by Dane Huckelbridge. I found it a wonderful source for further study.

Finally, I would like to thank those readers who have made it all the way to this final note. I hope you've enjoyed the journey. And should you ever make a trip to the Bluegrass Region, and Lexington in particular, please stop by Magee's for a warm greeting, a fine cup of coffee and a wonderful almond croissant. You'll find it right on East Main, directly across from the white house that sits adjacent to the school district's Central Office. You may also enjoy some fine food downtown at Saul Good or a great steak at Malone's. And if you make it to Coffee Times Coffee House, be sure to have some of the delicious Southern Pecan coffee they grind and roast right on the property. Finally, I would really appreciate it if you would visit my dear friend, Marcos Valdez, at his fine establishment, Papi's Mexican Restaurant. Without his help, all the Hispanic flavors that wind their way through this series would probably turn out to be more like Spanglish than authentic Mexican dialogue. While you're there, go ahead and order a "Sonia's Special." I think you'll enjoy it.

fjm

ABOUT THE AUTHOR

After a long career as a professional musician and educator, having written several instructional texts along the way, Frank Messina turned his attention to writing fiction in 2016. He holds bachelor's and master's degrees in Music Education and a Doctor of Education degree from the University of Massachusetts at Amherst.

A native of Long Island, New York, Frank moved to Lexington, Kentucky in 1978. Having lived there for over forty years, he now considers Lexington his home and is excited about sharing the beauty and culture of that wonderful little city as he leads readers through the exciting, albeit fictional, world of Sonia Vitale and the ladies of Bluegrass Confidential Investigations. ***The Bluegrass Files: The Bourbon Brotherhood***, is the third in a multi-volume series.

Follow f j messina at:
fjmessina_author on instagram
@fjmessina on twitter
@fjmessina on facebook

ALSO BY F J MESSINA:

The Bluegrass Files: Down The Rabbit Hole

The Bluegrass Files: Twisted Dreams

The Bluegrass Files: Mirror Image Coming Soon!

Curious About What Sonia Does Next?

Wondering about her relationships with Brad and Jet?

Would you like to know a little about the future of

Bluegrass Confidential Investigations?

Check Out:

The Bluegrass Files: Mirror Image

Pharmaceutical misdeeds, unrestrained greed. Sonia Vitale and her team race to solve a crime, protect thousands—and rescue a romantic rival!

Sign up for an email alert at fjmessina-mysteries.com

Or . . .

Follow Sonia at facebook.com/fjmessina

Made in the USA
Middletown, DE
26 March 2019